JUST A
BOY *and a* GIRL
in a
little CANOE

JUST A BOY *and a* GIRL *in a little* CANOE

SARAH MLYNOWSKI

HARPER TEEN
An Imprint of HarperCollinsPublishers

HarperTeen is an imprint of HarperCollins Publishers.

Just a Boy and a Girl in a Little Canoe
Copyright © 2020 by Sarah Mlynowski

ISBN 978-0-06-239710-2

Typography by Jessie Gang
20 21 22 23 24   PC/LSCH   10 9 8 7 6 5 4 3 2 1
❖
First Edition

For Jessica Aflalo Rubin,
my new camp BFF

JUST A
BOY *and a* GIRL
in a
little CANOE

PRE-CAMP: STAFF TRAINING SCHEDULE

	THURSDAY	FRIDAY	SATURDAY	SUNDAY
8:00 - 8:45 A.M.	BAGGAGE DROP-OFF PIER 40, NYC			
8:45 A.M.	DEPARTURE FOR CAMP	WAKEUP	FLAGPOLE	BREAKFAST
9:00 A.M.		BREAKFAST	BREAKFAST	DAY I PROCEDURES/ T-SHIRT DISTRIBUTION
10:00–11:00 A.M.		EMERGENCY PROCEDURES	BEACH PROCEDURES, SWIM TEST	SECTIONAL MEETINGS
11:00 A.M.– 12:00 P.M.	ARRIVAL AT CAMP/ UNLOAD BAGGAGE	WELCOME SIGNS/ CLEANING WHEELS	DOCTOR TALK	FINAL CLEANUP
12:00–1:00 P.M.	CON'T. UNLOADING BAGGAGE	LUNCH	LUNCH	KIDS ARRIVE
1:00– 2:00 P.M.	LUNCH	REST HOUR	REST HOUR	

	THURSDAY	FRIDAY	SATURDAY	SUNDAY
2:00–3:00 P.M.	SETTLE INTO BUNKS	CPR TRAINING	UNPACKING CON'T.	
3:00–4:00 P.M.	ICEBREAKERS	SECURITY PROCEDURES	SPORTS AND GAMES WITH SECTION HEADS	
4:00–4:15 P.M.	MILK & COOKIES	MILK & COOKIES	MILK & COOKIES	
4:15–5:15 P.M.	TEAM BUILDING	UNPACKING	CLEANUP	KIDS ARRIVE
5:15–6:15 P.M.	DINNER WASHUP	DINNER WASHUP	DINNER WASHUP	
6:15–7:30 P.M.	DINNER	FRIDAY NIGHT DINNER	FLAGPOLE	
7:30–8:30 P.M.	STAFF MANUAL/ DAYS OFF/OD	FREE PLAY	DINING HALL PROCEDURES AND DINNER	
8:30–9:30 P.M.	ROLE PLAYING/ SCENARIOS	BONFIRE	SECTIONAL SONG PREP	
9:30 P.M.	FREE PLAY		MOVIE	
12:45 A.M.	CURFEW	CURFEW	CURFEW	

Pre-camp

I can't believe I came back here.

The wooden bridge, the leafy trees, the white sign that says Camp Blue Springs in chipped blue paint.

Last time I was here was eight years ago. I was eleven. Eleven! I had braces and had never kissed a boy, despite my nickname.

Oh, wow, that nickname.

I was tortured, *humiliated* by my nickname on these very grounds. And yet, I am here again. Willingly. I must be some kind of masochist.

There's a small green building, the camp office, to my left, and a gate blocking the road in. A guy—skinny, seventeen, maybe eighteen, spiky dark hair—steps off the porch and meanders over to my car.

"Heeeeeeeey," he says, scratching his goatee. "Are you staff?"

"Yup," I say. "Checking in. Samantha Rosenspan."

"I'm Eric. Would you like to park in the lot just after the gate, mayyyybe?" He draws out his words, sounding slightly confused.

"I would love to park in the lot just after the gate, Eric," I say.

"Fannnnnntastic! You're going to Bunk"—he looks at his clipboard—"Six?"

No way. That was my cabin last time. I'm in the same bunk! "Six for the win," I tell him.

"Let me grab your bags for you," he offers.

"Thanks." I pop the trunk of my dad's twenty-year-old Honda Civic, which lives in my parents' driveway, and which I am borrowing for the summer. My dad can't drive anymore anyway.

The late afternoon sun warms my cheeks and I take a deep breath of the fresh pine air. It really does smell good up here.

Eric pulls one of my black duffel bags onto his shoulder, and I take the other. "Let's just leave them by the stairs," he says. "The Tank will drive them to your bunk."

I don't know if the Tank is a machine or a person, but I like that it/he will handle my heavy lifting. "Thanks. Do I just walk to Bunk Six after I park?"

"Yep."

I wonder if it's still in the same spot as it was eight years ago. "Near the flagpole? Lower Field?"

"Sounds right. I'm new."

I get back in the car. He opens the gate with his sandaled foot, and I drive through. There are about fifteen other cars in the parking area. The clock on my dad's dashboard says 5:05. The rest of the staff got here yesterday afternoon, but I told them I had an exam and couldn't drive up until today, which was only a half lie. I did have an exam, but it was last week. My boyfriend, Eli, is leaving for Europe tonight. Since he's going to be traveling for five weeks, we wanted to spend as much time together as possible. I basically moved into his parents' basement in Greenwich for the last week. He slept upstairs officially, but crept downstairs as soon as his parents fell asleep.

We met my second week at NYU. I was trying to get into my room, jamming my key in over and over, holding a plastic bag. He opened the door. Turned out I was on the wrong floor. His dorm room—the one I was unwittingly trying to break into—was directly below mine. He asked me if I had anything good in the bag. He'd been studying and wishing he had cupcakes, so he wondered if I was the cupcake fairy. Regrettably, all I had in the bag was a new bottle of shampoo, since mine had somehow exploded all over my shower bucket.

I apologized and went back upstairs.

But since I was trying hard to be Brave College Sam, I went back the next day holding another bag. I knocked on the door. "Cupcake fairy!" I said.

With the exception of a few family holidays, we've been glued together for ten straight months.

Until today.

Eli's cousin Yosef just got out of the Israeli army—and wanted Eli to travel with him.

I get it. I do.

A summer of traveling in Europe is objectively awesome. I told Eli he should go.

So then Eli suddenly had summer plans, and I realized I had no idea what I was going to do. Stay in New York on my own, in the dorm? Get an apartment? A job? Go back to Rhode Island? My besties from high school wouldn't be in Providence over the summer. And my friends from NYU, Lauren and Emily, weren't staying in the city. I tried to find an education-related summer job, but had no luck. I could maybe get a restaurant or retail job, but rent was so expensive, I wouldn't save anything. The prospects seemed bleak.

Then in March, I saw Danish on the subway. I hadn't seen her in years, since she'd been my counselor in training at Blue Springs a million years ago.

We bumped into each other. Literally. We were on the 6 train, and it was crowded. We were both standing and she smacked me in the arm with her bag before recognizing me.

"Sam! Is that you?"

It took me a few seconds to place her. She used to wear her hair short and striped with blue, but now it was all brown and down to her waist.

"It's me! Daniella Morganstein! Oh wow, it's been years!"

"Danish?" I said. That had been *her* nickname. I have no idea why. Did she speak Danish? Or eat Danish?

I hadn't seen anyone from camp for years. On purpose.

She nodded, her head bouncing like a bobblehead. "Yes! It's me! Do you live in the city now?"

"Just moved in September. NYU. You?"

"I'm at the New School. But my girlfriend is a senior at Tisch! What are you studying?"

"I'm majoring in education," I said.

"What are you doing this summer?"

"I'm not sure, actually."

"Really? Oh, oh, oh! Come back to camp! I'm unit head for the little kids! The juniors! They're so cute! I need another counselor for the eight-year-olds! Staffing for these kids is impossible! Please be my counselor for the eight-year-olds! You would be perfect!"

"I would?"

"Yes! You were one of the good ones. Nice. And sporty! Didn't you play softball? And you want to be a teacher!"

"Yeah, but . . ." I hesitated. "I mean, I didn't have the best time there."

She slapped her hand over her forehead. "Shit. I just remembered. Zoe Buckman. She was in your bunk, right?"

"Yes," I said, my cheeks flaming.

Zoe Buckman. My absolute nemesis.

First Zoe had glockshmeared me—that's when someone

7

pours bug juice on you when you're sleeping and covers you in baby powder.

Then she found my diary and read it to everyone in the bunk.

Then she stole my white bra and hung it on the flagpole.

And then came the shower incident. Which led to the nickname.

And then came the overnight. Where I got my period. For the first time. Before anyone else in my bunk.

"Zoe was *horrible*," Danish groaned. "Your whole bunk was the worst, actually."

"It was?" I felt oddly gratified. I hadn't been "too sensi-tive." It wasn't "in my head," like my mom said.

"Yes! But! None of the girls your age from that year came back. None of them!"

"None? Ever?"

"Well, they came back as campers, but none of them were asked back as staff. Some of the guys, but *none* of the girls. Botts is head of inters. He's your age, right?"

Seniors were the oldest campers—twelve- to fourteen-year-olds. Inters were ten- and eleven-year-olds. Juniors were seven- to nine-year-olds.

I nodded. I remembered Botts, aka Daniel Bottsman. Botts was short, funny, red-haired, and freckled. He had played on the twelve-and-under softball team with me. I'd hung out with him a lot that summer, actually. We'd been friends. The girls in my bunk *had* been horrible, Danish was

8

right about that. So I'd spent a lot of time with the softball team. Botts included.

"He's exactly the same. Still a sweetie. He's our youngest head staff member, but he's great with the kids and started going when he was six. You'll actually know a lot of people. Priya Singh is head of seniors; you remember her, don't you? She was a year ahead of you. Josh Gold is head counselor. Jill Wiseman is head of CITs. They met at camp and now they're married! Marissa Levkoff, who happens to be my ex, is head of waterfront. Don't worry, it's not awkward. Anyway, you would be *so* perfect. Consider this an official job offer. You'll make about two grand, which I know is less than you'd make working in the city, but it includes all food and lodging! And it's only six and a half weeks including pre-camp! And we'll have a great time. Camp as a counselor is way more fun than camp as a camper, promise. So will you come? Say yes! This is my stop."

I held on to the pole. Should I? If I didn't take it, I would probably have to go home for the summer. And I was not looking forward to listening to my parents' constant bickering.

And I may have been a loser as a camper, but I knew I could be a good counselor. No, a *great* counselor. I could make sure the kids in my bunk had an incredible summer. The summer of their dreams! No one would call *my* campers horrible nicknames.

And I hadn't hated *everything* about Blue Springs.

I loved the lake, the endless stars, color war.

I just hated Zoe Buckman and her minions. I had nightmares about them occasionally, even as a college student, which was ridiculous since so much time had passed. Why couldn't I get over it already?

But Zoe was gone. Gone and not coming back.

I could return to camp and *like* it. Maybe I could even love it! I could erase the bad memories! And it would even look good on my résumé to have hands-on experience with kids.

What else was I going to do all summer?

How often did a job bump into you on the 6 train? If this wasn't serendipity, I didn't know what was.

The train pulled to a halt. We both lunged forward and then back. "Well?" she asked.

I smiled at her. "I'm in."

Tiny rocks crunch under my feet as I walk down the road into camp.

Two girls, teenagers, are huddled together talking. Both are wearing shorts and T-shirts. I'm wearing a black cotton dress and my J.Crew ballet flats. I can see that ballet flats were a mistake. They are mesh, and the holes are already filled with camp dust.

The girls smile at me, and I smile back, feeling out of sorts. I'm not sure if I should introduce myself or not, so I don't.

I'm off to a flying start.

I take out my cell phone to text Eli and tell him I arrived. He was worried I'd get lost, but I knew Google Maps would do its job.

I type: Made it! Have only been attacked by three bears so far, but otherwise all good.

I wait for the text to send. When nothing happens, I study the bars. No service. Dead zone. Super. I was told that counselors, unlike campers, are allowed to have phones, as long as we don't use them in front of the kids. I assumed that meant that using them would be an option.

"Rosenspan!" I hear. My head snaps up.

It's Botts! Softball team Botts! Botts who is now head of the inter section.

"Hey, stranger," I say, smiling. He'd always called me by my last name. Never by my terrible nickname. He's walking with another guy who looks familiar.

Botts looks older. His shoulders have filled out. But I'm looking into the same eyes I did when I was eleven. "So the rumors are true!" he says, light brown eyes shining. "You're back! You missed us, didn't you?"

"Only you," I say. "Did you ever leave, or have you been here since the last time I saw you?"

"I haven't moved. I've been standing in this exact spot for eight years."

"It's good to see you," I say, and I mean it.

He pulls me into a hug. "I wondered what happened to

you. It's great you're back." He squeezes my shoulders. "And you're all grown up."

I *am* all grown up. I am no longer the awkward eleven-year-old I used to be, trying to hide my hips, boobs, and braces. I am now happy to have these boobs and hips—*and* my perfect teeth, thank you very much. And I'm not just a hick from Rhode Island anymore. I live in New York City. In the Village! I get my haircut in Soho. I am glamorous. I am cool. I am freaking awesome, so go to hell, Zoe Buckman.

"You know Gav, right?" Botts asks.

"I'm not sure," I say. No, wait. I do know him. I *definitely* know him. Gav is Gavin Lawblau.

No way.

Tall, lean, clear skin. Dark hair. Black T-shirt, blue board shorts. He's wearing dark sunglasses. He was the cool guy when we were eleven, and it seems like he's still the cool guy now.

"I think I remember you," I lie, but my cheeks flush. I hope he doesn't remember me.

"You look kind of familiar, too," he says, a lazy smile on his face. "What section are you in?"

"Juniors."

"Me too," he says. "But I'm a specialist. I sleep in Bunk Five with the Junior boys, but I teach sailing."

"The most psychotic kids at camp," Botts says.

"They are *totally* psychotic. Last year I found one sleeping on the roof. And another shit into a taco."

"Oh my God! That is disgusting," I say, laughing. "Please tell me no one ate it."

Now he laughs. "No, the smell gave it away."

I make a face, hoping that it's still a cute face.

"I believe you're Bunk Six, and your co-counselor is Talia?" Botts asks.

"I guess. Was she here when I was here?" I ask quickly. I hope not. The fewer old faces the better. Less people who might remember my nickname.

"No, she started as a senior. And Janelle is new this year. But Lis was here when you were."

Lis. I search my brain for a flutter of recognition. Nothing. "Um, great?"

"Can't wait to catch up later, but we're heading to the office. Do you remember where you're going?" Botts asks.

"I do," I say, adjusting my backpack. "I guess they switched Bunk Six from inters to juniors?"

He nods. "We did. Helps to have the little kids closer to the flagpole."

A loud voice comes over the loudspeaker. It's Eric the office guy. "Attention, all counselors. Attention, all counselors. It is now the beginning of Dinner Washup. Please go . . . um . . . please go . . . please go . . . wash up? Thanks." Then we hear a loud crash. And then, "Oops."

Botts looks up at the sky. "Am I imagining it, or does Eric sound high?"

Gavin nods. "He definitely sounds confused. He sleeps in

my bunk, and I'm pretty sure I heard him wandering around the cabin in the middle of the night."

Botts rolls his eyes. "He better not be high. Last year we found a huge duffel bag of amphetamines under the office girl's bed. I do not have the strength to deal with that again."

"You did?" I say, shocked.

"It wasn't a duffel bag," Gavin says.

"Okay, fine, it was more of a carry-on size. But still. It was a headache. I'm going to give Eric a warning just in case. See you later, Rosenspan. Glad you're back."

I smile as I keep walking up the hill. Botts is exactly the same. Everything here is exactly the same. It looks the same, it smells the same. The pool that I pass on my right is the same. It's an indoor pool, surrounded by glass, with a green lawn outside. I can practically smell the chlorine.

Everything is exactly the same, except me.

To my left is Upper Field. It's a big clearing with a gaga court, a Newcomb ball court, which is actually the same as a volleyball court, and a baseball diamond. I played on the softball team and got my first home run on that field. It went right over Bunk 10.

Now I'm walking down the hill. There's a cabin to my right. Bunk 9. I can see that the tennis courts are still behind it, with the plexiglass-walled athletic center called the Skydome behind that.

Next is the Rec Hall, where we sang songs on Friday nights. Counselors played guitar and piano, and the lyrics were displayed on a screen. It was one of my favorite parts of camp.

I keep walking. To the left is the walkway to the lake. Below I see the sandy beach and a bunch of staff members setting up sailboats and Windsurfers.

The road turns into another hill.

"You made it!" Danish calls out from underneath a leafy tree. "I am so thrilled."

"I made it," I say. "Sorry I'm late."

She's wearing Teva sandals, blue sweat shorts, a gray tank top, and she's holding both a walkie-talkie and a clipboard. "Oh, it's fine," she says. "I'm just glad you're here. You're such a great addition to my section." She looks at her clipboard. "Do you want me to introduce you to your co? I'm sure you guys will get along." She glances at her watch. "I need to be at the Arts and Crafts in like minus five minutes, but I can run."

"I can introduce myself," I say, although I'm suddenly nervous. "Don't worry about me."

"Yeah? Great. There's some issue with the paints. I'll see you at dinner, 'kay? You know where you're going?"

"As long as you didn't move Bunk Six." I want her to think I know what I'm doing. I want her to have total confidence in me. I can manage finding my bunk! I can manage a bunch of kids! I'm going to be a teacher! So of course I'm going to be a great counselor!

Hopefully.

"Ha! Okay, bye!"

I keep walking. There is *so* much dirt in my ballet flats. I really need to put on my sneakers. What was I thinking wearing these? I spot the flagpole next, which also marks the beginning of Lower Field, where the majority of the cabins are. There are six to my right, all in a line. There are four bunks to my left. Straight ahead is another baseball diamond and a basketball court. There's a path behind the basketball court that leads to the CIT village, but I never spent much time there since I was only here for one year and I wasn't a counselor in training.

Bunk 6. Right here.

There are two pretty girls my age standing on the porch. One looks familiar—I bet she's Lis, the one who was here when I was a camper, too. She's Asian American, with light smooth skin, and she's wearing her straight black hair in a low ponytail. The other girl is shorter, tan, super thin, and has spiral curls in a loose bun on top of her head. They're wearing tank tops and ripped jean shorts. They both look sweaty. They study me as I step up the stairs.

"Hi," I say, trying to make my voice sound extra cheerful and not at all nervous. "I'm Sam."

"I'm Talia," says the curly-haired one. "Your *co*-counselor." I can feel her looking me up and down, glaring.

Why is she looking at me like that? Does she know about my nickname? Do they all know? Do they not like me already? *Get it together, Rosenspan.*

I cross my arms tightly and then try to force myself to

16

relax. "Nice to meet you," I say. I push my sunglasses to the top of my head. I feel a bit like I'm standing in front of them in my underwear. The back of my neck feels tight.

"I'm Alissa," the familiar-looking girl says. "But call me Lis. You've been here before, yeah?"

"I was here for one year as a camper," I say quietly. Hopefully she doesn't remember me.

I study the porch. There are already four brightly colored towels hanging over the railing. There's a poster on the left side that says "Welcome, 6A!" in bubble letters and glitter. Then it says "Counselors: Talia and Sam" and lists a bunch of girls' names. "Francie. Shira. Emma C. Emma F. Lily. Prague."

I guess I'm in 6A.

"Prague?" I ask. "Is that a nickname?"

Lis laughs. "No! It's one hundred percent real. Her brother's name is Barcelona."

"No it's not."

"It totally is," Lis says. "He's in Bunk Eight. Senior."

I laugh. Talia doesn't. Her arms are crossed and she's still kind of glaring at me like I've done something to offend her, even though I just met her ten seconds ago.

On the left side of the bunk there's a second poster that says, "Welcome, 6B! Counselors: Lis and Janelle," and lists five names.

"We have one less kid than you," Lis says. "Although two of our kids are only seven, so it sucks to be us."

"I'll show you where you're sleeping," Talia says tightly, and opens the door to the cabin.

Great. She hates me already. I follow her.

"Danish has her own room on the right, since she's head staff and apparently needs her privacy, unlike us. The four of us are here." She pushes aside a hanging white bedsheet and steps inside the counselors' room, which is narrow and long. In the front part, there are two parallel single beds on metal frames, about three feet apart. One has a sleeping bag on it already and is under a window. "You and Janelle are here," she says.

"I guess that one is mine?" I ask, pointing to the bare one.

"Yes," Talia snaps.

Seriously, what the heck is up with her? Did I run over her cat on my way into camp?

In the far back of the room, there's a bunk bed pushed against the wall. The mattresses are both made up with sheets and pretty comforters.

"So why were you late?" Talia asks as Lis steps into the counselors' room behind her.

"I told Danish I had an exam," I say. "But honestly, it was because my boyfriend is leaving for Rome today. Don't tell?" Eli had convinced me that missing a day of pre-camp wasn't a big deal. And I'd wanted to spend the extra night with him. But I didn't want Danish to know I had blown it off. I wanted her to like me. I wanted everyone at camp to like me.

"We won't," Lis says, biting her thumbnail. "How long have you been together?"

"Almost a year," I say.

"Oh wow, forever," Lis says. "So why's he going to Europe without you?"

"He's traveling with his cousin. And I don't have the money."

"Pictures, please," she says.

I see Talia glare at her. Is she mad that Lis is not being a bitch to me?

I pull up a selfie that we took last night and show them. His brown eyes are squinting as he smiles at the camera. Our cheeks are pressed against each other.

"OMG, you guys are adorable together. He's so cute," Lis says.

"He's cute," Talia concedes, but her arms are still crossed.

"Yes," I say, smiling. "He is."

"Did you print any out?" Lis asks. "You should hang them by your bed."

"I forgot to," I say, wishing I were the type of girl who remembered to do stuff like that. "But he promised to send me postcards. I'll hang those."

Eli promised a postcard from every stop. And we are still going to talk all the time. And text. As much as we can.

"So you used to go here?" Talia asks, moving into her section of the room. Lis follows behind her.

"Um. Yeah. Just for one year." I sit down on my mattress. It sags.

"Wait, how old are you?" Lis asks. "One year older than me?"

"Nineteen. Yeah. I'm at NYU now," I add, trying to distract her. Nickname? What nickname? Look over there, a squirrel! "Where are you two going next year?"

"I didn't get in anywhere good, so I'm taking the year off to work at my mom's office—she's in real estate—and then I'm going to reapply. But Talia's going to Penn. She's a smarty pants. Do you like NYU?"

"I love it," I say. I love my classes. I love my boyfriend. I love my friends. New York has become home. I look around the room. "I guess I should make my bed. What are we supposed to be doing now exactly?"

"It's Dinner Washup," Talia says. "So, nothing. Then after dinner we have a bonfire. You missed most of the unpacking."

"The kids' stuff is already here?" I ask.

"Yeah, we got their duffels on Thursday."

"Oh yeah. I remember that. But the staff unpacks everything for them?"

"Just for the juniors," Talia says. "You don't want them unpacking themselves; they're a mess. They can barely remember to brush their teeth."

"You should show her the rest of the cabin," Lis says, biting her thumbnail again.

"I was in Bunk Six when I was a kid," I say. "But my memory is foggy."

"Come on," Talia says. She pushes through the white sheet, disappearing into the main hallway.

The cabin is divided in half with a wall down the middle: 6A on one side, 6B on the other. Both sides have beds in them and windows on the outside wall. I follow her to the left.

Four of the eight 6A beds are made. Their mattresses are all decked out in colorful comforters and little welcome mats by their beds. Most of them are Disney. Elsa. Anna. Moana. I'm hoping Shira has a She-Ra: Princess of Power comforter, but she doesn't. She went Star Wars. I love Star Wars, so I give her a mental thumbs-up anyway.

"Oh, wow," I say to Talia. "You did so much!"

"Yeah," she says. "I *did*."

I hadn't known that coming late would mean more work for my co. I just thought I'd be skipping the get-to-know-you games.

So *that's* why she's being such a bitch to me. She hasn't heard anything about me as a camper, she's just pissed. She had to unpack all by herself. I feel like a jerk. I *am* a jerk. Here I am wanting to impress everyone, and I'm making enemies already.

"I am so sorry," I say, my cheeks burning. "Seriously. I completely forgot that we had to unpack the kids. And you did them all! How can I make it up to you?"

Her face softens. "It's okay. There are still two kids left."

"I'll do them now. You go relax! Take a nap or something. Or a shower."

Talia raises an eyebrow. "I look that great, huh?"

21

I flush. "Oh, I just mean—"

"Kidding. I know I look like shit. After a day of camp my hair has puffed up. But anyway, we have more unpacking time tomorrow. After swim tests. I'll take a nap then. And you can make the chore wheel."

I shudder. Swim tests. As a camper I came up with every excuse possible to avoid going in the water. Headache. Earache. Not because of swimming—I'm a good swimmer—but because I knew I looked different from the other girls in my bathing suit, and during the test, all eyes would be on me.

"I forgot about swim tests," I say.

"Swimming is the worst. But the counselor tests are in the pool, at least. Come on," she says, and leads me into the cubby room next. It's a windowless room with a door out the back. Almost all the wooden cubbies are filled with tiny clothes, perfectly folded into squares.

"You did an amazing job," I say.

"Thanks," she says, looking pleased. "Lis and I had the nine-year-olds last year, but I remember some of these kids from Bunk Three. Prague is adorable. She's a riot. Seriously cute. I don't know Emma C., it's her first year, but her cousin is here and Emma is supposedly a super athlete. She's here on scholarship. Her dad died a few years ago and they had no insurance and she applied and the camp took her for free. Emma F. is new too, but her brother is a senior. She's adopted, he isn't. Fancy was here last year and is a total witch. Mean girl in the making. Just look at her clothes." She

22

points to the cubby across from us. "She brought Dolce and Gabbana T-shirts. To camp! She's eight!"

"Her name is Fancy?" I ask.

"It's really Francie. But come on. That was such an easy nickname."

I am not giving *any* kid a nickname.

"Who brings Dolce and Gabbana T-shirts to camp? They'll be covered in blue paint and chocolate pudding in four days max."

I laugh.

"You laugh now, but these kids are *gross*." She cracks a smile, and I see she has two dimples. She has a perfectly round face. Like a doll.

"The bathroom is right there?" I ask, pointing to the next room over.

"Yeah," she says. "Warning, we got the teeny-tiny kid toilets. Ugh, I wish they'd given me my kids from last year. Or any inters. Or even seniors. *Any* seniors. Juniors are the worst."

There are three stalls on one side of the room, and two sinks and two mirrors on the other. Counselors share with the kids.

"Be right back," I say.

The stall *is* small. And the toilet is definitely lower than a regular toilet. I feel a bit like Snow White.

There are names all over the back of the bathroom wall from previous years.

CS + TH forever.

Kayla Novak was here but now she's gone.
She left her name to carry on.
Those who knew her knew her well.
Those who didn't can go to hell!

Lis Katzenberg was here!

Lis! I'm not sure if Lis already wrote her name on the first day of pre-camp or if it's from last year.

I flush and head to the sink. Talia is already gone. I turn on the hot water handle and feel the shock of cold. Oh, right, there is no hot water, only cold. How had I forgotten about that too?

I head back to the staff room and step inside. Lis and Talia are stripping off their clothes.

"We're running to the showers before dinner," Talia says with a teasing grin. "Since *you* think I need one."

"I don't! I—!"

"She does need a shower," Lis says. "So do I."

"Enjoy your city look, Sam," Talia says. "It'll be gone in an hour!"

My "city look." Funny. I blew my hair straight this morning. I probably won't be able to get it this way again for the rest of the summer.

"When's dinner?" I ask.

"In an hour," Lis says.

Eli's flight leaves at seven, which means he'll be boarding soon. I need to say goodbye. I look at my phone. Still no service. "Wait, guys, is there Wi-Fi? I'm not getting cell service here."

"Only in the office," Talia says. "Not in the bunks."

"Crap," I say, tensing. "I want to reach my boyfriend before he takes off."

"You can get a signal by the showers," Lis says. "A faint one, but better than nothing. I'll show you in a sec."

"Still no showers in the bunks, huh?" I ask.

Talia shakes her head. "The senior girls have one. I can't believe we got stuck with juniors again."

I sit back on the bed and wait for Lis and Talia to put on their bathrobes and flip-flops.

"So where's Janelle?" I ask.

"She said she wanted to take a swim," Lis says, and snort-laughs, looking at Talia.

I raise my eyebrow. "What's her story?"

Talia picks up her shower bucket. "Let's just say I lucked out."

"Talia!" Lis says.

"I did," Talia says. "Sam seems totally normal and Janelle is . . . well . . . a little freaky?"

Me. I'm normal.

They have anointed me as normal.

Woot!

Still, I remember what it was like to be called freaky.

"What is normal, exactly?" I ask, trying to keep my voice calm. "Is there such a thing?"

"There definitely is," Lis says, lowering her voice. "And she is *not* it. Look what's in her cubby! Tube tops!"

"What's wrong with tube tops?" I ask. "I don't have any, but why do we not approve?"

"She doesn't shave her armpits," Lis says, and wrinkles her nose.

Plenty of my friends at college aren't so into shaving. "Maybe she's making a statement?" I say.

"A gross one," Lis says, and cackles.

"Lis," Talia says. "For all you know, Sam doesn't shave her armpits either."

Lis turns to me. "Do you?"

I admit, "I got them waxed in New York."

"Smart," Talia says. She sits down beside me. "In all honesty, we were worried. But I can tell I like you." She smirks. "Even if you made me do all the unpacking so you could hook up with your boyfriend."

I smile. "It was really good hooking up. Like, amazing."

Talia laughs.

The truth is, the best part of the last week wasn't even the hooking up. It was staying up late, my head on his chest, while he drew shapes on my back and we whispered and watched the sun rise. Then he'd sneak back to his room before his parents woke up.

Talia swings her shower bucket. "C'mon. His flight is going to leave any minute. You gotta move."

"Thanks," I say, and follow them out the front door and around the cabin toward the showers, which are between bunks 3 and 4, girls on the right, boys on the left.

"If you stand just beside that tree, you'll get service," Lis says. "Don't ask me why."

"I'm going in," Talia says, leaving me. "There better not be a line."

"Thanks," I say. And then I'm on my own and staring at the showers.

There are about twenty stairs to get up to them.

The incident that inspired my nickname occurred on stair seven, three from the top.

I tripped on my flip-flop.

I tripped, and then I tumbled down, down, down, and my bathrobe opened and my nether regions were exposed to everyone standing on Lower Field—girls *and* boys.

Including Zoe Buckman. Who just stood there, laughing.

"Porn star!" she shrieked. "Sam is a porn star!"

It didn't help that I was the only girl in my bunk who already had boobs and hair on those nether regions.

I stood up and covered myself as quickly as I could. My right elbow and left knee were skinned. And I had bumped my head.

By the time I got back to the bunk, Porn Star had morphed into Porny. I guess Porn Star was too much of a mouthful?

27

They called me that for the rest of the summer.

Porny.

I shiver.

I will not trip again.

No.

No one will call me Porny again.

No one. Will call me. Porny. Again.

This summer will be *great*.

I am not the same person I used to be: I am no longer quiet. I am no longer shy. I am no longer eleven. I have a 3.9 GPA!

I live in freakin' New York City!

And I am normal, dammit!

Totally, utterly normal!

And I have a super hot boyfriend!

I press Eli's name on my phone. It's ringing! Ringing . . . ringing . . . Connecting! Woot!

"Sam?" he says.

"Hi!" I say, filled with relief at the sound of his voice. I turn away from the stairs. "Yay. I'm glad I caught you."

"I'm at the airport!"

"I know! I'm at camp!"

"I tried calling," he says. "Did you see my texts?"

"No," I say. "Service here sucks. Apparently, I can only speak to you from deep in the woods."

"I guess you'll be spending a lot of time in the woods."

"I love the woods. That's where the ticks are."

Eli knows I am terrified of ticks. My mother had Lyme disease a few years back. She was in bed for months. Now

28

she refuses to go into the backyard.

"Good thing you bought a hundred bottles of bug spray," he says.

"It *is* a good thing," I say. "And you packed your money belt?"

"Oh, yeah, wearing it right now."

He's teasing me. But his mom bought him one to keep his money and passport safe. You're supposed to wear it under your clothes so you don't get pickpocketed. I don't think it's the worst idea. "Did you even pack it?" I ask.

"I did. But we both know I'm never going to wear it."

A mosquito lands on my arm and I swat it. "Apparently you have to put the bug spray on for it to work."

"Who knew?"

A counselor comes out of the showers and rushes down the steps. I want to tell her to slow down so she doesn't slip.

"So what are you doing?" I ask.

"Waiting for them to call my group. First class is already on. I'm going to miss you," he adds. "Why did I think leaving you for the summer was a good idea?"

My throat tightens. "I don't know. I'm pretty sure it was a terrible idea."

"It was," he says. "It really was. I wish you were coming with me. Oh. Wait. Hold on. They're calling my group. Finally. Okay, I'm up. I better go. I'll call you when I get to Rome. Actually, it will be the middle of the night there, won't it?"

"I don't care. Call me anyway. I don't think the phone

will work, but leave a message. I want to hear your voice."
I need to hear your voice. I swallow hard. "I'll call you back as soon as I can. I miss you already."

"I miss you, too. I love you, Beautiful."

"I love you, too."

He's the first guy I have ever said "I love you" to. He is my first everything. I always felt awkward with guys when I was younger. Maybe because I'm an only child, maybe because I was so terrified of my nickname coming true—but I mostly kept away from boys. I started flirting senior year of high school, but it wasn't until college that I finally felt confident enough to put myself out there for real.

I waited seven months to sleep with Eli. He called me "Beautiful." No one had ever called me that before.

"Have an amazing summer," he says.

"You too," I say. "Don't get pickpocketed."

"Don't get Lyme disease."

"I love you."

"I love you."

"I'm going now," he says. "I have to find my passport."

"That's why you need your money belt."

"Ha! Bye for real."

"Have a safe flight," I say, and wait for him to end the call.

He does.

I stare at my phone. He's going. He's really going.

I watch as his texts from earlier spill onto my screen now that there's service.

Eli: Did you make it? How are the ticks?

Eli: Going through security! Bomb jokes, yea or nay?

Eli: Made it! They loved the one about two terrorists walking into a bar.

Eli: You're not lost wandering around somewhere in the Adirondacks are you?

All his texts make me feel slightly out of breath. Like I'm treading water and can't feel the ground.

Crap, do I really have to take a swim test?

Talia and Lis step out of the showers. They are both wearing bathrobes and towels tied around their hair.

They take the stairs slowly.

"All good?" Talia asks.

"Yup. Just catching up," I say. The tension in my neck is back.

A new message flashes across my screen.

"I'll meet you guys in the cabin," I say.

They hurry to the bunk while I look back down at my phone.

Mom: I just ran into Jennifer Katz at the Fresh Market who has a daughter going to your camp! What age do you have again?

I write back:

Me: Eight year olds!

Mom: Oh! The girl is eight. I think her name is Francie.

Me: Fancy!

Mom: No, Francie!

Me: Yes. They call her Fancy. She's in my bunk.

Mom: Ah. How's camp? All good?

Me: Yup. Just got here. All good there?

Mom: Your father is driving me crazy but that's nothing new.

My father is always driving my mother crazy and my mother is always driving my father crazy. They've been married for twenty-five years. I'd say they are an adorable old married couple, but they aren't. Sometimes I catch them looking at each other like they genuinely despise each other. They've been together since they were sixteen. They sleep in separate rooms. My mom says it's because my father snores, and he does snore, loudly and horribly, but I don't think that's the only reason. I think they just don't like each other. Honestly, I don't know why they don't get divorced. I always thought they would once I went off to college, but so far it hasn't happened.

My dad had a brain tumor three years ago—his second—when I was in eleventh grade. The surgery got it, and he's in remission, but now he has to walk with a walker and doesn't want to go anywhere and he can't even drive. Maybe my mom feels bad about leaving him. Maybe he's too tired to leave her. Maybe it's less scary to stay and be miserable than to face the unknown.

There is a clacking over the loudspeaker. A loud squeak and then, "Attention, all counselors. Attention, all counselors. It is now time for dinner. Please head to the office. I mean the Dining Hall. Sorry. The Dining Hall." *Crash*.

There's a new text from Eli.

Eli: Hi. On plane. Taking off soon.

I type back: **Miss you. Love you.**

Eli: **Love you. Miss you.**

My throat tightens again and my eyes fill with tears.

I feel a prick on my arm and see another mosquito. I flick it away, but realize it's too late. I've already been bitten.

"These meatballs are better than I remember," I say, taking another scoop.

Meals are served family style. Talia got the tray for us from the kitchen even though she isn't eating any.

"I'm a vegetarian," she explains, squeezing a glob of hand sanitizer in her palm. "I pretty much just eat the soy-butter-and-jelly sandwiches all summer."

In addition to the main dish, there's a salad bar with veggies, bread, and soy butter and jelly outside the kitchen. A pitcher of water has already been set out by the kitchen staff at every table.

"Last year I gained ten pounds at camp," Lis says. "It was ridiculous. This year I am making friends with the salad bar."

"There's so much walking though," I say. "I'm starving already and I've only been here, like, an hour."

The three of us are sitting on the end of one of the wooden Dining Hall tables, against the wall. The Dining Hall is a long rectangle and divided into three sections. Juniors, inters, and seniors. Our section has six tables in it since there are six junior bunks.

Lis is sitting with us even though she should be at the

next table over. I'm not sure why, but Janelle isn't here yet so maybe she just doesn't want to sit alone.

I spot Gavin walking into the room. He waves at me.

I wave back.

"How hot is *he*?" Lis whispers.

"Pretty hot," I say back.

Our section is closest to the kitchen and salad bar.

The walls are covered in various plaques. Superbowl plaques. Color war plaques. Activity plaques, dating back to the 1970s, when the camp first opened. There's even an old big Star of David over the door. Way back in the 1970s, the camp was religiously affiliated and all the staff and campers were Jewish. But even eight years ago, when I'd been here, the owners had been trying to make the camp more inclusive. What had once been called Shabbat Dinner for the first fifty years was now called Friday Night Dinner; and instead of serving kosher food, meals were now just kosher style: meaning no shellfish, pork, or cheese on hamburgers.

I look around at the counselors. Out of the seventy people, about a third look familiar. I'd guess about 60 percent of them are teens who once upon a time were campers here. The staff seems only slightly more diverse than when I was a camper though; there's Lis of course, although I'm pretty sure she's Jewish, and Priya, who is Indian American, and I spot a few African American counselors who I haven't met yet. For the most part though, camp is still mostly Jewish, and mostly white, which is weird to see after living in a place like New York City. Seems like someone should tell the owners that if they really want camp to be more diverse it's going to take more work than renaming the meals.

I help myself to another meatball.

"What's for dessert?" I ask.

"Chocolate pudding," Talia says.

Lis groans. "Are they trying to kill me?"

"No one's forcing you to eat it," Talia says.

"Yes they are. Anyone who says no to chocolate pudding is a weirdo," Lis replies.

"Speaking of weirdos," Talia says under her breath, "here she comes."

I look up to see a tall busty blond, in a green tube top and leggings, skipping over to us. "Hi, ladies! How are the meatballs? They look AMAZING."

"They're great, Janelle," Lis says.

She plops into the seat beside me. "Hi!" she says. "You must be Sam. Welcome to camp! We're so happy to have you here! It's the best, eh?'

I catch Lis rolling her eyes.

"Nice to meet you," I say, and smile.

She smiles back—it's a huge smile. Her eyes crinkle and her mouth opens wide. I can see that one of her front teeth is twisted, like she never had braces. She's about a head taller than me, and wider. She is wearing a small silver cross around her neck.

"It's great to meet you! Do you need help unpacking? Let

me know if you need anything. We're all in this together!"
She grabs a paper plate and dumps a scoop of meatballs onto
it. "I am so thirsty, my mouth is a desert. Where's the bug
juice?"

"We just got water," Lis says.

She wrinkles her nose. "They didn't have bug juice?"

"I didn't see it," Talia snaps.

"Not to worry, I'm on it—be right back," she says, jumping back out of her seat and hurrying off to the kitchen.

Lis skewers a piece of lettuce. "She's been here one day
and she acts like she owns the place."

I can already tell what the problem is. Janelle is *too* happy.
Too eager. *Too* confident. *Too* different. Girls like that either
take over the place or get eaten alive.

She comes back a few minutes later with a large jug of
pink juice. "Look what I got! This place is amazing! And
how funny is it that the kitchen staff is all Australian? Maybe
I'll go to Australia next summer. So, who wants *bug juice*?"
She overemphasizes the words, then says to me, as an aside,
"I thought it was just Kool-Aid. Camp is so awesome."

"We taught her a new term." Lis rolls her eyes. "I'm good,
thanks."

"Me too," says Talia.

Janelle smiles at me, unfazed. "Sam?"

"Sure," I say. "Water's boring."

She fills up my cup and I gulp it down in one shot. So
sweet. But so good. Kool-Aid but better. "It tastes like childhood," I say.

Janelle laughs. "It does! It really does!" And she takes another forkful of meatball.

"I'm done," Lis says, picking up her plate. "Going to say hi to Allie."

"Me too," Talia says.

They drop their plates in the nearby garbage and head to the senior section, laughing to each other the whole way.

I resolve not to be bitchy just because they're being bitches.

I turn to Janelle. "So this is your first year?"

"Yes! And I love it! I've never been to camp in my life."

"Where are you from?" I ask.

"It's a long story," she says. "Do you want the short version or the long version?"

"Um, long, I guess."

"I was born in Saskatchewan but then I moved with my mom to Calgary. Have you ever been?"

"No," I say.

"No one here has! So strange. It's the Canadian prairies."

"Got it," I say.

"I only lived there until I was six. Then I moved to Prince Edward Island. Have you heard of PEI?"

"Of course. *Anne of Green Gables*!"

"Right! That's what I told Lis and Talia, but they've never read it. I lived there for a few years, but then—you're not going to believe this part—my biological father, who I hadn't even met, tracked me down. He had another kid—Michelle, my little sister—and my sister had AML. It's what comes before leukemia. Have you ever heard of it?"

"I haven't," I say. "But it sounds horrible."

"I know, eh?" She takes a scoop of rice.

"Anyway, he wanted to test to see if I could be a donor. 'Cause siblings make the best donors. So of course, I got tested."

"Wow. Were you a match?"

She shakes her head. "No. I wasn't. But they found a match in Oklahoma! Can you believe it? And she's great now. My sister is great." Janelle's eyes are filled with happy tears.

"That's . . ." It's a lot. I don't know what to say. "Wow."

"I know." She nods. "Do you want some pudding? I'm going to get us pudding." And with that she's off.

Wow. I can't imagine going through all that. So much to deal with.

Lis and Talia slide back into their seats beside me. "She told you about her half sister, didn't she?"

I nod.

Talia shakes her head. "She tells every person she talks to. She told the kitchen staff at lunch."

"It *is* a crazy story," I say.

"Yeah. Exactly. Crazy." She makes a *loco* motion with her fingers.

Lis points to Talia. "You are so fucking lucky you got the normal one."

Talia just laughs.

* * *

The head staff make announcements after dinner, and then we all head back to our cabins.

I unzip my duffel and make my bed, and then start to organize my clothes. I know they won't stay that way, since I have never been known for my neatness. I hope I'm not expected to tidy up after the campers, because I can barely tidy up after myself.

I glance down at my phone, but have no service. It's not like I would hear from Eli anyway, since he'll be on the plane for the rest of the night. It feels strange to be so out of touch. To know that even if I want to reach him, I can't.

At eight thirty, Eric's voice comes over the loudspeaker and announces that it's time to go to Upper Field for the campfire.

"It's getting cold out," Lis tells me. "You better put on something warm. Do you have Uggs?"

"People still wear Uggs?" I ask.

"They do at camp," Talia says.

Lis bites her pinkie nail. "Wait. We need to bring towels to sit on."

"I haven't unpacked those yet," I admit. "But let me try and find one."

"You can share mine," Talia says, grabbing a dry one off the porch.

"I'll share too," Janelle says.

I catch Lis and Talia give each other a look.

The four of us meander our way back down the dirt road,

picking up other counselors as we go. The sun has already set, but it's still light out.

I meet Mike, who is wearing red earmuffs. Everyone calls him Muffs. His co-counselor is JJ, who has wildly puffy blond hair.

"Nice to meet you," I tell them.

"Actually, I remember you," Muffs says. "I was here when you were here, but a year younger. I'm Lis's age."

I freeze. But he doesn't bring up the Porny nickname, so either he doesn't remember or he's being nice.

When we get to Upper Field, I see the smoke wafting up into the sky. A bunch of the counselors are sitting in a circle on their towels around the fire.

Danish is holding a stick over the fire with a marshmallow on it. "Hi, all!" she says. "Grab some sticks! We're making s'mores!"

"OMG, amazing!" Janelle cries. "S'mores are the best! I live for marshmallows."

Lis and Talia spread out their towels and sit down side by side on the ground. Janelle runs off to look for sticks. I stand still, debating what I want to do. I am not that into s'mores, but I love a perfectly roasted marshmallow.

Gavin pulls his stick out of the flames. His marshmallow is on fire. He blows it out in a massive, showy huff. "You look confused," he says to me, pulling his charred marshmallow off his stick. "Want me to make you one?"

Eleven-year-old me would not believe that hot Gavin

was offering to make me a s'more. Every girl in my bunk had a crush on him. If I remember correctly, he went out with Zoe Buckman for two weeks, then dumped her, which made her act like even more of a bitch, and him even hotter.

"No thanks," I say. "You kind of killed yours."

"What? Killed it? Are you kidding? I did that on purpose!"

"You burnt it to a crisp on purpose?"

"Absolutely did!"

"I do not want a burnt marshmallow. But I would like to borrow your stick."

"What, you don't trust me?"

"I am very particular about my marshmallow roasting," I say.

He lets out an exaggerated sigh and hands it to me.

I reach for the bag of marshmallows and spear one on the pointy end of the stick. I gently hold it over the fire, careful not to let it burn.

I watch it slowly turn gold. Gavin is standing beside me.

"Good technique," he says. "Are you all settled in?"

"Don't distract me," I say. "I'm focusing."

"Watch out for the flying bat," he says.

"I don't believe you," I say.

"Now there's a flying cat," he says.

"Now you're just rhyming."

"I'm a poet and I didn't even know it."

I laugh and turn to look at him. He's smiling. He has a nice smile. Always did.

When I look back, my marshmallow is on fire. "Crap!" I yell, and he laughs again.

I attempt to blow it out. Finally, the fire is gone. My marshmallow is burnt, but not terribly. I wait for it to cool, pull it off, and pop it in my mouth. Mmm. Gooey.

"Good?"

"Not bad. A little charred." I smile at him.

"Sam, come sit!" Talia says.

I hand Gavin back his stick, wave, and scooch in beside her. We're only about a foot back from the fire, and the flames warm my face.

"What should we sing?" Botts asks.

Janelle is sitting beside him.

Priya is sitting on the other side of him with a guitar in her lap. She starts strumming the opening cords to something that sounds familiar.

"Oh! Good call!" Botts says. *"A long, long time ago—"* he sings.

The staff jumps in. *"I can still remember how—"*

My lips feel sticky from the marshmallow, but I sing along to "American Pie" too.

We sing "Hey There Delilah," "Wonderwall," and "Leaving on a Jet Plane." The night gets darker and the smoke gets higher and we run out of marshmallows. At around eleven, a chill sets in. Janelle is deep in conversation with one of the swim staff, but Lis says she's getting cold, so the three of us head back.

I stare up at the sparkling sky as we walk. The stars are everywhere, like white paint splattered across a black canvas.

"I missed the stars," I say. "There are no stars in the city."

"What do you mean?" Talia asks.

"Too much light pollution," I explain.

"No stars! That's the saddest thing I've ever heard," Lis says. "We have a ton of stars in Long Island."

"North Caldwell, too," says Talia.

"It is pretty sad," I say. "You don't even realize it, though, until one day, you do. It's hard to see the moon too. Not as hard, but it's always hidden by buildings."

Before going back to the bunk, I stop at the secret spot by the showers to send a quick text to Eli.

Me: Good night! Good morning! I hope you had a great flight.

I sang songs by the campfire. Miss you. Love you.

I read through my other texts too, and write back to my friends from NYU, and my mom, and my dad, and then head back to my cabin before I get eaten by a bear. Kidding. I'm sure there aren't actual bears at camp. Mosquitoes, yes; bears, no.

Hopefully.

I'm in bed when Priya sticks her head through the door sheet. "Everyone here?" I take a moment to admire her perfectly arched eyebrows.

"Aye," calls Lis, from her bed.

"Yeah," I say. "Janelle is in the bathroom. Not sure where Danish is."

"She's in the head staff office answering some parent emails," Priya says. I remember the head staff office being by the Dining Hall. It's the office above where the doctor lives. "Good night, ladies. See you in the morning."

Her head disappears and then the front door slams behind her.

I look at my phone one last time before bed. No signal. I'm glad I sent a text, though, so Eli will arrive to a message from me. I wish I could say good night from bed. At school, he lucked out with a very absent roommate, so I slept over almost every night. But whenever we weren't together, we would text each other good night, or a kissy emoji. I plug in the phone beside my bed and leave it on a shelf. Lis and Talia are getting changed and climbing into bed.

"Hey there," Janelle says, joining us. "Did someone come in?"

"It was Priya checking on us," I say. "Do they always do that or was she just worried one of us fell into the bonfire?"

"They always do it," Lis says. "One of the head staff comes around every night to make sure all the staff members are tucked into our cabins and not out gallivanting around the camp."

"Got it," I say.

"Janelle, will you turn off the lights?" Talia asks.

"Just gimme a minute," she says, and strips off her pants. She takes off her bra, and climbs into her sleeping bag in her tank top.

"You forgot to turn off the lights," Lis says.

"Oh! Right! Sorry!" She gets out of her sleeping bag and turns them off. The room is dark, but the porch light is still on.

"Outside one too?" Lis asks.

"Oops!" Janelle says. She runs outside without pants and runs back into her sleeping bag. "Done!"

"Thank you," Lis says.

"Wait, Danish is still out," I say.

Janelle laughs. "On it!" She runs back outside again.

She's a trooper, that's for sure. I pull my comforter up to my chin.

"I love this place," Janelle says, getting back inside her sleeping bag. "I'm so glad I'm here. I'm glad you guys are here too. Are you glad you're here?"

"Sure," I say, because I don't want to be a downer. The fire was nice, but my mattress is saggy, I miss my boyfriend, and I'm cold. And it's hard to fall asleep in a new place. I know in a few nights, it will feel normal, but right now it still feels strange. Right now, I can't help but wonder if I made the right choice coming here. What if I hate it and I'm not good at being a counselor?

"It's going to be an excellent summer," Janelle says happily.

"I hope so," I say.

My phone lights up. A text from Eli? I reach over to see. But it's nothing. Just a phantom light. My heart sinks. He'd still be on the plane anyway. I turn over the phone so it's facedown, close my eyes, and try to fall sleep.

"Good morning, ladies!"

I open my eyes and see that our room is bathed in light, since apparently, the white sheet hanging over our window is not the world's best shade.

Danish has the door sheet to our room pulled back. "Rise and shine! Flagpole in fifteen!"

This room could really use blinds—and doors.

My cheeks are ice cold. It's freezing. I forgot that camp mornings were cold, especially at the start of the summer. Need coffee. What time is it? I click on my phone. It's eight thirty.

No texts. No signal.

Eli is in Europe! He landed! It's after lunch there! I hate that I have no signal.

I get up and start rifling through my cubby.

Janelle groans from her bed. She's facedown, with the pillow over her head.

"Everyone just wears their pj's in the morning," Talia tells me, securing her curly hair into a bun on top of her head. "So don't feel the need to get fancy."

"I remember that," I say. "Vaguely."

"Although Janelle should probably put on some pants," she adds.

I stand up and throw a red zip-up hoodie over my shirt. I keep on my sweatpants, and find my sneakers under my bed. Just need to brush my teeth and I'm ready to go. I'm not looking my most glam, but it's just camp breakfast.

Cold toilet seat. Cold water. Cold teeth.

I head back to our room and Janelle is still under her pillow. "Hey," I tell her. "Janelle? Time for flagpole."

No response.

"Janelle?"

"Grrrst," she mumbles.

"C'mon, she'll meet us out there," Talia says, and pushes her way out of the room.

I head out onto the porch, and see that a group of counselors are already standing around the flagpole area.

"Morning, everyone!" says Botts. He's wearing jeans and a zip-up sweatshirt, and his reddish hair is wet, like he's already showered or gone for a swim. "Welcome to our first flagpole! Woot! When the kids are here, please make sure they get into their bunk lines as quickly and quietly as possible so we can start. Then we'll call up a camper to raise the flag in the morning and lower it at night. We sing the national anthem in the morning and 'Taps' at night. Today, we'll have"—he looks around at all of us and stops at me—"Rosenspan! Rosenspan's here! Do you all know Sam Rosenspan? She got here last night, but she was here with me when we were kids. Welcome back, Rosenspan! She's a counselor in the junior section. Everyone say hello to Sam!"

Oh no. Please, no.

"Hello, Sam," everyone mumbles.

"Come raise the flag, Rosenspan," Botts says.

Oh God, I'm not even wearing a bra! What the hell? Why am I not wearing a bra? It's like I'm asking for Porny to come back!

But no one says anything. No one seems to be pointing and whispering either as I shuffle to the flagpole.

Just in case, I make sure to have my back to the counselors as I tug on the rope.

I find coffee immediately. It is hot and it is free-flowing and it is located right inside the kitchen. Great coffee it's not, but it is strong enough to get the job done. Once I find the Splenda, I am good to go. Ah.

There are also slightly soggy waffles, melon, bananas, and Greek yogurts in all types of flavors. Also every table is given two different boxes of sugary cereals and a container of milk.

"I haven't had Froot Loops since I was seven," I say. "But I am looking forward to changing that immediately."

"Yesterday we got Lucky Charms," Talia says. "Those were fantastic."

"Bunk Seven has them today, if you miss them," Lis says.

"I do miss them," Talia says solemnly. "I really do. But I am too lazy to stand up. I will just hope that the box returns to us at some point in the future."

"Keep the faith," I say.

I am halfway through my bowl of sugar when Janelle marches through the doors.

"These mornings are killers," she says, standing by our table. She's not wearing a bra either. She's *also* not wearing a sweatshirt, just a thin T-shirt. Her boobs are everywhere.

"Wait till the kids get here," Lis says. "They're up at, like, six."

"Ugh," Janelle groans. "So what do we have after breakfast? Nap time?"

"Swim test," Talia says.

"Noooooo!" Lis cries.

"Yes," Talia says. "And I have worse news."

"What?"

She sighs. "It's in the lake."

"This is cruel and unusual punishment," Talia huffs as I push myself to the dock for the tenth time.

"It's like an ice box," I say.

"It really is," Marissa calls out. She's the head of swimming. I remember her from when I was a camper—she was a CIT with Danish. Maybe that's when they dated. Marissa is wearing a bright yellow one-piece and a whistle around her neck. "I'm sorry! But there's something wrong with the chlorine in the pool, and we can't get off schedule—"

"We better not be the only section taking the swim tests in the lake!" Lis cries.

"The juniors always get screwed," grumbles Talia.

"No we don't," says Danish, who is swimming beside me. "It's going to be terrific to be a counselor for juniors this year! You'll see! Terrific! Go, juniors!"

"It doesn't seem terrific," Lis says. "It seems freezing."

"I am actually finding the water refreshing!" Janelle says as she glides across the lake. Her strokes are long and fluid. Unlike the rest of us, she is an excellent swimmer.

I like swimming, I just haven't done it in a while.

"Janelle, you're done," Marissa says.

"Wahoo!" she cheers. She steps up onto the ladder and grabs her towel from the dock.

"Danish, you have two left and the rest of you slowpokes have four," Marissa says.

"I hate you right now," Talia says. "Just thought you should know."

Cold, cold, still cold. Will this ever end?

Four laps later, we plant our feet in the sandy shore.

"Way to go, ladies!" Marissa says. "You passed. You are allowed to do all boating activities and swim in the deep section of the lake!"

"What if we hadn't passed?" Talia asks. "Would we get to skip all those activities?"

"Bunk Five!" Marissa calls out. "You're next!"

"Janelle!" Lis cries. "Can you get us our towels?"

Janelle is at the top of the beach talking to the guys.

"She's a flirt, huh?" Talia mutters. "JANELLE! Janelle has too many letters. We need a nickname for her. Nelly? Belly? Ohhh, Jelly?"

I can't tell if that's an insulting nickname or not. "Let's just call her Janelle," I say.

50

"Jelly is a really good nickname," Lis says.

Janelle looks over at us.

"Jelly! Janelle! Would you bring us our towels?" Lis cries. "We're freezing!"

"Of course!" Janelle calls back and runs back down the hill to the waterfront. She picks up our three towels and brings them to the edge of the water. "Here you go, m'ladies."

"Thanks," Lis says, shivering. "Are my lips blue? They feel blue."

I thank Janelle for my towel as she hands it to me with a smile.

The guys from Bunk 5 walk down the beach with Janelle. Muffs and wild-haired JJ. JJ is tall, thin, and pale. Muffs is shorter, tanned, muscular, and still wearing his earmuffs.

"So what came first?" I ask him. "The nickname or the headwear?"

"The headwear," he says.

"And why do you wear earmuffs during the summer?" I ask. "No judgment. Just curious."

"It's kind of my thing," he admits. "I have cold ears."

"Or maybe you have really nasty ears," Lis says. "And you just don't want to show anyone."

"That is absolutely a possibility," he says. "I am not a fan of Q-tips. I'm going to take the earmuffs off to swim, though. So you can check them out." He turns to me. "So why did you stop coming?"

"Huh? You mean to camp?"

"Yeah."

"I just . . ."

"Oh, there was that horrible girl in your bunk! Zoe Buckman!" JJ says. "Was it because of her?

I nod. "Sort of."

"Bennett is a senior," Muffs says.

"Who's Bennett?" I ask.

"Her brother," he says.

"Her brother still goes here?" I ask. Ugh. Not that I'd recognize her brother. Or he'd recognize me. And anyway, he would be too young to have been here eight years ago.

"My cousin was in your bunk," Muffs says. "Kara Fortnoy?"

"No way!" I say. "I remember her."

"She was a bitch too," he says.

"Nah," I lie. She had been the one to notice my blood-stained sweatpants on my overnight. Then she told her BFF Zoe Buckman.

"She totally was. It's okay. She still is. So why'd you come back? Because they're gone?"

"I just missed the camp mac and cheese," I say.

He laughs.

"And my boyfriend was going away and Danish offered me the job on the train. I'm studying to be a teacher, so it all worked out."

"Does that mean you're going to take being a counselor, like, super seriously?" Lis asks.

"Well, I want to do a good job," I say. "Doesn't everyone?"

"Maybe you can do a great job for both of us," Talia says, and everyone laughs.

I think she's kidding?

"So are you still with the guy?" Muffs asks.

"Of course," I say. "We didn't break up because he went away."

He laughs. "Good luck with that. Relationships never last at camp."

"What a terrible thing to say," Lis says, swatting him on the arm. "Relationships last."

"No they don't," JJ says. "Name one."

"Trevor had a girlfriend last year!"

"He did?"

"He totally did."

"Didn't he hook up with the office girl?"

"The druggie?"

"No!"

"Yes!"

"I don't think so."

"Look—" I interrupt, feeling a squeezing in my chest. "My relationship is going to last. We've been together a long time. Almost a year. And he's the best. A summer apart is not going to make a difference."

Everyone's quiet. "If you say so," Muffs says. He readjusts his earmuffs.

"Don't be an ass," Lis says to him.

"Where did he go, anyway?" Muffs asks. "Your boyfriend who's the best."

I laugh. I can't help it. "Europe."

"No way," Muffs says. "Gavin's girlfriend is in Europe too."

We all turn to the water, where Gavin is on a sailboat.

"Is she backpacking too?" I ask.

"I have no idea," Muffs says.

"I'm not the only one at camp with a significant other, then, huh?"

"Nope."

"There you go."

"You guys can go hunt for Wi-Fi together," Talia says.

It might be nice to have a friend in loneliness.

After swimming, we meet Dr. Harris back in the Dining Hall. She wears her blond hair in a tight bun and shows us how to use an EpiPen.

We practice jabbing each other in the thigh.

Post a lunch of make-your-own tuna sandwiches, I sneak over to the cell signal spot to try to call Eli. I know I won't be able to do this when the kids are here, since they aren't supposed to see us on our phones, but today is fair game. A bunch of texts from him pour in, but I dial right away. My heart starts to thump as I wait for him to answer.

He answers on the first ring. "Hi!" he exclaims.

"You answered!"

"I did!"

"Hi!" I can't stop smiling. "How's Rome?"

"Hot."

"What time is it there? Where are you? Are you with your cousin?"

"It's eight p.m. here," he says. "And I'm at the hostel. And his plane lands at nine, so I'll see him soon."

I wish I had met Yosef. I have no idea what he's like. Or what he's going to want to do. "Are you exhausted?" I ask.

"I just woke up."

"Did I wake you?"

"Maybe."

"Oh, I'm sorry."

"No, no, no, it's good you did. I need to shower and I slept for five hours anyway, which is way too long. How's camp?"

"Good. Better than the last time I was here, at least."

"No one called you any sexy names?" he says with a laugh.

"It wasn't sexy," I say quickly.

"I'm kidding," he says. "I know how much that name bothered you."

I've told him about being called Porny. It was one of the reasons I waited seven months before sleeping with him. I felt so much shame about my body, about having sex, about being "Porny."

Eli was so patient, too. He never pressured me, even though he had slept with his high school girlfriend regularly.

He waited until I was ready. Until one Thursday night, when we were just lying in his bed, my head on his NYU T-shirt, talking about where to go that night, when I told him I wanted to.

He ran to the pharmacy so fast, I told him he should try out for track.

I don't know what changed in that moment. I just knew that I felt safe with him. And that I wanted to do it.

"So no one's being a jerk?" he says now.

"No," I say. "We've mostly been settling in. My co-counselor was mad that I was late, though."

"But you were spending time with me," he says. "And it's only the first few days."

"I guess," I say. "She had to unpack the kids without me."

"Just bring her some cupcakes," he says. "She'll forgive you."

"I'm not sure where I would find cupcakes," I say. "So what's the hostel like?"

"It's like the dorms, but grungier."

"Sounds . . . gross?"

"Yeah. It's fine. It was cheap at least."

"What did you do today?"

"Took the train from the airport. Dropped my bag off. Wandered around in the heat. Took an epic nap." He yawns in my ear.

"How was the flight?"

"Fine. Watched a movie and passed out."

We stay on the phone, trading stories, until Eric comes over the loudspeaker.

"Attention, all staff. Attention, all staff. It is now the end of Rest Hour. Please go . . . um . . . unpack."

"What was that?" Eli asks.

"Announcement. I have to go."

"I should shower anyway. When will we talk next?"

"I'll text you tonight, and will call around this time tomorrow? Good?"

"Yup. Not sure where I'll be, but I'll have my phone on me and I spent extra to have the best possible international plan."

"Okay. Good. I miss you. Have fun with Yosef. But not too much fun," I add.

He laughs.

"Have fun with the EpiPens," he says. "But not too much fun."

I head back to the cabin and unpack the last kid.

Their clothes are little and adorable. The mini Converse are my favorite.

After dinner with Talia and Lis—Janelle is MIA—I change into my bathrobe, put on my flip-flops, grab a towel and my soap bucket, and head to the showers.

I climb the steps very, very carefully.

The shower room is pretty much how I remember it. It's a wooden cabin aboveground. There's a bathroom stall in the

57

front, and then ten shower stalls in total, five on either side. Each stall has a yellow shower curtain, and I yank mine open.

I let the hot water blast over me. At least there's hot water in here. I don't think I could handle six weeks of cold showers.

It feels good to have a minute alone. I wonder what Eli's doing.

"Sam?" I hear Talia say. "You here? You almost done?"

I jump. Guess I'm not alone.

"Five minutes!" I say. "You should go ahead!" I would prefer to walk down by myself this first time.

"We'll wait for you!" Lis shouts back.

Crap. I hurry up and turn off the water. I wrap myself in my towel, dry off, then wrap it around my head and slip into my bathrobe.

I grab my stuff, and carefully—very carefully—walk down the stairs.

"You okay?" Lis asks me. "You're walking like a weirdo."

"I . . . I don't want to trip."

"You guys, when I was a camper there was this one girl who fell and then . . ." She stops mid-step. "OMG. Was that you? That was *you*, wasn't it? You're Porny!"

Of course the name is coming out just as I'm standing on the stairs. It's like my childhood nightmares are coming true, and I'm powerless to stop them.

"Porny?" Talia asks.

Shit. What happens now?

"I tripped on the stairs," I say. "I flashed everyone."

"And Zoe Buckman took it from there," Lis finishes for me.

"She did," I say. "Could we not spread my former nickname around camp? It wasn't my favorite."

"No kidding," Talia says. "Don't worry, we won't tell. *As long as you're nice to us.*"

"That was super creepy," I say.

"I was joking!" she cries.

I blink. Hmm, why do I only kind of believe her?

"I need something that rhymes with wet your bed," Muffs, still wearing his earmuffs, says.

"No bed-wetting jokes, please," Danish says.

We're back in the Dining Hall, and we're divided by cabin. We are each supposed to rewrite a verse from the song "A Whole New World" from *Aladdin* to make the junior section song. Right beside us is Gavin and Muff's table. I'm still annoyed by Muff's comment at the lake. I know he's wrong, obviously, but still. It's possible to stay in a relationship if you're at camp. Of course it is.

"You ready, Bunk Six?" she asks.

Lis whoops. So far she hasn't mentioned my old nickname, thank goodness. Neither has Talia.

We have the first verse. I feel nervous.

We all stand up. Janelle, our transcriber, holds the paper in front of us and we sing.

"We can show you Blue Springs
The lake, your bunk, a can-oooooe.
C'mon, juniors, it's time for you to
Have the best of times."

Everyone cheers.

Not a Grammy winner, but it will hopefully do?

"Wahoo!" Janelle cries.

When the song is over, Danish instructs us to head over to the CL—the Counselors' Lounge—to watch a movie.

"What's the movie?" Lis asks.

"*Wet Hot American Summer,*" Danish tells us.

"Fitting," Muffs says.

We all file down out the back door and climb down the stairs. It's dark out already, and there's a chill in the air, so I zip up my fleece sweatshirt.

"Maybe I'll stop at the office first," I say. "For Wi-Fi."

"I'll show you where to go," Gavin says.

"Thanks," I say.

We all walk together past the lake and up the hill. Talia starts humming the tune to "A Whole New World."

"Oh no, you don't," JJ says.

"*No one will tell us no, or where to go!*"

"*Or say we're only dreaming,*" Lis finishes.

"Maybe we should ask to watch *Aladdin* instead," Muffs says.

"Yes!" Lis says. "We totally should."

"I know all the words to 'Let It Go,'" Janelle says. "My

half sister, Michelle, is a big *Frozen* fan." She turns to Muffs. "Did I tell you about my half sister?"

We come to a fork in the road.

"We go this way," Gavin tells me.

"See you guys soon," I tell the girls.

Gavin and I continue up the hill.

"Texting your girlfriend?" I ask him.

"I am," he says. "How did you know I had a girlfriend? It's not written on my forehead, is it?"

"It totally is," I say. "In big black letters. I think Muffs did it while you were sleeping."

"That wouldn't surprise me in the slightest," he says. "He has already written his name on every surface of the cabin."

"Lis too! I know about your girlfriend because Muffs gave me a hard time at the beach. About having a boyfriend. Oh, wait—he said they're together! Well, not *really* together, but your girlfriend is in Europe too."

"Yep. Both of our significant others are off in Europe, while here we are, together, walking in the moonlight." Gavin smiles. He looks like the bad-but-lovable character in a TV show. He's definitely the hottest guy at camp.

"Is your guy in Paris?" he asks.

"Not Paris," I say. "Or I should say, not just Paris. He's backpacking. Currently in Rome. What's your girlfriend doing in Paris?"

"She's working at an art gallery."

"Wow. Impressive."

"Yeah. She's living there for the summer."

"You didn't want to go too?"

"I mean, yeah, sure, I would have gone to Paris. I've never been to Europe. But I've been coming here forever. And I don't think her parents would have loved it if I'd crashed at her place the whole summer."

"Got it," I say.

"What about you? How come you ended up back here instead of backpacking through Europe?"

"I wasn't invited," I say. "He went with his cousin. I couldn't have afforded it anyway. I already have a ton of debt from school."

"Well, they're in Europe, and we're not. Big deal. Who needs macarons when you have mac and cheese?"

I laugh. "Exactly. I love camp mac and cheese."

"Me too. You missed it yesterday, but it was super cheesy with just the right amount of bread crumbs. Here we are."

We are suddenly standing outside the office.

Oh well. I guess that's the end of our conversation. Too bad. Maybe we'll get to walk back together? Gavin's just so nice to look at . . .

I shake my thought off. Ha! Maybe my nickname should be Horny instead of Porny.

Anyway, calling Eli. That's why I'm here.

"So where's the Wi-Fi?" I ask.

"We have to go inside," he says.

We climb up the three stairs and open the door.

Eric the office guy is sprawled across the gray couch eating raisins. Very, verrrrrrry slowly.

Oh, he is definitely stoned.

I turn to see if Gavin is seeing this, but he's already typing on his phone.

"Network is CampBlueSprings?" I ask.

"It's . . . um . . . um . . ." It takes Eric a few seconds, but he eventually shares the password.

I wait for my texts to download.

One from Emily asking if I made it to camp.

One from my mom asking if I'm having fun.

Finally one from Eli:

Hi! Going to bed. Yosef made it. We went to a bar. Italian drinks are strong. Love you. Good night, Beautiful.

Oh wow, I miss him!

I flip over to his Instagram account to see if he posted anything.

Nothing. I write back:

Hey babe! I misssssssssssss you. This time difference sucks. Wish you were awake! Wish you were here! Wish we were naked in your bed! Ignore that, I don't want to get you all hot and bothered on the other side of the world.

I look over to see if Gavin is still writing. But he's looking at me. "Wanna walk back to the CL?" he asks.

"Sure," I say. "Give me one sec."

He nods.

I look back down at my phone and type:

I love you. Have fun!

I slip my phone back into my sweater pocket. "Done," I say. I turn to Eric. He is still eating slowly. "Enjoy the raisins."

Gavin snort-laughs.

"How stoned was he?" Gavin asks as we head back to the CL. "On a scale of one to ten?"

"Eleven," I say. "Maybe twelve."

"I'm not into raisins, personally," he says. "Grapes, yes. Raisins, no."

"Not even if they're covered in chocolate?"

"That's a different situation entirely."

I laugh and then we're both quiet for a few steps.

"So how long have you and your girlfriend been together?" I ask.

"Since February," he says. "Not that long."

"You go to school together?"

"Yeah. University of Maryland," he says. "You?"

"NYU."

"Kat is from New York," he says. "She grew up in the city."

"Where?"

"Upper East Side."

"I live downtown," I say. I want him to know that I'm a downtown kind of girl, aka, fun and cool. Upper East Side girls are prim and proper. Or so the TV shows tell me.

The CL is right in front of us.

"I'm kind of excited to go in," I admit.

"To see the movie?"

"No, I've seen the movie. To go into the CL! I was a camper here, but we were never allowed inside because it was the—"

"Counselors' Lounge."

"Right. So what happens in there exactly?"

"Oh, it's magical."

"It is, isn't it?"

"There are strobe lights. And trampolines. And secret passageways."

"I knew there'd be secret passageways! Do they go right to the Dining Hall?"

"Right to the kitchen. To the freezer where all the ice cream is."

"I had a feeling."

He smiles at me. "Should we go in?"

"We should."

"I'm afraid you might be disappointed."

"Story of my life," I say, and he opens the door for me.

The lights are off and the movie is already on. There are no disco balls or trampolines. Probably no secret passageways, although I can't say for sure. The paneling on the wall does look a little loose. It's basically just a large room with a wood floor, a few rugs, and old couches. There's a big TV against the far wall. Counselors are lying all over the place. There are two big bowls of popcorn in the back of the room and everyone has small cups of it.

Talia waves to me and points to an empty spot next to her.

"Have fun," Gavin says to me. He opens the door.

"You're not staying?" I ask.

"Nah. I've seen this." He pushes the door and disappears. Hmm. Mysterious. I wonder where he's going. I snake my way through the spread-out counselors and find my spot between Talia and Lis.

It's after midnight, and my face is washed and I'm in my pajamas and tucked into my covers. So are Lis and Talia. Janelle is in the cubby room. Our front door opens and there's a knock next to the curtain. "Everyone decent?" It's Botts's voice.

"Yes!" I say. "Come in!"

Botts opens the curtain. He's wearing a fleece sweater zipped up over his chin. He has a walkie-talkie clipped to his belt, and he's holding a big black flashlight.

He plops down on the corner of my bed.

"So how're you holding up, Rosenspan?" he asks.

"All good," I say. "Were you in the CL?"

"No, I had some admin stuff to do. But tell me about you. Are you glad you came back?"

"So far," I say. "It's fun to see the magic behind the curtain. I didn't realize how much work went into everything when I was a camper."

"Wait until the kids get here," he says.

"Right," I say. It's weird, because it feels like so much has already happened while the kids *aren't* here. It's like maybe, when you're a counselor, the kids aren't the only important part?

Lis sits beside him. "You didn't tell me she was Porny!"

Ugh. Really?

"I have no idea what you're talking about," he says with a shrug.

Aw, what a sweetie.

"How's Janelle doing?" Botts motions his chin toward Janelle's sleeping bag.

"She's nice," I say. "How did she end up here? Are there always international staff members? Not that Canada is *that* international."

"A lot of camps have an exchange program with international students who want the experience. Plus, it's a job. And they get to come to America. Everyone wins."

"Not everyone wins," Lis says. "I don't think Jelly uses deodorant."

My back stiffens. "She doesn't smell. And we're not calling her Jelly." I turn back to Botts. "What do you do on rounds exactly? Chitchat with everyone?"

"I check on everyone, but I only stop and chat with killer softball players I haven't seen in eight years."

"What do you do if someone is missing?" I ask.

"I find them," he says. "But no one's missing now, since they know I'm coming around. People sneak out later."

"Really?" I ask. "Where do they go?"

"To hook up," Lis says.

"Where?" I ask. "There's not much privacy in these rooms."

"That never stops anyone," Botts says. "When we were

CITs, Dee literally fell out of Baker's top bunk with her bra half-on."

"Nip!" Lis cries out. "They all called her that."

"I never called her that," Botts says.

"Do we get a CIT?" I ask, changing the subject.

"No," he says. "We don't have enough for everyone. And we can't work them too hard because they pay to be here. And they're barely in camp. They go on a lot of trips."

"Do we go on any trips?" I ask.

"Just a canoe trip to New Beach."

Ugh. New Beach.

The worst day ever.

New Beach is actually part of camp property, but it's across the lake, so you can take a boat there and make it seem like you're actually going somewhere far away. Thank goodness it *is* actually in camp, because after Kara noticed that I had bled all over my sweatpants, and told Zoe, and all the girls started shrieking, "Porny is disgusting!" "Porny smells!" "Porny's gross!" like a scene out of *Carrie*, my counselor Jennifer took me back to camp to shower, get a pad, and change clothes. We had to return to sleep at New Beach, though, and of course the rest of the girls were still up to whisper insults at me as the tent sagged above my head.

I couldn't do any water sports for the rest of the week. Jen offered to teach me how to use a tampon but I was too terrified.

I can do without going back to New Beach. Ever.

Janelle pushes the curtain open. "We have company!"

Botts gives her a high five. "Janelle! I was about to send out a search party for you."

"Don't be silly, I was just taking my time."

"I was telling them about your upcoming trip to New Beach," he says.

Her eyes widen in delight. "Nude Beach?"

Lis snorts. "No! New Beach! New!"

She laughs. "Nude Beach sounds more fun."

"It really does," Botts says. He stands up. "All right, ladies, tomorrow is a big day. The kids arrive at noon. I'll let you get some sleep."

He closes the door gently on his way out.

Lis turns to me. "So, did you and Botts stay in touch?"

"No, not at all," I say. "But we were friends when I was here. He's a nice guy."

She sighs. "He is, right?"

Talia laughs. "Lis has had a crush on him forever!"

"Ooooooh," squeals Janelle.

Lis turns bright red. "I have not!"

"Have so!" Talia says. "Since you were like a junior, right?"

"Okay, fine," she says, biting her thumbnail. "Maybe a tiny crush."

"You guys would be cute together," I say. "Do you want me to put out some feelers?" If I help her with Botts, maybe she'll bury the Porny nickname somewhere deep.

"Okay. But without making me look desperate. Because I'm not. I'm just . . . interested. Maybe."

"That's the understatement of the year," Talia says. "Although there's always Muffs . . ."

"I'm not interested in that guy and his kind-of-sexual nickname and his weird earmuffs!" Lis says.

"Muffs is in love with her," Talia tells me.

"He is not," she says. "Besides, he's like my brother! We go to—went to—high school together!"

"I have my eye on someone too," Janelle says, waggling her eyebrows. "Actually two someones."

"Ooh, tell us," I say, turning back to her.

"Well, JJ is adorable," she says. "And he looks good in a bathing suit."

Lis bursts out laughing. "JJ is gay," she says. "He came out when we were CITs. Sorry to burst your bubble."

"Dang," she says. "Okay, then. The hot tennis teacher. He's smokin'. Is he straight?"

"I believe so. But did you really just use the word *smokin'*?" Lis asks.

"I did." She makes a sizzling sound. "What's his story?"

"Who's the tennis teacher?" I ask.

"Benji Rhee," Lis says. "He's tall and has amazing shoulders and was wearing a Red Sox hat in the CL. He *is* smokin'. And I think he's the only other Korean American at camp. But his you-know-what is probably smokin' too because he hooks up with everyone."

"Oh, I noticed him," I say. "He is hot."

"And a player," Janelle says. "I like players!"

"Not me," Lis says.

"What's your type then?" Janelle asks her.

"I like nice guys. Although my bubbe would prefer if I marry a nice Jewish guy."

"What's a bubbe?" Janelle asks.

"Jewish grandmother," she explains. "I'm adopted. In case you're wondering."

"Cool," she says and turns to Talia. "What about you? Interested in anyone?"

"No," she says quickly.

"She never likes anyone," Lis says. "Something's wrong with her."

"Nothing is wrong with me! I come to camp to relax, not to hook up with guys."

Janelle giggles. "I came completely to hook up with guys!"

We all laugh.

"What about you, Sam?"

"I guess to make some money, and be around kids," I say.

And to put my Porny days behind me once and for all.

WEEK 1 SCHEDULE—BUNK 6A

	SUNDAY	MONDAY	TUESDAY	WEDNESDAY	THURSDAY	FRIDAY	SATURDAY
PERIOD 1 10:00–10:45		DANCE	WRESTLING	SI	NEWCOMB	DRAMA	BASKETBALL
PERIOD 2 10:45–11:30		CANOEING	SAILING	DANCE	BASKETBALL	SI	SAILING
PERIOD 3 11:30–12:15	KIDS ARRIVE	BASKETBALL	TENNIS	GYMNASTICS	SI	ARCHERY	SI
12:15–12:30	LUNCH WASHUP	LUNCH WASHUP	LUNCH WASHUP	LUNCH WASHUP	LUNCH WASHUP	LUNCH WASHUP	LUNCH WASHUP
12:30–1:00	LUNCH	LUNCH	LUNCH	LUNCH	LUNCH	LUNCH	LUNCH
1:00–2:00	REST HOUR	REST HOUR	REST HOUR	REST HOUR	REST HOUR	REST HOUR	REST HOUR
PERIOD 4 2:00–2:45	SWIM TESTS	SOCCER	DRAMA	BAKING	KAYAKING	ART	NEWCOMB
2:45–3:15	MILK & COOKIES	MILK & COOKIES	MILK & COOKIES	MILK & COOKIES	MILK & COOKIES	MILK & COOKIES	MILK & COOKIES
PERIOD 5 3:15–4:00	SOFTBALL	SI	ARCHERY	TENNIS	SOCCER	WATERSKI	ARCHERY
PERIOD 6 4:00–4:45	GYMNASTICS	A&C	GS	GS	GS	GS	GS

72

Week 1

"Here they come!" Botts yells. "Get ready!"

We are waiting on the side of the dirt road for the arrivals.

Indeed, here they come. At least a dozen gray buses, the fancy kind, are all headed toward us. The first one stops just in front of the camp sign, and the others all line up behind it. The buses kick dust up everywhere and I shield my eyes, wishing I had my sunglasses on.

The doors open and my heart starts to race. I can do this. I can do this!

I hope I can do this.

"Sam! Talia!" Danish calls from the door to one of the buses. "Come get your campers!"

Oh, wow. Here we go. For real. I hurry up to the bus and stand by the door.

She sends our campers out one by one.

"Fancy, meet Sam and Talia!"

Fancy? Oh, right! Fancy! With the Dolce and Gabbana T-shirts. The one whose mom my mom saw at the Fresh Market.

"Hi, Fancy!" Talia says.

"Hi, Francie!" I say.

"It's *Fancy*," she says to me.

Okay, then.

Fancy is a small redhead covered in freckles. She is wearing a Chanel backpack that is bigger than she is. She has designer sunglasses perched on her head.

She seems to live up to her nickname.

"Shira, meet Sam and Talia!"

"Hi, Shira!" we chant.

Shira steps off the bus. She's tall, thin, pale, and darkhaired. She is missing two of her front teeth. Her hair is in two buns, Princess Leia style.

"Shira! Like She-Ra, Princess of Power! Are *you* the princess of power?" I ask.

She gives me a fake, toothless smile. "All the teachers at school use that joke."

Whoops. But yay—I am making the same joke as the teachers! I am clearly a born educator.

"Emma F., meet Sam and Talia!"

Emma F. is almost as tall as Shira. She's holding a fuzzy stuffed lion and is dressed all in polka dots. She's African American and is wearing her hair in two braids with pink tips.

"Hi, Emma F.!" we chant.

"Emma C., meet Sam and Talia!"

Other Emma steps off the bus. She has curly blondish hair and light skin that is already a little sunburned. She looks like an athlete. She's wearing a Mets baseball hat, a Mets T-shirt, and gray sweatpants. A baseball lover!

"Hi, Emma!" we chant.

"Let's go, Mets!" I add.

"Lily, meet Sam and Talia!"

Lily steps off the bus. A cloud of big, bouncy curly brown hair frames her face, even though she's Asian. She's wearing a pink leotard and purple cartwheel shorts.

"Hi, Lily!"

"And the final girl in Bunk Six A is Prague!"

Ah, Prague.

Prague looks exactly like a mini Kim Kardashian, with jet-black hair that she clearly got blown out. She's wearing a rhinestone headband, jeggings, two layered tops, and heart-shaped sunglasses. She flips her hair. Her nails are painted lavender and covered in rhinestone decals.

Oh, brother. She's fancier than Fancy!

She takes one step off the bus and trips, falling on her hands.

We all freeze.

"Omigosh, are you okay?" I ask, bending down. Danish, Talia, and I crowd around her.

Her sunglasses fall off, and her big brown eyes fill with tears. "Ouchie," she says.

I help her up. Her arms are shaking.

"Way to make an entrance," Talia says.

Prague laughs but then sobs.

"Oh, sweetie, I'm sorry." I hand her back her sunglasses.

"I'm okay," she says. "Really. That was just. Ugh. So embarrassing. Like, seriously." She brushes off her hands and knees and links her arm through mine.

"You sure you're not hurt?"

She nods.

I look at the rest of the girls. All six of them are staring at me, waiting for instructions. I'm not sure what to do. I look at Talia. She's done this before, right? "Do we go back to the bunk?" I ask.

"Sure," Talia says. "Let's all go back to the bunk!"

"To the bunk," I say. "Bunk Six A! You're going to love it. I was in the same bunk when I was a kid."

"When's lunch?" Fancy asks. "I'm hungry." Her voice is unexpectedly low and gravelly, like a smoker's. It almost makes me laugh.

"Me too!" says Shira.

"Lunch is in thirty minutes," I say. "We're just going to drop your backpacks off at the bunk, and then head to the Dining Hall."

Fancy wrinkles her nose. "But I'm *hungry.* Can we get a snack?"

"I . . . I don't know," I say. Do we make the call about whether or not they get snacks? I think we do.

"I have cupcakes," Lily says. "You can have one." She puts down her backpack and starts searching through it.

Cupcakes! I think about Eli. I miss Eli.

"Let's just do this back at the bunk," I say, flustered. Other kids are getting off the buses and we're kind of in the way.

"I have chips," says Emma F. "Barbecue chips! Do you like barbecue chips? They're my favorite!"

"I have salt and vinegar chips!"

"Me too!" says Shira.

"I have candy!" says another one. "So much candy!"

"I have cookies *and* candy," Prague says. "Also brownies."

How much food did these kids bring? "Let's just go to the bunk," I repeat. I steal a glance at Talia.

"Come on, girls. Honk!" Talia says. "You're getting in everyone's way!"

I motion to the girls and start walking back over the bridge.

"Honk, honk!" I cheer. "Let's move 'em out!"

Yikes. Stressed already. I wonder if I can have a brownie.

As soon as we get to the bunk, it's a whirlwind. The girls all squeal as they find their made-up beds and reunite with their belongings. They hug their pillows and stuffed animals and kiss their parents' pictures on the walls.

Aw. They're cute. It's easy to forget how young they really are.

"Let's have a junk party!" Fancy cries, taking out a piece of licorice.

Now? Oh no.

"Guys?" I say. "We're going to have lunch really soon. Maybe we shouldn't have candy right now?"

"I have candy necklaces," Lily says, talking right over me and jumping on her bed like it's a trampoline. "One for each of us."

"That is so adorable," Prague says. "We'll all match!"

"Guys?" I try again. "Lunch is in ten minutes. No candy now, okay?"

None of them listen to me. None of them even look at me. It's like I'm not here. They are pooling their junk in the middle of the floor.

Where is Talia?

Shira has an entire brownie in her mouth. And I can see it all between her missing two front teeth.

"I have M&M's," Fancy yells. She takes out the M&M's. A yellow bag.

The peanut kind.

"STOP IT RIGHT NOW," I yell.

All their heads swirl to me.

"No peanuts," I say, taking my voice down a notch. "You guys are not allowed to have peanut M&M's." I walk over to Fancy and take the M&M's out of her hand. "Sorry."

Fancy glares at me. "But . . . but . . . no one in our bunk has a peanut allergy."

"You're right that nobody in the bunk has a peanut

allergy," I say. "But other kids in the camp do and we're not taking any chances."

"That's so unfair," she whines. "My parents paid for these."

"Talia?" I call out. "Where are you? Help!"

"Just changing!" I hear. "There in a sec!"

"How do you know that no kids in the bunk have a peanut allergy?" I ask.

"My mom called and asked," she says, her voice extra low and gravelly. "*Obviously.* I'm not *psychic.*"

Psychic, no; a tiny jerk, yes.

Do not call the children tiny jerks. Do not call the children tiny jerks. "Listen, everyone, it's almost lunch," I say, trying to remain calm. "We're leaving here in five minutes. There'll be lots of food there."

"But I'm hungry now," Lily says.

"Can we have the candy after?" Shira asks.

I hear Eric's muffled announcement in the distance. "Attention, all counselors. I mean, attention, all counselors and . . . and, uh, campers. Yeah. Campers. Attention, all campers and counselors. It is now time for lunch. Please go . . . please *proceed* to the kitchen. I mean Rec Hall. Dining Hall! Yes, Dining Hall. Thank you."

"It's a good thing you're hungry, then," I say. "Because it's lunch! Hooray! Come on, kids, let's go eat."

"But what about the candy? We can eat it afterward?" Emma F. asks.

"Do we have to wash our hands?" Emma C. asks.

"Yes, you have to wash your hands," I say. "It's lunch washup. So you should absolutely wash your hands."

"I don't want to wash my hands," Fancy says.

"So don't," I snap. "Eat your lunch with grimy bus hands. Your call." *Yikes.* The kids have been here an hour and I'm already losing it. I take a deep breath. I force a smile. I cannot lose it. I want to be good at this. I *need* to be good at this. "Everyone meet on the porch in three minutes, 'kay?"

"I'm not washing my hands," I hear Fancy say as I turn around.

"You can use my sanitizer," Talia says, stepping out of our counselors' room. "It smells like cinnamon."

I keep walking, all the way to the porch. And then I realize I forgot to wash my own hands.

Lunch is soggy grilled cheese and cold french fries.

Not that I have time to eat. I am too busy getting food, finding ketchup, pouring bug juice, and cleaning up bug juice.

Shira spills it all over the table when she tries to pour herself a cup. Then she starts to cry. Which is how I become the Designated Pourer.

As for the meal itself, the kids seem to be divided into two groups. Half of them help themselves to two sandwiches, multiple plates of fries, and piles of ketchup, as though they've never seen food before, while the other half barely eat.

"Do you want something from the salad bar instead?" I ask.

Shira shakes her head. "I'm not hungry."

Maybe she shouldn't have eaten that entire brownie. At least she's not crying anymore.

Fancy goes to take a look at said salad bar and comes back with a scoop of tuna that she then just moves around her plate.

Awesome. I lean over to Talia. "What are we supposed to do? Force-feed them?"

"I guess they'll eat when they're hungry," she says, shrugging. She leans closer to me. "Do you want to call it?"

"Call what?" I ask.

"Freeze," she whispers, and waggles her eyebrows.

I had forgotten all about freeze. Oh, how I hate-loved freeze as a camper. "Okay," I say. "I'll call it. One. Two. EVERYONE FREEZE!"

Prague giggles and freezes. Fancy and Emma C. freeze too.

"Huh?" says Lily.

"You all have to freeze right now," I say. "First one to move cleans up the table!"

"You move, you stack!" Talia says.

They are all frozen. Prague has her cup up to her mouth. Some of them are holding up forks. Some of them are mid-smile. Some are mid-chew. Shira was about to stand up. She's kind of crouching there. She does not look steady. She does not look steady at all.

And she moves.

"Shira's gone!" I call out.

Shira bursts into tears.

"Crybaby," Fancy says.

"Hey!" I say. "Don't call people names."

I promise Shira that the bright side of stacking one meal is that it means she does not have to stack the next one. When the rest of the kids freeze, she can continue eating, she can try to make them laugh, she can pick her nose, she can do whatever she wants.

But she does not stop crying.

"Is everything okay?" Danish asks, walking up just as the snot drips down Shira's nose.

"Noooooo," she cries.

"She has to stack," I explain. "I called freeze."

"Maybe we shouldn't call freeze at the very first meal," Danish says.

Right. Oops. "No freeze. Forget freeze!" I tell the girls. "Counselors stack!"

"I'm not stacking," Talia grumbles.

"I'll stack," I say, but Danish has already moved on to the next table.

I am really nailing it.

Rest Hour: We help the girls get settled.

Swim Tests: Someone pees in the pool. We don't know who, but we know there are warm spots. So. Someones, plural, peed in the pool. Fantastic.

Milk and Cookies: Twice a day we get snacks in the dining

hall. This is called Milk and Cookies even though today they only serve fruit, and no cookies. But I get to see Gavin in a bathing suit and his abs are . . . not terrible to look at.

Softball: Hurrah, something I'm actually good at! And so is Emma C.! She sends the ball flying through camp! "Way to go, Slugger!" I cry out.

"Can that be my nickname?" she asks.

Maybe nicknames are okay if they're good nicknames? "Okay, if that's what you want us to call you!"

"Yes, please!"

"Sure thing, Slugger!"

"Then I get to be Emma!" Emma F. calls out. "No more F! Actually, never mind. I want to be Em. Can I be Em?"

"Why not," I say.

Gymnastics: Lily is a superstar. Like Olympic-level. Okay, maybe not Olympic-level but really, really great. I try to walk on the balance beam but fall off. Talia does a pretty good headstand.

Finally, we have Dinner Washup.

Time for a fifty-five-minute break. I am exhausted. I lie on my bed. My campers are being kind of quiet, which I'm guessing means they are eating candy.

When the fifty-five minutes are done, we gather the kids on the porch and head to the flagpole together.

"Get the kids in bunk lines!" Josh, the head counselor, hollers from beside the flagpole, where all the head staff is huddled.

"Come on, girls, bunk lines!" I call out.

"Bunk lines," Talia repeats, but with less gusto. She is not that animated a counselor, I think.

I see that Gavin, JJ, and Muffs already have their kids lined up in a row, so I try to get my kids to do the same. But they keep talking to each other and hopping around like little bunnies.

Yup, they were definitely sneaking candy.

It takes a good ten minutes, but finally the whole camp is here and the kids are lined up. Josh calls up Bennett Buckman to lower the flag because it's his twelfth birthday.

Yes. *Bennett Buckman.*

He has the same perfect nose and dark hair as his sister.

I try not to give him the evil eye.

"Thank you," Josh says as "Taps" ends. "Now walk— don't run—to the Dining Hall!"

The kids all run.

Lis, Talia, Janelle, Muffs, wild-haired JJ, Gavin, and I all trail behind.

"Juniors are exhausting," Muffs says.

"They so are," Talia says. "I'm going to nap again at Free Play."

"I was going to hit some tennis balls," JJ says. "Anyone want to come?"

"I do!" Janelle squeals. "Hello, Smokin' Hot Benji!"

"Don't tell me he's straight," JJ says.

"Don't tell me he's not," she says.

"I'll come and be the line judge," Muffs says. "Lis? Gav?"

"Sure," Gavin says.

"I really need to shower," Lis says.

"I really need a nap," Talia says.

"I really need Wi-Fi," I say. Which actually means, I really need to text Eli. My cell phone is hidden in my sweatshirt pocket and I can't wait to hear how his trip is going.

Immediately after yummy Chinese food for dinner, it's Free Play.

I sprint over to the office.

I missed two calls and about ten texts from Eli.

What's up?

I miss you.

Did you lose your phone?

Oops. I was supposed to call him hours ago.

I dial his number.

He answers on the first ring. "Heyyyyyyyy," he says.

"Hi! Am I waking you?"

"Yes," he says. "But it's okay. I want to hear your voice. What happened? You said you would call five hours ago."

"Sorry," I say. "I couldn't get away."

"Oh," he says. "Busy there, huh?"

"So busy."

"Having fun?"

"Kind of?" I say. "I'm exhausted."

"So tell me what you're doing."

"Running after the kids, mostly."

"Are they spoiled brats?"

"What? No! I mean, Prague spends her Augusts summering in the Hamptons. Yes, she used summer as a verb. But Emma C. is amazing at softball—I nicknamed her Slugger!—and Em—previously known as Emma F.—carries a stuffed animal everywhere she goes. And Shira is missing her front teeth. And Lily is, like, amazing at gymnastics. You would not believe what she can do on the uneven bars."

"I wish you were here with me," he says.

"I wasn't invited," I say.

"Wait, what? You could have come!"

"I would have been such a third wheel. And anyway, I need to make money, not spend it."

We have an awkward silence.

"Maybe we can do something together next summer," he says.

"Sure," I say. I like that he assumes we'll still be together then.

"Hey! Sam!" Eric says. "I gotta call the period, 'kay? So shush."

"Already?"

"Yessssss," Eric says.

"Sorry, Eli," I say. "I have to go."

"But you just called me!"

I close my eyes. "I know. But I have to get the kids all the way on the other side of camp and take them for Evening Activity."

He sighs. "Okay. I get it. I just miss you. When can you call again?"

"I'm not sure," I say. "Maybe Rest Hour tomorrow? Or Free Play. That might be too late for you. But I'll try."

"I love you," he says.

"I love you too." Then I take a deep breath and run back to camp.

"Okay, girls, pajamas on, please!" I call out, still out of breath. I am on OD, which means On-Duty, which means, I am responsible for watching the kids from nine until midnight, when all staff have to be back in their bunks. So being on OD means you have to do bedtime. There are also Free Play ODs, but for that only a handful of counselors are scattered at posts throughout camp, so I won't have that assigned too often. Anyway, tonight I know Lis, Talia, JJ, and Muffs are on their way to Slice, the pizza place down the road. Apparently, that's where the staff goes to hang out at night when they need a break from camp. Rumor has it they are not that strict with the drinking age. Although the head staff have made it very clear that any staff members who are caught drinking on nights out will be sent home immediately.

Janelle has gone to watch a movie in the CL.

Which leaves me with the girls, aka the wild animals. Apparently, they do give out cookies at night for Milk and Cookies. Fabulous. Just what these kids need before bed, more sugar.

Am I really supposed to get all these girls to go to sleep? How will I do that? And it's not just my side of the bunk. I'm responsible for both sides. Twice as many kids!

"Just slip Ambiens in their lemonade," Talia told me as she cheerfully waved from the porch, hair blow-dried straight and lipstick on. She was wearing clean jeans, boots, a cute black top, and her hair down.

"Ha," I said, hoping she was kidding.

Now the kids are running around both sides of the bunk, music blasting.

"Can we have a candy party?" Em asks me.

"No," I say. "Come on, everyone! Why don't you get into bed and we'll play a game or something!"

"Please can we have a candy party? Pretty, pretty please?" they all say at the same time.

I sigh. "Pajamas on. Then one piece of candy each," I say. "And then you brush your teeth!"

"Can we keep the candy the whole summer?" Slugger asks.

"I think you get a few more days with it," I say. "But I'll ask Danish. We can't keep it for too long."

"Why not?" asks Fancy.

"We'd get raccoons!" I say.

They all gasp.

"In the bunk?" Shira asks.

An image comes back to me and I start to laugh. "True story," I say. "When I was in this cabin, one night I woke up to go to the bathroom and I saw a raccoon eating a bag of . . ." I hold for extra reaction. "Gummy bears!"

Some of them gasp and some of them laugh. "Did you scream?" Prague asks me. "I totally would have screamed."

"I totally did," I say, nodding. "And then I woke up some of the other girls and they started screaming and then all of us were screaming and the counselors came into the bunk and they started screaming and then one of them got the broom and chased the raccoon out through the front door."

"Did he take the bag of gummy bears?" Prague asks.

"He totally did."

"You really slept in this bunk when you were a kid?" Lily asks.

I nod.

"Is your name on the wall?" Em asks.

"I don't think so," I say. I had wanted to erase my name from this place, not engrave it.

"Can we have candy now?" Lily asks.

"Okay, girls, pajamas and then one piece of candy each! Let's go!" I clap my hands and stand up. "Everyone to the cubby room!"

The girls follow me. I'm not sure how the cubby room has already become a total disaster, but it has. Clothes are everywhere.

"Put your dirty clothes in your laundry bag!" I remind them.

"Where's my laundry bag?"

"I can't find my pajamas!"

"Have you seen my slippers?"

I do my best to help all eleven girls find their stuff. By the time we're done, the cubby room looks about ten times worse than it did before. Awesome.

"Candy time!" Fancy yells at the top of her lungs.

"Just one each!" I holler. I take a few minutes to try to organize and then go back into the bed area.

Danish, Jill, and Josh are standing in the middle of it.

The girls are all *stuffing* their mouths with candy. What happened to one piece each? This is a disaster.

"How's it going?" Josh asks me, eyes darting around the room.

"Just getting them ready," I say, trying to keep the panic out of my voice.

"Maybe no candy tonight?" Danish says.

"They're only allowed one piece each," I say.

"Francie, are those peanut M&M's?" Jill asks.

What is Jill even doing here? Isn't she in charge of the CITs? We don't even get a CIT!

Fancy has about ten in her hand and ten in her mouth. Plus she is giving them out to other girls.

"Are you kidding me?" I say out loud. "Are you trying to kill someone?"

Fancy's eyes widen.

Everyone stares at me. "Sorry," I say. "That came out wrong. I thought I got rid of the peanut stuff before."

Josh confiscates the offending chocolates.

"Sorry," Fancy says.

"Sorry," I say.

"Try and get them into bed soon," Josh says. "Tomorrow's a big day. And get rid of the candy by end of day tomorrow, okay, Sam?"

I nod, mortified.

"I'll come back and check in on you in a couple hours, 'kay?" Danish tells me.

Please, I think, please let them be asleep by then.

An hour later, ten o'clock, the candy has been eaten, and almost all the girls have brushed their teeth. All the girls in 6B are in their beds.

Could it be? Are all my kids almost in bed too?

Em, Slugger, Shira, Fancy, Prague, and . . . missing one. Who am I missing?

Lily. Where's Lily? I check the cubby room. Nope. Sinks. Nope. "Lily?"

"In the bathroom!" she says.

"Okay," I say. "Lights out in two."

"Be right there," she says.

"Does everyone have their flashlights?" I ask. I am almost done. Woot! I am almost done!

I wait two more minutes. I head back to the bathroom.

"Lily?" I say softly. "You okay in there?"

"Just trying to poop," she tells me.

Excellent. A little TMI, but I guess I should get used to it.

A few minutes later she finally flushes, comes out, and washes her hands.

"Did you already brush your teeth?" I ask.

She shakes her head.

"Then brush your teeth, 'kay?" Omigod, forget brushing teeth, this is like *pulling* teeth.

She spends at least five minutes finding her toothbrush and then her toothpaste and then brushes her teeth for what must be a world-record amount of time. At least fifteen minutes.

Finally, finally, she is in bed.

"I'm turning out the lights now," I say. "Everyone have their flashlights?"

They all turn them on.

"Lights off!" I say, and flip them. Some of them giggle.

"I can't believe I'm really here," Em says. She hugs her fuzzy lion.

"Me neither," Slugger says.

I silently add, *Me neither.*

I change into my own pajamas—checked flannel ones that are adorable—and then wash my face and brush my teeth. I even floss. I tell the girls they have five more minutes to turn their flashlights off, and then five minutes later, I tell them to turn them off for real. Then I get into my bed. I look at my phone, even though I know I won't have another message. I scroll through my pictures of Eli and find my favorite, when he was sitting on a bench in Washington Square Park. It's the look he's giving me that I love, the one that says *I love you and I want to kiss you immediately.*

I wish he were here. It would be fun to have him at camp. I'm not sure if he'd be a good counselor or not, though. Everyone likes him, but he's not exactly an early riser. He kind of does whatever he wants to do whenever he wants to do it.

Today's conversation wasn't great. It was rushed; he was obviously annoyed.

Maybe I can sneak away and call him after breakfast, during cleanup.

There's a knock on the counselors' doorframe.

"Yes?" I say.

The curtain opens. It's Fancy. "Sam?"

"Yes, Fancy?"

"Shira is crying *again*." She rolls her eyes.

I get out of bed. "She is? How come?"

"Who knows?"

"Okay, I'll come back," I say. I follow her into the room and hear that Shira is indeed crying. She's facedown on her pillow but I can see her little shoulders shaking.

I sit down on the edge of her bed. "Hey, sweetie," I say. "What's wrong?"

Her shoulders shake again. "I miss Tamara," she says.

"Who's Tamara?" I ask. I look at the family picture taped to the wall. "Your sister?"

"No," she sobs. "My sister is Maya. Tamara is my dog. And I miss her so much. She sleeps in my bed every night! She's probably really lonely!"

"I'm sure she misses you too," I say, but that just makes Shira sob harder. "But maybe . . . maybe . . . maybe she went to sleep with Maya! Because I'm sure Maya misses you too and this way they're keeping each other company!"

She turns over to look at me. Her eyes are dripping with tears. "You think she's sleeping in Maya's bed?"

"Yeah! For sure!" I say.

Her sobs escalate. "Noooo! What if she wants to stay sleeping with Maya even when I get back?"

I open my mouth but no words come out.

"What if when I get back she loves Maya more than me?"

Good Lord.

The next thing I hear is more sniffling. But not from Shira. This time it's Slugger.

"I miss my mom," she says.

Oh no.

"So do I," sniffs Em, hands trembling around her lion.

It's like dominoes! They're all going down! How do I stop this? They're going to dehydrate!

"What's happening in here?" one of the 6B girls asks, popping her head around the dividing wall. "You guys are being super loud."

"We're all homesick," Em says.

"You're acting like five-year-olds," Fancy says. "It's embarrassing."

Shira sinks back in her bed.

"Hey," I tell Fancy. "Don't be mean. It's totally normal to feel sad tonight."

"It is?" Slugger says.

"Of course it is," I say.

"Were you ever homesick?" Lily asks.

"Are you kidding me? Definitely." I think back to the first night I spent at camp. I hadn't wanted to come, but that's when my dad had his first tumor and my parents thought it would be better to have me away for the summer. "I remember lying in bed and staring at the ceiling and feeling so . . . weird. Do you guys feel weird?"

They all nod.

"Me too. Because it's not my bed! I love my bed at home! It has clean sheets! And at camp the beds are so small and saggy!"

They giggle.

"And at home you sleep by yourself with the door closed," I say.

"I sleep with the door open," Prague says.

"Me too," two of them answer at the same time.

"I share a room with my sister," Shira says.

"Lucky," Prague tells her. "I'm on my own floor and I hate it."

"Your own floor?" Slugger asks in disbelief.

"But you want to know something?" I ask, plowing ahead. "What?"

"This is the hardest part. Tonight. Sleeping in this bed for the first night. But if you get through the weirdness of sleeping in this new place tonight on these saggy mattresses— then after this, it's a breeze."

Lily wipes her eyes with the back of her hand. "Really?"

"It's true," Fancy says.

"Really," I say. And then I think about what I used to do when I would lie in bed and hear my parents fighting.

"I'm going to teach you all how to keep the nighttime weirdies away, 'kay?"

"How?" Em asks.

"Like this," I say. And then I turn around on Shira's bed and lie flat on my back and put my legs up against the wall. "Everyone copy me! That's a counselor's order."

There's some giggling, but I see all the girls turn around and place their legs against the wall. Shira is right beside me, and I can see that she's smiling a perfect toothless smile.

"Is everyone in position?" I ask.

"Yes," they say.

"Okay, now we're going to drum our feet against the wall like this—"

I get a good rhythm going. *Thump thump thump.* They all follow along. "Now we'll go around the room and everyone has to say one thing they're excited about for this summer. I'll start. I'm excited for . . ." What am I excited for? "Sing-Song!" I say.

"What is Sing-Song?" Em asks.

"On Fridays, we all go into the Rec Hall and sing songs. They put the words up on the screen so we can all see them."

"What songs?" Lily asks.

"Great ones," Prague says. "Like 'Leaving on a Jet Plane.'

'Summer Nights' from *Grease*. Old ones, but they're fun."

"I'm excited for the ten-and-under baseball team," Slugger says. "I play on a traveling team at home."

"I was on the twelve-and-under team!" I offer her an air high five. I look to the bed next to us. "Okay, Fancy, what are you looking forward to?"

"Visiting Day," she says.

Everyone laughs.

"Not *just* to see my parents. It's 'cause my mother brings snacks on Visiting Day. She brings cupcakes from Magnolia in New York. Have you ever had them? They're my favorite."

"I have had Magnolia cupcakes," I say. That's where I got Eli's! "And they are delicious. So now I'm excited about Visiting Day too. Excellent. Something else to look forward to! Lily, you're next."

"I'm excited to make new friends. My dad came to this camp when he was a kid. And he's still friends with the guys from his bunk. Best friends. And they're really old."

"Aw," says Prague.

"That could be us," Slugger says.

"It really could," I say, and my throat feels choked up. Maybe I don't speak to anyone from my bunk, but this bunk, these kids, they could be different. They could be friends for life.

"Okay, ladies," I say, after everyone has said something they're excited for. "Time for everyone to get back under the covers. You okay?" I ask Shira.

97

She nods. "Can you tuck us in?"

"I would love to tuck you in," I say.

I hear them the next morning. Early. Very, very early. They are laughing and running around, and I distinctly hear the word *licorice*.

The clock on my phone says it's only six forty-five. We don't have to be at flagpole until eight fifteen. I pull the covers over my head and pretend not to hear them for over an hour.

Eventually, I hear the front door open and Priya pops her head into our room. "Morning, ladies! Flagpole in fifteen!"

I sit up. The other counselors are still dead to the world. The room is cold, so I put on an extra sweatshirt, and since the floor is cold too, I step into my slippers. Then I push through the curtain-door and go see what the little monsters are up to.

"Morning, girls," I say, standing in the doorway. They are in the middle of the room. Their mouths are stuffed with brownies, gummy bears, and of course, licorice. At least I don't see any peanut M&M's.

When they see me, they all shriek and laugh and dive back into their beds.

"You're all getting cavities," I tell them.

They are giggling uncontrollably.

"Can we save a little room for breakfast?" I ask.

They are still giggling.

I am giggling too.

We get the girls to flagpole on time. I am even wearing regular clothes instead of pajamas, in the hopes that I can make it to some cell service after breakfast. In the Dining Hall, I bring the kids a tray of scrambled eggs, toast, jam, and a pitcher of orange juice. There is a small accident with the ketchup.

I have a large cup of coffee. It tastes terrible but hits the spot in the best way possible.

I call freeze. Slugger and Lily start laughing at the same time, so we decide they will stack together.

There are no tears the entire meal, which I take as a personal win.

I have my phone in my hoodie pocket. "Can you take the girls back to the bunk?" I ask Talia. "I want to check in with Eli."

"No problem," she says drowsily. Her coffee hasn't kicked in yet.

As soon as the kids are released, I make a run for it. I know I don't have that much time, but I just want to hear his voice. I want him to know that I'm thinking about him.

The Wi-Fi kicks in as soon as I step inside the office. Hurrah! My phone is flooded with texts.

Hello, Beautiful! I'm in Florence! It's about 100 degrees.

There are a few other texts from him but I can hardly wait to write him. I type:

Hi!

I just ditched the kids to run to the office to try you. I am going to call you!

I dial his number and wait while it rings. Ringing . . . ringing . . .

"Hello?" he says.

"Hiiiiiiiiiiii!"

"It's you!"

"It's me! I snuck away to call you early!"

"Hooray! I miss you!"

"I miss you too!"

I laugh and tell him *everything*, the words gushing from my mouth. He tells me all about what he's doing there. The museums. His cousin. The pizza. I ask a lot of questions about the pizza. The connection is clear. The connection is perfect. It's like he's standing right beside me.

We talk and talk and talk until I have to go again.

"When can we talk next?" he asks.

"I don't know. I can get back here at seven p.m. But maybe it's too late."

"I don't care! Wake me up! Call me!"

"You sure?"

"Yes!"

"Okay. I love you."

"I love you too."

And we hang up.

I gotta go. I sprint back to my cabin, making my calves burn. I glance at my other texts while I run. There's a number I don't recognize.

Hi, Sam! I got your number from your mom! I'm Francie's mother! Mandy! Small world, right?! We are so thrilled you're her counselor this year! How is she doing?

I can't write back now anyway, but remind myself to do it later. As I step onto the porch, I hope that all the kids are ready for their activity, which is dance.

But when I step inside, I see that the kids are still half dressed and the bunk is a total mess. Like a disaster mess. Like I can barely see the floor. It is covered with clothes and candy. But there's no time to clean up because we have to get to dance.

"Girls, we gotta go," I say. "Talia? Lis? Janelle?"

Both sides of the bunk have dance. It seems like a lot of our activities are both sides of the bunk.

"Coming!" I hear, and Janelle comes out of the counselors' room. "Girls! Come on!" she says, and steps into her side of the bunk.

"On the porch!" she yells. "Wear your dancing shoes!"

"And by that she means sneakers!" I add.

Lis and Talia step outside too, just as Danish steps on the porch. "Hi, guys!" she says. "How'd you do with your first cleanup? Will you be getting a ten?"

Uh-oh. I forgot that the section heads give all the bunks a cleanup score after cleanup. They write the daily scores on a sheet on the wall. That is not going to make us look good at all.

The girls look stricken. "A ten?" Shira shrieks. "Is it out of a hundred?"

There is a lot of snickering.

"Oh, I'm sure you did a great job," Danish says. "You guys better hurry to dance, though. The period already started."

And off we go as Danish steps into our bunk to check out the disaster.

By the time we get to the Rec Hall, dance is almost half over. But the girls get into lines and practice some moves and then what seems like a second later, Eric's voice comes back on the loudspeaker, telling us it's time to go to second period.

"What do we have next?" Janelle asks.

"Canoeing," Talia says, and then mutters in my direction, "Can she not read a schedule?"

"Okay, we'll go straight to the beach," I say, ignoring her. "Is that Gavin?"

"No," Lis says. "He's sailing."

"Are they wearing their bathing suits?" I ask.

"Not sure," Lis says.

"Don't they have to wear their bathing suits on the beach?" I ask.

"Right," Talia says. "Forgot about that."

"Girls? Any of you wearing bathing suits?"

"No!" the girls call back.

"Awesome." I guess that's the last time I go make a call during cleanup.

We herd the girls back down the road to the bunk and instruct them to put on bathing suits quickly.

"What else do they need?" I ask.

"Towels," Lis says. "In case they get wet."

"Bring towels!" I call out. "And sunscreen! Wear sunscreen!"

I pass the cleanup score on the way to change. Two out of ten. Crap.

We arrive late to canoeing. The sailboats, kayaks, and windsurfers are already in the water. I see Gavin on the other side of the lake with some of the older kids.

"Come on, girls!" calls the canoeing teacher. We have to get each of you in a life jacket." She has a thick British accent.

After fitting them for life jackets, we start canoeing safety training, which involves learning what to do if the canoe flips over. This involves all of us getting wet. This leads to a lot of eight-year-olds, shrieking. And some counselors shrieking.

"I didn't want to get this shirt wet," Lis grumbles, biting her pinkie nail.

"Too bad, so sad," Fancy says. I try not to laugh.

When the period is called, we run back to the bunk, change out of our wet bathing suits, put on shorts, T-shirts and sneakers, and herd them to basketball, which luckily happens to be on Lower Field, not far from our bunk.

"We made it!" I say. I plop down on the bleachers. I pray Trevor, the basketball specialist, will let me sit for a minute and catch my breath.

"Girls, where are your hats?" Trevor asks.

Argh. Freaking hats.

"Our counselors didn't tell us to bring them," Fancy says.

Way to throw us under the bus, Fancy.

"You need hats," Trevor says. "It's sunny. Maybe your counselors can run back to the bunk to get them?"

"Not it," says Talia.

Surprise, surprise. "I'll go," I say.

"I'll come with you," Janelle says, and the two of us sprint back to the bunk to collect a hat for each of them. I'm lucky enough to find one by each of their beds.

"I have no idea if these belong to the right kids, but they'll have to do," Janelle says.

We hurry back to the court and pass out the hats.

"Thanks," Trevor says. "Next time tell the girls to wear socks and sneakers, too."

"They are wearing socks and . . ." My voice trails off as I notice that only Slugger is wearing socks *and* sneakers. The others are either wearing flip-flops, Crocs, or sneakers without socks. Lily is wearing a leotard, no shorts.

"Sorry," I say, and sit back down on the bench beside Talia. It's hot. I wish *I* had grabbed a hat.

While Trevor teaches the girls to dribble, I close my eyes and let the sun warm my cheeks. Ah. That feels good.

"Um, guys?"

I look up to see Danish standing in front of us.

All four of us are on the bench doing nothing.

Crap, crap, crap.

"You really need to be *involved* in the activities. It encourages the girls to be involved too. You have to lead by example!" She looks at me while she says it.

But I was! I canoed! I swam! I got hats! I just took a one-second break. "Sorry," I say, and jump up off the bench.

The other counselors do the same.

"And today's cleanup was a disaster. Have you made a chore wheel? That will help. And from now on you really need to be helping them clean up in the morning. A clean bunk in the morning makes for a better day." I was supposed to make a chore wheel, wasn't I?

"Aye, aye, Captain," Talia says, saluting her.

"Thanks," Danish says.

"Water break!" Trevor calls out.

The girls all look at us.

"Where's our water?" Em asks.

Danish sighs. "Did they not bring their water bottles?"

Oops. I want to be good at this, but there is too much to remember!

"They have to carry them with them at all times," Danish says. "Their water bottles and their sun hats. It's hot out here. We don't want them dehydrating."

"Got it," I say. "I'm really sorry."

"It's just the second day," she says. "We're all learning."

"I'm thirsty!" Fancy says.

"Me too!"

"Me too!"

"So am I!"

"Okay, why don't you all run back and get your water bottles," Danish says. "And maybe one of you should go with them."

"I'll go!" I say in my best I-can-handle-this voice, and I run.

It's seven p.m. and I am back at the office. Today kicked my ass, and it's not over. There is still Evening Activity and bedtime. I'm not on OD, but I am so wiped out I think I'll just go to sleep early. But first I get to speak to Eli again!

I dial his number. It rings. And rings.

I get his voice mail.

He told me to wake him up, didn't he?

I try again. Voice mail again.

My heart sinks. I guess his ringer is off. Or he's just sleeping through it. I text instead.

Me: Hiiiii! Are you still up? Call me if you're still up! I'll hang out in the office for another five mins or so.

The door swings open and it's Gavin. He's wearing his sunglasses but no shirt. Once again I am not complaining.

"Hey," he says. "How's it going?"

"Great," I say.

"How's Eli?"

"Eli?" Oh. Right. My boyfriend. Look away from his abs. Away from his abs! "He's asleep. But I spoke to him

106

earlier today. So we're good. How's Kat?"

"I don't know. But I am hopefully about to find out."

Gavin's phone rings and he answers the call.

I guess his girlfriend waited up to talk to *him*. He's facing the other way, but I can see from the side of his face that he's smiling.

I can also see how smooth his back is. I wonder if he ever needs help putting on suntan lotion? I am very good at applying suntan lotion. Not on children, perhaps, but definitely on hot shirtless guys.

I look back down at my phone, text Eli good night, send quick hellos to my friends, wave goodbye to Eric and Gavin, who is still deep in conversation, and head back the bunk, just in time to see a raccoon run right out of it.

Shit.

I walk into a bunk of eleven screaming girls and three screaming counselors.

"We're getting rid of the candy!" I call out. "We're getting rid of it RIGHT NOW!"

"Okay, girls," I say after breakfast the next day. "We are getting a perfect ten at cleanup today, do you understand? A perfect ten! Not one sheet out of place."

"It's impossible," Talia says. "These girls are disasters."

"They just need our help," I say.

"I don't know how to make my bed," Slugger tells us.

"I don't know how to fold," Fancy says.

"Talia and I know how to do both!" I say. "We will teach you! And we are going to be ready for everything today!" I study our schedule. "Here's the deal. We have wrestling first, and then sailing, and then tennis. So we're going to put our bathing suits on under our clothes, with sandals. So we won't have to come back." Planning for the win!

"My mother told me not to wear a bathing suit all day," Lily says. "It makes my vajayjay angry."

Everyone starts laughing.

"You definitely shouldn't wear a *wet* bathing suit all day, Lily. But a dry one is totally fine. Your vajayjay will be a-okay-ay!"

They all laugh.

"I really wish they'd moved me to inters," Talia grumbles.

I'm starting to wish they had moved her, too.

Talia steps up and helps make their beds and fold their clothes, while I get them dressed. And we make it to wrestling on time wearing bathing suits under our shorts and T-shirts, and carrying towels. With sunscreen!

The wrestling specialist doesn't even mind about the bathing suits since they are apparently good to wrestle in. Yes! Winning!

Also, the wrestling teacher introduces himself as the Tank. Mystery solved.

When we get to the beach, Gavin ushers us into the boating house to fit us with life jackets.

His is bright yellow and nicer than all of ours—I'm guessing he brought it from home. I would too if I had to wear one all day. The one I'm wearing is red and soggy.

There are two other sailing counselors, and one sailing CIT, but since Gavin is the head of the activity, he talks to all of us about sailing safety. Then he divides us up into four groups, or four boats.

"Sam, your group is in my boat," he says.

I have Slugger, Prague, and Shira. I buckle my life jacket and make sure theirs are buckled too.

"I've never been in a sailboat," Slugger says, climbing on.

"It's the best," Prague tells her. "Can we suntan on the edge?"

"This isn't that kind of sailing," Gavin says.

He adjusts the straps and the wind catches our sail and we start to glide across the lake.

He jumps back and forth between the sides, holding on to all the strings, in command of the boat. He's wearing aviator sunglasses that are attached by a rope around the back of his head. I guess sailing instructors lose a lot of sunglasses to the water.

He's not wearing a shirt under the life jacket, and his arms are thick and already tanned. He's wearing red bathing trunks. I feel nakedish that I'm just wearing a one-piece under my life jacket, but all the girls are only wearing their suits and jackets—more clothes would have been weird. And probably would have gotten wet.

He explains a few things about the boat until he tells the girls that they can sit on the stern for a bit if they want to stretch.

I let my head fall back as we glide across the lake. "This is great!"

"Glad you like it. You can put your feet in the water if you want," he says.

"I'm not going to fall in?"

"You will not fall in," he says. He raises an eyebrow. "Unless you want to fall in."

I stick one foot in the water. It's nice. But still, cold. "I do not want to fall in," I say. I put my other foot in, too. The part of the lake we're in is calm, although we can hear the other kids on the other boats across the lake.

"So how's Kat doing?" I ask.

"Seems good. She's living the life, that's for sure. She's going to all these fancy French parties. And then she's running off to the Mediterranean for the weekend."

"Sounds glamorous," I say.

"She is definitely glamorous," he says. "She'll probably trade me in for a French billionaire or something."

"I doubt it," I say.

"Can we jump in?" Prague asks.

"If you want to," Gavin says.

"I kind of want to," Prague says. "Who's coming with me?"

No one answers.

"Okay, scaredy-pants—I will jump in on my own!"
And she does.

"Sammy!" she squeals to me. "You have to come in!"

Sammy? I don't hate it. "Well . . ." I hesitate. It is hot out. "Why not? Can I take off my life jacket?"

"Can you swim?" he asks.

"I can," I say. "I promise I won't drown. You won't have to give me mouth-to-mouth." Oh wow, did I really say that?

He raises an eyebrow.

I snap off my jacket. Now I really feel kind of naked. I jump in. If his girlfriend is flirting with French billionaires, then it's only fair that I flirt with him.

The water is a shock of cold, but feels amazing. "Gavin?" I say. "Coming in?"

"Me?"

"I know it's not the Mediterranean, but . . ."

He laughs. "Does anyone else want to swim?" he asks the kids.

They shake their heads.

"Okay. Coming in." He snaps off his life jacket—*abs*—takes off his sunglasses, and dives off the boat and into the water in a perfect arc.

He pops up beside me, his hair dripping. "You okay?"

"Perfect," I say.

"And you're sure you don't need mouth-to-mouth?" he asks, smiling.

"Pretty sure," I say.

It's a little naughty, but totally harmless.

And I'm kind of liking it.

Back in the bunk, as the kids change quickly, I sneak a peek at our cleanup score. Eight! We got an eight! That is so much better than a two! We do not have to clean with the campers during Rest Hour with an eight. We can nap! *I* can nap!

"Don't forget sneakers!" I yell. "And socks! And sun block! And hats and water bottles!"

We make it to tennis, which is all the way across camp near Upper Field, and we're only five minutes late. I am impressed with myself.

I am also impressed with Benji, the smokin' hot tennis teacher. He is indeed smokin'.

Are camp guys always so attractive, or am I just finding them all attractive because I am not allowed to have any of them?

The girls do drills, which mostly involve them lining up and Smokin' Hot Benji lobbing balls at them, which the girls try to hit with their rackets. They take water breaks every four minutes.

It's at least a hundred degrees out. Everyone misses most of the balls, except Shira, who is actually pretty good.

"He's straight, by the way," Janelle whispers to us, doing the eyebrow waggle again. Then she turns back to him. "Benji? Can you help me with my backhand?"

"Sure," he says.

She runs toward him and he stands behind her, showing her the moves, his hands on her shoulders.

Now his hands are on her waist.

Now *her* hands are on *his* waist. She is making a move on Smokin' Hot Benji!

"I feel like we're watching something we shouldn't be," Lis says under her breath. "Maybe they want to get a room?"

Eric's voice echoes over the loudspeaker, calling an end to the period.

"Come on, girls," I say, leading them back to the bunk.

Benji and Janelle stay in their positions.

"We'll see you at lunch!" I call out.

"She's after your nickname, Porny," Lis says to me. "Gross."

"At least someone's getting some action," I say.

The girls are whiny as we head back to the bunk. They're hot and hungry.

"Can we never have tennis again?" Fancy asks.

"I like tennis!" Shira says.

"'Cause it's the only thing you're good at," Fancy barks back.

Shira turns bright red.

"That's not true," I say. "Shira is great at a lot of things."

"Like what?" Fancy asks.

"Like folding."

"And crying," Fancy says.

I stop walking and crouch next to her. "Fancy, stop it. I am not going to stand by while you hurt Shira's feelings. Do you understand? Enough is enough. Think about how you would feel if someone said something like that to you. Would you like it?"

She bites her lower lip and she shakes her head.

"Then stop. And it would be nice if you apologized."

"Sorry," she mutters to Shira, her face flaming.

"It's okay," Shira says.

"Thank you, Fancy," I say, and take Shira's hand. "Let's sing a song."

"That's a good idea," Prague says. "What song?"

I think back to cheers and songs I sang in camp. "Okay, girls, repeat after me. *We're going on a bear hunt!*"

"*We're going on a bear hunt,*" Prague and Shira say.

"I meant everyone!" I call.

"*We're going on a bear hunt!*" they all sing.

"*We're gonna catch a big one!*" I say.

"*We're gonna catch a big one!*" they repeat.

"*A big grizzly bear!*"

"*A big grizzly bear!*"

"*Well, I'm not scared!*"

"*Well, I'm not scared!*"

We go through the rest of the song all the way to the bunk. They get louder and louder with each line. Other campers stop to stare but our kids keep going.

They're smiling and singing and swinging their hands. Even Fancy.

I realize I've lost Talia and Lis along the way. Not that I'm surprised.

"You're a *really* good counselor," Em tells me.

Maybe I am.

I plan on calling Eli at Rest Hour, but it turns out all the kids have to write letters home, and it's my job to supervise them.

Prague has preprinted fill-in-the-blank camp stationery and is finished in a minute.

The stationery says:

Dear _____ , Hello from Camp _____. My favorite activity is _____. My least favorite activity is _____. My favorite meal is _____. My least favorite meal is _____. The counselors are _____.

I read over her shoulder and am pleased to see that she filled in *great* for the counselor one.

Look at me! I am great!

I help the rest of them write return addresses, explain where the stamp has to go, and help them spell *canoeing*.

I never make it to the office.

But I do make it to archery.

"Look at me, I'm Katniss!" says Slugger. Considering she couldn't spell *canoeing*, I can't believe she's reading *The Hunger Games*, but then I realize she probably just saw the movies.

"Want to try?" the archery teacher asks me.

"I do want to try!" I say. After all, I *did* read the books!

I get into position, pull the bow back, and aim for the target.

I miss. Spectacularly.

"Try again," the teacher says.

This time I get it on the target. Woot!

"You're a natural," she says. "Want to go for the bull's-eye?"

"Let's let the kids have another go," I say.

Slugger actually gets a bull's-eye, putting me to shame.

And then so does Talia.

"I am also shockingly good at bowling," she says.

I don't make it the office for the rest of the day. Prague skins her knee at Dinner Washup, and since I am somehow covered in lake water from GS (General Swim), I decide I need to shower at Free Play.

It starts to pour during Evening Activity, and it's too wet and dark to venture to the office.

I miss Eli. I miss his voice.

I don't care if I have to take a boat to get there, tomorrow I'm getting to the office.

The next day, I finally, finally make it to the office at Dinner Washup.

There are many texts from Eli.

UGH I can't believe I missed your call! I fell asleep! The phone was right by my head! I don't know how I didn't hear!

SORRY!

OK, will make sure to have the phone nearby tomorrow at 1 your time! I miss you!

Hi! It's one! Waiting!

1:10.

It's 1:30 now. Maybe you're stuck somewhere. Going to a bar in a few. Not sure if I should wait or not.

I gotta go. Busy day, I guess.

You have not called in a while. Everything OK?

Then nothing today.

I call him.

He answers on the first ring.

"Hi! You're alive!"

"Sorry," I say. "It's so busy here!"

"I'm busy too," he says. "But I still have time to text you."

"Ah, but you have Wi-Fi access," I say, suddenly annoyed. "I don't."

"I know," he says.

"And you're on vacation," I snap. "And I'm working."

"I know," he says again. "I just miss you."

I sigh. "I miss you, too. I'm sorry. I'm trying to get to the office as often as I can."

"I'm sure you are," he says, and there's a pause.

"So how were your last two days?" I say.

"Good," he says. "We went to some museums. How were yours?"

"I did not go to a museum. I schlepped children from one

117

end of camp to the other." I decide to give him a little bit. "But I also went in a canoe."

"You did? I love canoes!"

"Me too." I don't tell him about swimming with Gavin or sailing with Gavin or Gavin splashing me when I was in the water.

We talk for another twenty minutes until I hear him yawn. "Can you call me tomorrow?" he asks.

"I can try for Rest Hour or Dinner Washup. But sometimes something comes up and then I feel terrible. Like letter-writing day."

"Just do your best, I guess," he says. His voice sounds a little bit condescending, but I decide to let it go.

"Will do," I say instead. "I love you."

"I love you, too."

The next two days are busy, but I manage to make it to the office every day. We get more eights at cleanup. I make a chore wheel. I get people into the right clothes, wearing the right shoes. Talia French braids their hair and we try to teach her how to make Princess Leia buns.

I play soccer. We sing more camp songs. I put sun block on everybody.

I catch the raccoon making a run for it from our bunk with a package of SweeTarts, so we spend our Rest Hour searching for all the candy that the campers have taken pains to hide from us in their underwear bags and under their beds.

Finally, it's Friday night, and we all change into white shirts for Friday Night Dinner. That is part of our not-Shabbat but kind-of-Shabbat tradition.

Dinner is roasted chicken and veggies, and we all get grape juice, which seems like a bad idea with white shirts. But! Tradition! Not-Shabbat!

After Free Play is Sing-Song, my favorite camp activity. We all cram into the Rec Hall and the screen comes down, and while the camp owner plays the piano and Priya plays the guitar, we follow along with the lyrics and sing all the regular camp songs.

Then we go into "Leaving on a Jet Plane," "House at Pooh Corner," "Hello Muddah, Hello Fadduh," "Hey There Delilah," "Closer to Fine," "One Tin Soldier," "Summer Nights," "Breaking Up Is Hard to Do," and "Wonderful Tonight." Finally, we sing "Stay (at Camp)," the final song. Everyone sings their parts.

"Why can't we stay at camp,
Just a little bit longer.
We want to make our friendships,
Just a little bit stronger . . ."

It's like time hasn't passed at all. I feel like I'm eleven all over again. Except this time, I am sitting next to Janelle, I have Lily on my lap, and they are both singing as loud as I am.

Botts is sitting on the edge of the stage singing his heart out, too.

Where's Gavin? I spot him in the back of the room, chatting to the Tank. He spots me looking at him and winks.

I wink back.

It's okay, it doesn't mean anything. Right?

After Milk and Cookies, I'm on OD again. I change into sweats and a cozy shirt, and then tuck the girls into bed one by one.

"Good night, Prague," I say, patting her on the head.

"Good night," she says, closing her eyes.

"Good night, Em," I say.

"Good night."

"Good night, Shira," I whisper.

"Good night, Mommy," she says.

Everyone laughs, including me.

"Oops," she says, blushing.

"I don't mind," I say.

"You're kind of like our mom here."

"More like a big sister," I say, and kiss her head.

The next day is a whirlwind. Tommy, one of the junior boys, has an unfortunate run-in with a canoe paddle and has to go see an emergency dentist.

His family lives in Miami, so Danish has to take him.

She grabs my arm at lunch. "Sam? I need a favor," she says.

"Of course, what's up?"

"I'm not sure I'll be back for Evening Activity. Priya will cover me at GS but can you take over tonight, running the activity?"

"Sure," I say, suddenly nervous. "What is it?"

"It's Family Feud," she says. "Have you seen it?"

"Of course," I say. In the real *Family Feud* they ask a hundred people a question, like name the best dessert. Then the top five answers are put up on a board. Contestants have to guess the top five answers.

"You'll have to finish putting together the surveys. It's pretty easy. I have the questions, I just need you to ask twenty kids for answers. Hopefully I'll be back for the activity, but if not, just run it. Make sure to do a bunk check and see that the kids all leave to get to Milk and Cookies on time. Sound okay?"

"Um . . ." I hesitate. Running an activity? That sounds scary. But I can do it. Teachers plan activities all the time.

"Sure," I say eventually. "No problem."

She squeezes my shoulder. "Awesome. You're the best. Thank you!"

Now what?

During Rest Hour I head to Bunk 4 in search of non-junior campers to interview. I ask them questions like name a Disney princess. Name a magical power. Name a camp dessert.

The answers range from Moana and Tiana to flying and invisibility to s'mores and chocolate pudding. I spend Free Play writing all the answers out on poster boards and then carrying them across camp to the Rec Hall.

I stand onstage.

"Hi, guys!" I say. "I'm running the activity tonight!"

"Who are you?" asks one of the junior boys.

"I'm Sam!"

"Sammy!!!!" my whole bunk cheers. I wave.

"Danish can't be here tonight, because she's with a camper—"

"Toothless Tommy!" one of the Bunk 5 boys yells, and the kids laugh.

"Is he really toothless?" one of the nine-year-old girls calls out.

"Is the tooth fairy coming?"

"There's no such thing as the tooth fairy!" a boy yells.

"Shhhhhhhhh," I say, giving the stink-eye to his counselor. I do not want to shatter anyone's innocence at my first nighttime activity. "Tommy is going to be fine! But first let's do a bunk check. Bunk One—"

"Is there a mic? We can't hear you!" someone yells from the back.

"Oh, um, I don't know. I can talk louder?" I raise my voice.

"There's a mic on the piano!" Janelle calls out.

"Oh. Okay. One sec." I hurry off the stage. It doesn't look too far from the ground, so I decide to jump off, but I land weirdly on my foot, which kills.

I wince.

I hobble to the piano, pick up the mic, and try to figure out a way to turn it on. Omigod. I am totally messing this up.

"There's a button on the side," one of the counselors says.

Ah. Got it. I turn it on. "Testing?"

There is a ton of interference. Great. Um. I turn it off.

"You're too close to the speaker!" someone else calls out.

Omigod. I'm like one minute away from people throwing tomatoes at me.

I try to calm myself down and carefully climb up the stairs. I kind of feel like all my camp nightmares are coming true. I'm not wearing a bathrobe, am I? Or am I bleeding through my pants?

I take another deep breath and try the mic again. "Hello?"

It works. Yes! Small miracle.

"Let's start over," I say. "Bunk One!"

"Check!"

So far so good. "Bunk Two!"

"Check!"

I go through them all.

"Bunk Five!"

"Check," say JJ and Muffs.

"Six A!"

"Check!" says Talia.

"Six B!"

"CHHHHHHHECK!" says Janelle. "Go, Sammy!"

"Awesome," I say. "We're all here. And tonight we're playing Family Feud!"

The room is quiet.

"Can I get some excitement, please? Tonight we're playing Family Feud!"

The counselors clap.

"Tonight we're playing FAMILY FEUD!"

This time everyone claps.

"That's better! We're going to start with Bunk One versus Bunk Five! Counselors, you can help organize but no giving answers, 'kay?"

A little girl from Bunk 1 and a boy from Bunk 5 come up.

And here we go.

Bunk 2 wins, but everyone seems to have had a great time.

"Nice work," Gavin says to me as I send the kids off to Milk and Cookies.

"Thanks," I say.

"Heading for a Wi-Fi run?" he asks.

Oh crap. I haven't had a chance to call Eli today. I guess I could go now. But I really need a shower.

"I am going to try and squeeze in a shower," I say. "I've been interviewing kids and making posters all day. And it's not like he's awake anyway. . . ."

"Good point. You going for pizza tonight?"

"Yes," I say.

"Great," he says. "See you there."

Huh. I smile. I guess I'll see him there.

"Thank you so much," Danish says, back in the bunk later that night. "I heard you did a good job."

"Thanks," I say. "How is Tommy?"

"Not actually toothless," Danish says. "Although I suspect the nickname will stick."

"Yikes." I wince. "It's a bad one."

"Keep up the good work, Sam."

It's completely uncool, but I know I am beaming. "Will do."

Janelle is OD, but I tuck all the girls in and say good night before leaving.

"Are you coming for pizza?" Lis asks me. "We're getting a ride."

"Yup, coming!"

I think about school. Eli is usually the one everyone invites to parties. I am the one who goes along. He's the one everyone likes, and I'm the plus-one.

So who am I? Porny or Plus-One or Pizza Party Girl?

Here at camp, I'm feeling more and more like the last one.

It's nice to be the one everyone likes.

It's nice to be me. Known for who I am.

It's nice to be here.

WEEK 2 SCHEDULE—BUNK 6A

	SUNDAY	MONDAY	TUESDAY	WEDNESDAY	THURSDAY	FRIDAY	SATURDAY
PERIOD 1 10:15–10:45	POTH PRACTICE	TENNIS	A&C	SI	NEWCOMB	DRAMA	TENNIS
PERIOD 2 10:45–11:30	POTH PRACTICE	DRAMA	GAGA BALL	KAYAKING	SHOWERS	SI	SI
PERIOD 3 11:30–12:15	POTH PRACTICE	DANCE	SAILING	DANCE	SAILING	CANOEING	SAILING
12:15–12:30	LUNCH WASHUP	LUNCH WASHUP	LUNCH WASHUP	LUNCH WASHUP	LUNCH WASHUP	LUNCH WASHUP	LUNCH WASHUP
12:30–1:00	LUNCH	LUNCH	LUNCH	LUNCH	LUNCH	LUNCH	LUNCH
1:00–2:00	REST HOUR	REST HOUR	REST HOUR	REST HOUR	REST HOUR	REST HOUR	REST HOUR
PERIOD 4 2:00–2:45	POTH PRACTICE	WRESTLING	SHOWERS	BAKING	KAYAKING	ART	ART
2:45–3:15	MILK & COOKIES	MILK & COOKIES	MILK & COOKIES	MILK & COOKIES	MILK & COOKIES	MILK & COOKIES	MILK & COOKIES
PERIOD 5 3:15–4:00	SHOWERS	SI	NEWCOMB	TENNIS	SOCCER	SOCCER	WATERSKI
PERIOD 6 4:00–4:45	GS	GS	GS	GS	GS	GS	GS

Week 2

After a full day of POTH—Putting On the Hits—a lip-syncing contest where we lose, I am getting ready for our first staff party.

I am wearing my nicest jeans, my low-heeled sandals, and a cute black shirt that's open in the back. I have a black sweater with me too, for when it gets chilly. I have blow-dried my hair and put on makeup. This is as glam as I can get at camp. (Glamp?) Not that I care that much about looking good, since I'm not trying to impress anyone.

Well, not totally true. I want to look good. For me.

There's nothing wrong with that, is there?

Gavin will be at the party. We shared a pizza at Slice. Not just me and him; Muffs, Lis, and Talia had some with us.

All the counselors in the junior section will be at the party. The CITs are sitting OD so we can all go.

"The bus leaves in fifteen minutes," I say, lining my eyes with blue in Lis's mirror. "Are you ladies almost ready?"

"Yes!" Talia says. She turns to me. "I love your lipstick. Your whole look is so New York."

"Thanks," I say, almost done. "Bye, girls!" I call out, giving them all good-night hugs and tucking them in.

"You're looking hot!" Prague says.

"You are too young to use the word *hot*," I say. "Unless you're talking about weather . . . or soup."

She blows me a kiss.

The four of us say goodbye and hurry down the road to the office to catch the bus. We join and pick up some of the other counselors as we walk down the road. Everyone is so happy to be getting out of camp for a party. It's a nice night—the sky is inky black and the stars are bright and it's not too cold. Josh and Jill are staying behind to make sure nothing goes horribly wrong.

I climb onto the bus and take an empty row. Talia sits beside me. She's wearing her hair down and extra curly.

I'm not sure what to expect at the party. Will everyone be making out?

Sigh. Maybe there will be cell service?

At least Gavin will be there. Without anyone to make out with either.

"So what exactly happens at a staff party?" I ask.

"Dancing, mostly," Talia says.

"The counselors were always so loud when they came back."

"They were probably drunk," she says. "Mine always were."

"Ooooh, that explains it," I say. "But how? Everyone's under twenty-one."

"There's always some booze being snuck around."

I do not think I want to get drunk and risk being fired. That would not look good for future teaching jobs at all.

The engine turns on. There are woots from the back. The bus starts rolling down the dirt road.

More cheers.

When we turn onto a bigger street, the signal bars on my phone come on. I wish it were earlier so I could call Eli. We haven't actually spoken on the phone for like three days now. Talia is checking her phone too. My texts stream in.

Eli: Hi babe.

Eli: Look at me with David's Michelangelo!

Eli: Night, Beautiful. Hope you had a great day. Wish we could talk more.

"I love how much your boyfriend misses you," Talia says, reading over my shoulder.

"Yeah," I say, although to me the "Wish we could talk more" feels kind of like a dig. It says, *You are not trying hard enough to call me.*

He's in freakin' Europe! Isn't he having fun?

I wish we could talk more, too. I just can't run to the office every period.

I also have a few texts from Lauren and Emily. And then also from Fancy's annoying mom, which is how I've identified her in my phone. Apparently I give mean nick-names now too.

Fancy's Annoying Mom: Hi, Sam! I looked on the website and saw a group picture of Francie—she wasn't smiling. Is she unhappy?

"Group picture?" I ask Talia. "Do they post pictures of the kids somewhere?"

"Um, yeah. The pics that Jill is always taking? She posts them online."

"No way!"

"Yes way. What did you think they were for?"

"I don't know. A slideshow at the end of the summer?"

"That too. But she also posts like fifty pics online every night. The parents sit there and wait for them. Parents are crazy."

Fancy's Annoying Mom: Her cheeks also look a little flushed. Is she wearing her sunscreen?

Fancy's Annoying Mom: Also wondering if she is using conditioner in her hair? Please make sure she does. Her hair gets tangled. It looks tangled in the picture.

Fancy's Annoying Mom: Hello?

Fancy's Annoying Mom: I would really appreciate if you responded.

Three dots appear on my phone and I drop it in my lap hot-potato style. Stalker!

"OMG," I say. "Fancy's mother keeps texting me."

"Oh no!" Talia says. "How did she get your number?"

"She met my mom at a grocery store . . . long story."

"She's the worst. She calls Josh twice a day. She complains about everything! What did she say?"

"That Fancy looks unhappy in the pictures."

"Just ignore her. Do not engage. Do not engage! The worst kids always have the worst parents. And the worst parents always tip the worst at Visiting Day."

"Tip?" I say. "Parents tip?"

"The nicer ones do," she says.

"There's no way my parents tipped," I say.

"Then they're assholes."

I laugh. "But I was a good kid. I think?"

"I was a bitch," she says, and goes back to her phone.

I flip to Instagram. We're not allowed to post while we're at camp, but I can still see what Eli is up to.

I flip to his stories and see that he posted a picture. He's with a group of people—girls and guys. So many people I don't know. He hasn't tagged them. Guys. Girls. Girls holding beers.

Pretty girls holding beers.

The drinking age in Europe is only eighteen. My shoulders tighten at the idea of him on the other side of the world drinking with random pretty girls.

I flash back to a keg party, his hand under my skirt.

He better not put his hands under any of these girls' skirts!

I study their outfits. They are all wearing sundresses. I hate them all.

I really should call every day.

Now I'm the one being needy.

I click off my phone and put it away. I am not going to worry about Eli hooking up with someone in Europe! Sure, he's probably flirting with other girls and that's fine! I am flirting with other boys! There is nothing wrong with flirting!

But I should call more. Should I call now?

No. It's the middle of the night there.

Everyone cheers when we pull into the restaurant's parking lot. The door is open and the music is already blasting even though no one is inside. There's a table filled with cupcakes.

Aw. Cupcakes.

After about ten minutes or so, people start dancing. All the lights are on, so it feels less like a party and more like an awkward sixth-grade social.

"Hey," says Gavin, coming up beside me. "Can I buy you a drink?"

"I thought they're all free," I say.

"They are. I was trying to be chivalrous," he says with a smile.

"Ah," I say. "Well then, yes. I'll take a Coke."

"Two rum and Cokes," he tells the bartender.

The bartender raises an eyebrow. "It's a dry bar," he says.

"Boo," Gavin says. "Two Cokes, then."

Eli isn't drinking Cokes. Eli is drinking actual alcohol.

"Does it seem unfair to you that our significant others are out there guzzling Heinekens and French wine while we're drinking rumless Cokes?" I ask.

"It does," he says. "We can drink on our day off at least. Are you coming with us to Botts's?"

"What's happening at Botts's?"

"He has a cottage about thirty minutes away. We will drink Heineken and French wine. He told me he was going to invite you. For our day off. If you can take a Tuesday/Wednesday."

That's sweet. "Oh, thanks," I say. "He hasn't mentioned it. I was maybe going to see my parents . . ."

"Parents? Where are they?"

"Rhode Island."

"What? That's too far. And parents are no fun. Come to Botts's. Heineken! French wine!"

"Honestly," I say, "I don't even like Heineken."

He laughs. "What about French wine?"

"I can make that work," I say. "But in a taste test I would not be able to tell the difference between French or Italian wine. Or wine from New Jersey."

"Here's what I know about wine—white is served cold," he says.

I laugh. "Look at you, fancy pants."

I lean against the wall and look around. But not at Gavin's fancy pants. Which are actually jeans. Which encase a pretty nice ass.

Not looking!

"Want to take bets on who's going to hook up with who tonight?" he asks.

"That seems wrong," I say. "But yes."

We both spot JJ in the corner dancing with one of the swim staff. "That looks possible," I say.

"JJ has been eyeing that guy for weeks."

I spot Lis, Talia, and their friend Allie whispering to each other in the corner. She's tall, with long, wavy brown hair.

Muffs is trying to get Lis's attention.

"Does he have any chance with her?" Gavin asks.

"I don't think so," I say.

"Is it the earmuffs?"

"Possibly what the earmuffs are hiding."

"Lis likes Botts, huh?" he asks.

"I cannot reveal bunk secrets," I say. "But do you think she has a chance with him?"

He hesitates. "Maybe. He had a serious girlfriend for the last few summers. Cassie. But they broke up in the fall. And she didn't come back."

"Oh, that's sad."

Then he laughs.

"What?"

"I've been meaning to give you a heads-up—Eric has a thing for you."

"Eric?" I ask.

"The office guy!"

I blush. "The stoner? Seriously?"

"Yes. He says you spend a lot of time there."

"Yes, calling my boyfriend!"

"He's not picking up on your reasons for visiting."

"Can you tell him I'm not available?" I say. "He should like someone else."

"Feelings are feelings, I guess?"

Our eyes lock a moment longer than they should.

Just then Botts walks up to us. "Rosenspan! What are you doing for your day off?"

"Coming to your cottage!" I say. "Drinking French wine!"

Botts punches Gavin's shoulder. "He invited you already? Bastard. Stole my thunder."

"I did," Gavin says.

"So you're in?" Botts asks me.

"I am. As long as I can take the Tuesday/Wednesday. Let me check with Talia and Danish. And thanks for the invite."

I laugh and go find Talia, who is still whispering in the corner, laughing with Lis and Allie.

She waves me over.

"Our co-counselor is one second away from doing a pole dance," she says. The counselors beside her laugh.

I look over at Janelle. She's standing on a chair, dancing, in a hot pink tube top. Smokin' Hot Benji and Jamon, one of the Australian kitchen staff, are dancing beside her.

"She's drunk," Talia says.

"I think she's just naturally spirited," I say.

"No, Smokin' Hot Benji has a flask," Lis says.

"She's totally going to hook up with one of them tonight," Talia says.

"She's just dancing," I say. I think about Gavin. I think about Eli and the sundress girls. "Not all flirting is prelude to hooking up."

"We'll see," Talia says. "But my money's on Jamon."

"Mine's on Smokin' Hot Benji," Lis says. "They were almost making out the other day. Sam?"

"Since I have to be celibate all summer, and since I am hoping to live vicariously through you people, I am hoping for Smokin' Hot Tennis Benji."

"Okay, Porny," Talia says with a laugh.

I know she's joking, but my cheeks heat up, and I turn around before she can see.

I wake up in the middle of the night to the sounds of soft moaning.

I open my eyes for a split second and see two bodies in Janelle's bed, under the covers.

I put my pillow over my head and go back to sleep.

"Rise and shine, everyone!" Danish says. She's standing in front of our doorway. "Time to get up!"

Janelle groans. Unfortunately, I'm at this point very familiar with her groaning sounds.

At least the guy is gone. I saw Jamon leave just as the sun was coming up.

And I will be buying some earplugs on my day off.

Janelle pushes her covers off her face.

"Fun night?" I ask her.

"Oh yeah," she says, laughing. "Super fun. We didn't wake you, did we?"

"You woke me," Talia calls from the back room.

"And me," Lis says.

"And me," I add.

She laughs even harder. "I am *so* sorry! Why didn't you say something?"

"I didn't want to . . . interrupt?" Lis says.

"Next time just throw something at me," she says.

"Or maybe next time you could go to *his* bunk," Talia says.

"Totally," Janelle says. "I told him to come visit and he did! I wasn't sure he was going to come!"

"Oh, he definitely came," Talia says.

She laughs even harder. "Ha! We didn't have sex. But yeah, still fun. I'm totally going to be a zombie all day."

She jumps out of bed and heads to the bathroom.

"That was gross, yeah?" Lis asks, zipping up her sweatshirt.

"Yeah," Talia says.

"I just wish they could have gone somewhere more private," I say. I am *definitely* getting earplugs on my day off.

"Oh, Talia, before I forget, are you okay with me taking Tuesday/Wednesday for my day off? That means I leave Tuesday night and come back Wednesday?"

"Yeah, and that's fine. Lis and I were both going to take Friday/Saturday together. Will you be okay with just Janelle? Promise to be back before the Saturday overnight."

"Yeah. No problem." It's not like Talia and Lis do that much to help.

"If Janelle brings someone back, you can always try sleeping in my bed," Talia offers. "At least you won't be right on top of them."

I sigh. She has the top bunk. "I'm not sure I want an aerial view."

"Don't go! Don't go!" Em cries, wrapping her arms around my waist. The girls are walking to flagpole, and I am heading to the office where I'm supposed to meet Botts and friends. I am carrying a backpack with my clothes for the night.

"I'm sorry, girls!" I say, hugging them. "I'll be back tomorrow! It's just one day!"

"Don't leave me!" Talia cries.

I laugh. "You'll be fine."

"I doubt it," she says. "What happens if I call in sick?"

"Lis and Janelle have to watch all of them."

"I will kill you," Lis says, glaring.

"Will you bring doughnuts?" Fancy asks.

"Yeah! Bring us doughnuts!"

"The chocolate frosting kind," Fancy says. "The best counselors bring doughnuts."

"Is that a thing?" I ask Talia.

"You're asking if doughnuts are a thing?" she asks.

"Is it a thing for counselors to bring back something for the kids?"

She nods. "Yes. For kids and co-counselors. I like mine with sprinkles. Didn't your counselors bring you stuff?"

"I think I'm remembering Munchkins," I say. "But I'll see what I can do. Now line up, ladies! Have a great evening and I'll see you tomorrow night!" I readjust my backpack, blow them all kisses, and head to the office.

Gavin is already there. His backpack is slung over his shoulder. He is still wearing his sunglasses even though it's after six.

Emily would totally make fun of him for that. I kind of want to, but I don't.

"All good?" he asks. "Botts just left a few minutes ago with Lawrence, Brody, and Allie. Since we can't all fit in one car, I said I would drive with you. Also, I have no car."

"I don't mind," I say. Just the two of us in the car. Nothing weird about that. We're friends. Meaninglessly flirty friends. "And *six* of us are staying there? How many rooms does he have? Do we have to double up?" I don't really know Allie. I am not sure I want to share a room with a virtual stranger. Although as soon as I say the words, I worry he thinks I mean doubling up with him.

He laughs. "You have obviously never seen his cottage. There are a million rooms."

"A million?"

"Probably. It has wings."

I smile. "It's a flying cottage?"

He blushes. "No, I mean—never mind. You'll see." Gavin types the address into his phone.

"So tell me who the other people are who are coming tonight," I say.

"Allie and Lawrence were together last year. Brody is kind of a loner. He's the Arts and Crafts specialist."

"Oh, yeah."

"I heard he's doing the nasty with the archery specialist."

Doing the nasty? Emily would make fun of that, too. "How do you know that?"

"People like to gossip on sailboats," he says. "Allie's the biggest gossip, by the way."

"Oh. Okay." And why is he telling me this?

"She's friendly with Kat. They went to the same preschool or something in New York."

Ah. "Small world," I say. Is he trying to tell me that he's not going to flirt with me in front of Allie? That I shouldn't flirt with him?

Whatever.

After about twenty minutes, I pull onto a dirt road that leads us to a massive house.

"This is a cottage?" I say. "More like a village."

"A small village," he says.

It's seriously about the size of my dorm building at NYU. It looks like a wood cabin, but a massive one. To the left is the lakefront. Instead of a sandy beach, there is a perfectly manicured green lawn leading to a white dock. Docked in the water are a rowboat, a motorboat, and a canoe. The water is bright blue. "This is all his?"

"His family's," Gavin says quickly. "They're in Europe."

"Who isn't?"

"Us. We are not in Europe."

"With this house, maybe I don't mind," I say.

I turn the ignition off. I sneak a peek at my phone to see if there's service. There is!

I have ten new texts. Seven are from Fancy's Annoying Mom. One from my mom. One from my dad. One from Eli.

Eli: Call me! I miss you!

I should call him before he goes to sleep, but I really want to settle in. I drop my phone in my backpack and head for the house.

It's strange toggling between real life and camp. As soon as I get to the house, I take a steaming hot shower, without flip-flops, in my own private bathroom, in my own private guest room. It's a beautiful lilac-wallpapered room, with a crisply made double bed and painting of a lakeside sunset on the wall. After getting out of the shower, I climb into the freshly made sheets and finally text Eli.

Hi! On day off! I have Wi-Fi though! I just got here but call me tomorrow!

I play on Instagram for a few minutes, scrolling through his and everyone else's pictures.

Finally I get dressed in leggings, a tank top, and a zip-up sweatshirt. By the time I get outside, Gavin and Botts are already cooking, so I set the outdoor table.

Lawrence is just sitting there drinking. He's hot in an *I go to the gym too often* kind of way. He's the type of guy who stares at your boobs while you talk.

Allie is sitting beside him. I notice she has full lips, and a small gap between her two front teeth.

The whole house is gorgeous—there really are wings—but the outside is my favorite. There's a hot tub, and a perfect pool, and a dock swaying slightly over the water. The sun sets while I place the napkins around and snack on chunks of Brie and Botts's parents' wine.

He took out a white and a red from his parents' wine cellar.

"They won't mind?" I ask.

"Nah," he says. "They're Canadian. They think the drinking age should be eighteen."

I set the table using what Botts told us were the pool dishes, which just means not glass.

Botts stopped on the way and picked up burgers, steaks, beef salami, cheese, and stuff for breakfast. "I got some veggie burgers too," he tells me. "I didn't think you were a vegetarian, but I wasn't a hundred percent sure."

"You could have texted me," I say.

"I don't have your number!"

"Right." Another way camp is not the real world. We all talk to each other all the time, but never on the phone.

Gavin grills some salami to start and by the time the burgers are cooked, the stars are out in full force. Dance music is playing from the outdoor speakers. It's perfect.

"Who wants cheese on theirs?" Gavin asks.

"Me!" I call out.

"None for me," Botts says.

"I know, I know," Gavin says. "Botts keeps kosher."

"Really?" I ask.

"I try," he says with a shrug.

"Gavin, you make a great burger," Allie says, taking a bite. I'll have to tell Kat what a great cook you are."

"Oh, she knows," he says. "She especially loves my salami."

"I'm sure she does," Botts says dryly, and we all laugh.

The six of us are sitting at the table between the lake and the pool. It's so pretty under the stars! And we're drinking wine! A lot of wine!

And the more wine we drink, the louder the six of us get. Somehow Botts, Gavin, Brody, and Lawrence end up doing handstands on the dock.

"Behold the North American male and his unique mating ritual," Allie narrates in an overly formal tone.

"What?" I nearly snort wine out of my nose.

"They're showing off for us," she explains.

I pretend like I don't agree, but I kind of do. And I kind of love it.

After we finish our meals, and clean up the plates, and pour more wine, Lawrence suggests we make our way to the hot tub.

"I'll change into my suit," I say.

"Fuck it," Brody says. "I'm going in my boxers."

He strips off his clothes and goes in.

"In," Allie says.

"Um . . ." I should change into my bathing suit.

Botts takes off his clothes too. He's wearing Star Wars boxers. They are adorable. He goes in.

Lawrence goes in next.

I look at Gavin. He looks at me.

Am I going to do this? Going in a hot tub in my bra and panties isn't cheating, is it? I wouldn't tell Eli, obviously. But it's not *cheating*.

Gavin takes off his top.

Oh, those abs.

Okay, I'm going in. I unzip my jeans. I am wearing a good blue lace thong. The bra is beige and doesn't match, but it's not horrible.

I sink into the steaming water between Botts and Allie. Ahhh. Perfect.

Botts smiles when I sit down.

Everyone but Gavin—me, Botts, Lawrence, Allie, and Brody—is already in. I see that under the water, Lawrence has his hand on Allie's thigh.

"Nice out here, huh?" Botts says to me. "We're glad you made it to Camp Blue Springs this summer, Rosenspan."

"Happy to be here." I clink my pool wineglass with his.

"Any room for me?" Gavin asks, and Allie scoots over.

My breath catches as Gavin sinks in next to me.

He really *does* have a good stomach. Also shoulders. Also salami, I'm pretty sure. I feel my face heat up and it isn't from the hot tub. Or the wine.

It might be from the wine.

We're crowded in here and his knee touches my knee under the bubbling water. Accident or on purpose?

"Your co-counselor is a riot," Allie says.

"Talia?" I ask, trying to focus on her.

"I love Talia, but I meant Tube Top."

"Oh, Janelle," I say.

"Yeah. Her."

"I like those tube tops," Lawrence says.

Allie gives him a look.

Gavin's knee is *still* touching mine. It has to be on purpose. It has to be!

"I like her a lot," I say, trying to keep my voice calm. "She's a good counselor."

"I hear she's slept with half the male staff," Allie says.

"She hasn't slept with me," Botts says.

"Or me," Brody says.

"Or me," Gavin says.

"You have a girlfriend," Allie says, pointing her finger at

him. I notice that her other hand is on Lawrence's arm.

"I only slept with her once," Lawrence says.

"Lawrence!" Allie chides. Then she climbs onto his lap. "Don't you dare sleep with her."

He laughs.

Brody takes a joint out from somewhere and passes it to Botts. He passes it to me. I inhale and then pass it to Gavin.

I don't smoke often, and I've only ever done it with Eli. But if you're not going to smoke in a hot tub on a summer night on your day off from camp, when are you going to?

"She hasn't hooked up with that many people," I say. "There's been one guy. And anyway, she's single, so who cares?"

She's single. Unlike me. Even though I'm the one who is practically naked in a hot tub with four boys, none of whom are my boyfriend, one of whom now has his thigh pressed against mine.

Does he feel what's going on here? He must!

Should I move? I don't want to move.

I will not do anything stupid. I will not do anything stupid. I will not do anything stupid.

What if Allie sees? Will she tell Kat that some chick is hitting on her guy? Am I hitting on her guy? Is he hitting on me?

The joint comes back to me.

My head starts to spin.

I think I should go to my room before I do something stupid.

"I'm going to call it," I say suddenly.

"Already?" Botts says.

"Me too," Allie says. "Lawrence, help me out?"

I think they are calling it for a different reason than I'm calling it.

"I can stay a little longer," Gavin says.

I pull myself out of the hot tub, wishing really hard that I was not wearing just a soaking-wet bra and a blue thong. "Good night."

"Good night," they all say back.

I do everything I can not to look at Gavin as Allie, Lawrence, and I head back into the house.

"Hi," I say, answering my ringing phone. The sun streams through the window.

"Did I wake you?" he asks.

"No," I say groggily.

"Liar," Eli says. "Isn't it already ten there?"

"Yeah," I say.

"Where are you?"

"Botts's country house. Day off." I am proud of myself for behaving last night. Sure, I smoked pot and got drunk, was pretty-much naked in a hot tub, and had a guy's thigh pressed against mine, but I stayed loyal and that's what counts. "Where are you?"

"Berlin. In a hostel. Not a country house."

"Did you get bedbugs yet?"

"Probably. Did you get ticks or lice yet?"

"Probably." I scratch my head. "Are you traveling with other people?"

"We met some Aussies. They're fun."

I want to ask if the Aussies are male Aussies or lady Aussies, but I don't.

"The funniest thing happened last night, actually." He tells a whole story. I try to listen but kind of fall asleep. "But we forgot our umbrellas!" And then he laughs.

"That was the punch line," he says.

"Oh. Sorry. Ha!"

"I guess you had to be there."

"I'm just tired," I say. "I don't get a lot of sleep at camp." We pause.

"Yeah," he says. "So what did you do last night?"

"Um . . . Just a barbecue." I do not mention the pot, the hot tub, or the thigh. Which makes me wonder what he's not mentioning.

"Anything fun on deck for this week?"

"Um . . . our bunk is going on our overnight. To Nude Beach," I say, and laugh.

"Huh?"

"It's called New Beach. But Janelle calls it Nude Beach."

"Ah. Got it."

"I was kind of dreading it earlier in the summer, but it should be fine. We won't really be nude," I say. "No nudity of any kind. At least not mine. The eight-year-olds do like to run around naked."

I spot my wet thong and bra on the floor.

What was I thinking last night?

I get out of bed and peek through the blinds. There's someone in a kayak across the lake. Gavin, I'd guess. The water is a mirror reflection of the pale blue sky.

Botts is sitting on a sun chair on the dock, reading a book. I wonder what time they went to bed last night. I crashed pretty hard.

I hear a door open down the hallway, and hear Allie tell Lawrence that she'll meet him downstairs.

So I guess that happened last night.

"Do you have to go?" Eli asks me.

"No! Do you?"

"Well, a bunch of us are meeting at the bar."

"Oh. Okay." I hate it when people say "Do you have to go?" when really *they* have to go. For that matter, so does Eli. Or he used to. "Have fun," I say. "Remember your umbrellas."

"Ha. What are you gonna do today?" he asks.

"A whole lot of nothing, I hope. Day off."

"Have fun, Beautiful. Love you."

"Love you, too." I click the phone off and stare at it for a second. He's so far away. And for the first time, he felt it.

"Hey, Rosenspan," Botts says. The two of us are sitting in chairs, reading. Gavin, Brody, Allie, and Lawrence are playing Frisbee. We are all wearing the bathing suits that we didn't bother putting on last night. Allie is giggling all over the place. I guess she's happy with how things went after the hot tub.

"Guess what tomorrow night's Evening Activity is?" he asks.

"I don't know. Tell me!"

"Staff softball game!"

I throw my arm up. "Woot!"

"You're on my team—yes?"

"Of course," I say. "I play third base. Don't forget."

"I know," he says.

"I don't want you giving my position to the Tank or something."

"No way. And he's captain for the other team."

"We're playing against the Tank?" I scream.

"He's slow. Sturdy. But can't actually hit a ball. We're good. Do you think Janelle would play?"

"For sure."

"We could use some other ladies too. The other team has Priya and Marissa and they are fast."

"I'm fast."

"Oh, I remember."

"I'll ask around," I say. I wonder if Lis would play. I remember that I'm supposed to feel Botts out about her. "But speaking of ladies . . . have your eye on anyone this summer?"

He puts his hand on my chair. "Are you making a move on me, Rosenspan? What about your boyfriend?"

"I am asking on behalf of a friend," I say.

"Suuuuure," he says. "I'm just messing with you. I know you're out of my league."

I laugh. "I'm not 'out of your league.' I've just got a boyfriend."

He waves his hand. "But I have a feeling I know who you're asking for."

"You do?"

He shrugs. "One of your bunkmates, perhaps?"

"Perhaps," I say carefully. "Are you interested?"

"I don't know," he says. "Maybe? She's nice and funny and definitely pretty, but . . . I don't get the sense we're into the same things. What if we're not a good fit in the real world?"

"What are you into exactly?" I ask.

"Baseball. Camp. Skiing. Star Wars. Books." I notice he has *Jonathan Strange & Mr. Norrell* opened beside him and that it's half read.

"Any good?" I ask him, pointing at the book.

"Very good," he says.

"Well, she's definitely into camp," I tell him. "I'm not so sure about the others. But it's the summer! Why are you worrying about the real world?"

If last night is any indication, I don't seem to be worried about the real world.

"Good point," he says. "Ten for two!"

"Huh?"

"You've never heard that?" he asks. "It means you live ten months in the real world for two months at camp."

"Ten for two!" Allie says, plopping down on the empty chair beside us. "But maybe camp is the real world and the school year is the pretend one. That's how I like to think of it."

"What's real anyway?" Botts asks. "Is your guy the real deal?" he asks me.

"Eli?" I say. "Of course. I wouldn't be with him if I didn't think he was."

But then I wonder, *is* he the real deal? How do you know? And what if he isn't?

Am I just wasting an entire summer because we were too afraid to take a break?

I freeze. Where did that thought come from?

A Frisbee goes whizzing by my head and into the water.

"Oops," Lawrence says.

"I'll get it," Gavin offers. "I could use a swim." He shallow dives into the water, grabbing the yellow Frisbee with one hand outstretched. "Man, that feels great."

"Cannonball!" Lawrence jumps in after him.

"I'm burning up too," I say. Instead of jumping off the dock, I step onto the shore and wade into the water. The ground feels sandy and murky and sinks under my feet. "This is kind of gross," I say.

"That's why we jumped in," Gavin says.

"Thanks for the heads-up." I dive under the water and swim out toward him. "Hi," I say.

"Hi," he says back. "Glad you came?"

"It's no South of France," I say. "But it's not half-bad."

We call it a day at three, shower, pack up, and head back to camp. Gavin and I stop at Dunkin' Donuts on the way back. We both get a box of doughnuts for the kids.

I get *another* text from Fancy's mother.

Me: Hi! Am on my day off. Will check when I get back!

Fancy's Annoying Mom: You get days off from camp? How hilarious. If only moms got days off!

Um, if Fancy is here, doesn't she have the *whole summer* off?

We arrive at Dinner Washup exactly when the next crew is leaving for their days off.

I see Danish wearing her backpack on my walk to flagpole. "Feeling rested?"

"Very," I say.

"Good! I'm going on my day off. Don't burn the bunks down. Muffs is in charge."

Earmuffs? Why did she put him in charge instead of me? Did I not do as good of a job at Family Feud as I thought? "Where are you going?" I ask, trying not to sound jealous.

"Saratoga. Meeting Kirsten! Hooray!"

"Who's Kirsten?"

"My girlfriend!"

"Oh! I forgot you have a significant other outside of camp! Why do I never see you at the office making phone calls and using the Wi-Fi?"

"Because, my dear, I use the Wi-Fi in the head staff office, near the infirmary."

"Ahhhh, that is so much closer."

"It really is," she says. "Sucker."

I laugh. "Have fun!"

I hurry back to the bunk. I'm excited to see my girls.

"Hello?" I call out.

"Sammy!" I hear.

"She's back!"

"Hooray!"

At least ten arms wrap themselves around me.

"We missed you so much!"

"Don't ever go away again."

"Did you get us doughnuts?"

"Yes, my sweeties, I did."

Everyone cheers. Unlike their parents, they are so easy to please.

It's ten thirty p.m. and Lis, Talia, Muffs, JJ, and I are all sitting together at Slice.

Janelle and Gavin have OD.

"Did Botts say anything about me?" Lis asks as soon as Muffs and JJ get up to get drinks.

I hesitate. "He thinks you're pretty. And nice."

"He does? Really?" She smiles.

"I think he needs to get to know you. You should try to spend some time with him. Speaking of which, want to play in the staff baseball game tomorrow night?"

"Um, no," she says.

"Why not? It's the perfect opportunity to get to know him! And impress him!"

She bites her nail as she talks. "I'm not going to impress him when I drop the ball. That would un-impress him. But I'll come to the game and cheer for both of you, okay?"

"Fine," I say.

"Is your camp boyfriend playing too?" she asks.

"My camp boyfriend?"

"Yeah. Like a work husband. Camp boyfriend. Gavin."

I blush. "He's not my camp boyfriend."

"He totally is," Talia says. "He always puts you in his boat at sailing. Haven't you noticed?"

"Has he?" I have *definitely* noticed that.

"Does Eli know about your camp boyfriend?" Talia asks.

"There's nothing to know, it's perfectly innocent," I say. "He even has a girlfriend!"

"That's why it's so perfect," Lis says. "He has a girlfriend and you have a boyfriend! You're the only person he can flirt with without getting into trouble or giving anyone false hope. Last year he hooked up with three different girls, by the way. It must be killing him to stay loyal. But his girlfriend *is* gorgeous. She's a ten, for real. And not just a camp ten, a real ten."

"How do you know what she looks like?" I ask, my voice low.

"Um, Instagram," Lis says. "Have you not looked at his pictures of her?"

"No," I say. But now I want to see them immediately.

"She's not hard to find. I follow him, and he tags her. Ergo I know who she is." She pulls up his Instagram and hands me her phone. "That's her."

Definitely gorgeous. Stick-straight light brown hair with blond highlights. Amazing cheek bones. Big eyes. Glam. Yep, a real ten.

I spot Muffs and JJ returning to our table, and I quickly hand Lis back her phone.

Even when I was a camper, everyone wanted to get to know Gavin. He was the guy all the girls thought was hot.

And now that I know his girlfriend is gorgeous, for some reason, he is even hotter?

The score is 5–7. It's the ninth inning. We're losing. And I'm at bat. Botts is on first. Janelle is on second. Brody is on third. We have two outs.

I've had one walk so far, one out, and one ground ball. I haven't played in a while. Since high school. Funny that Eli has never seen me play.

"You can do it!" Botts screams. "Come on, Rosenspan! Take us home!"

"Go, Sammy!" my girls scream from the bleachers.

No pressure or anything.

Smokin' Hot Benji is pitching.

He tosses the ball.

I miss.

"Strike one!" Josh says.

Crap.

He tosses the ball again.

I miss again.

"Strike two!"

"You got this, Rosenspan!" Botts yells.

I look up at Gavin. He makes a swinging motion.

I got this.

The ball sails toward me and I swing and this time I smash it! The ball goes sailing in the air right over Bunk 11!

Everyone cheers and I run to first base, second base, third base, and home! I did it! I brought everyone home! Botts even dives into home right in front of me and then high-fives me as I step on the plate.

"Impressive," Gavin says, and our eyes lock. "Athletic and adorable. Quite a combo."

"Thanks," I tell him. Then my campers jump all over me, shrieking and cheering. The eye contact is gone.

"You're in my boat," Gavin tells me on Saturday morning when I bring my bunk down to the beach.

I'm glad Talia and Lis are on their days off or they would totally say *I told you so*. Also they would call me out for putting eyeliner on before boating.

Prague, Em, and Lily are in our boat too.

"It's a perfect day for sailing," Gavin says as I sit down beside him.

He says the same thing every time.

I laugh. "But there's no wind!"

He shrugs. "Still a good day for sailing. Sun. Water. A boat. Good company. What more could you want? I'm going to teach you how to jib the boat today," he says.

"I don't know what that means . . . but it sounds kind of dirty," I say, lowering my voice.

He laughs. "Oh yeah?"

"Totally."

"I'm also going to teach you how to tack," he says.

I fake fan my face. "Why, sir! You are being most inappropriate. I am a lady!"

He laughs again.

"Where did you learn how to sail anyway?" I ask when he finally sits down and we're halfway across the lake.

"Self-taught," he says. "I grew up in Annapolis, Maryland. Near the water."

"Speaking of water," Prague says, jumping into the conversation. "Can you try and get frog hunting on the schedule, Sam?"

"Frog hunting!" I cry. "I loved frog hunting!"

"Me too!" Prague says.

"What, exactly, is frog hunting?" Lily asks.

"We all put on Billy Boots and go to the marsh and catch frogs and put them in buckets," I say. "We did it when I was here. It was fun. I'll ask Danish. Want to come frog hunting with us, Gav?"

"No thanks," he says. "I prefer to keep my hands slime-free."

"But it's fun!" Prague says.

The boom comes across and he jumps to the other side of the boat. "Pass."

I'm surprised he's not up for it, but I guess chasing frogs in a marsh is not everyone's cup of tea.

"Fine," Prague says. "But you're coming with us to New Beach tonight!"

"You are?" I ask, surprised.

He nods. "I'm your tripper. They always send one of the boat staff to help out."

"That's fun," I say, flushing. I turn to Prague. "How did you know that?"

"I know everything," she says, and pokes Gavin in the side. "Are you cooking?" Prague asks.

"Yup. I'm in charge of the hot dogs."

"I had no idea we got a helper," I say. "I was wondering if anyone was going to instruct me on how to roast a weenie. Do you stay overnight too?" I keep my eyes down as I ask the question.

"Of course I stay overnight," he says, and my heart races. "It's *really far away.*"

He shakes his head at me. I realize that he's not staying overnight; he's just saying that for the girls' benefit since they are not supposed to know New Beach is a part of camp.

"Oh, please," Prague says. "It's right by Bunk Eleven."

I laugh. "You really do know everything, don't you, Prague?"

"I really do," she says, and turns back to the water.

"Come on, girls, we gotta go!" I call out from the porch.

"You're so lucky your camp boyfriend is coming on our overnight," Talia says.

I laugh. "He's not my camp boyfriend!" But then I think about my actual boyfriend, and realize that today was so busy that I forgot to text him again. Yesterday was busy too. I was on nighttime OD plus Free Play OD and couldn't get to the office. Staying in constant contact is harder than I thought it would be. And where are those postcards he was supposed to send me? He was supposed to send one a day while he was abroad. Why's he so busy that *he can't send me postcards*?

"I'm just jealous," Talia continues. "Everyone in camp is in love with him and he only talks to you."

"That's not true," I say, but it might be true, and I kind of like it.

I wonder what he's like as a real boyfriend. Is he romantic? Is he a good kisser? Is he the kind of guy who makes the first move? Would he take my hand first? Touch my back? Or just try to kiss me?

Inappropriate! I try to shake off the thought.

I wonder if Talia's really jealous, though. She doesn't seem interested in Gavin. Or any of the guys, for that matter. Or the girls.

"Come on, guys!" I yell again. "On the porch! Hustle!"

The girls trickle out, wearing their backpacks, which are hopefully filled with their warmest pajamas, a bathing suit, a towel, and a change of clothes for tomorrow. They are holding their water bottles and plastic garbage bags for storing their sleeping bag and pillow, to keep them from getting wet if they fall in the water. It better not rain.

I have my own backpack of clothes, my own sleeping bag and pillow, and an extra supply bag.

When the girls are finally on the porch, I lead the way to the beach. "We're going on a boating trip!" I yell out to the tune of, "We're going on a bear hunt."

They repeat after me, all the way to the water.

"Everyone get a life jacket!" I say, still in Bear Hunt mode. The girls chorus it back, and Gavin gives me a funny look.

"Ready?" Gavin says. He's standing by one of the rowboats.

"Oh yeah," I say.

I have a flashback to rowing over here when I was a kid. That was a terrible night. But now I'm in charge. And everyone is going to have fun.

We divide into two rowboats and push off. Talia goes with Gavin, since she claims not to know how to row. Luckily, it'll only take ten minutes to get there.

The lake is quiet and mirrorlike since it's Dinner Washup and we're the only ones on it. Each row sends ripples through the reflection.

I see the fireflies have come out too.

"Why are we taking a boat when we could walk?" Em asks.

"Because they want us to think it's really far away," Prague says. "They do this every year. Seniors get to go on actual canoe trips outside of camp."

"New Beach *is* really far away," Gavin says. His voice travels across the water.

"Liar!" Fancy exclaims.

Gavin and Talia's boat arrives at New Beach first. He rows as close to the shore as possible and then jumps out to pull it in. The girls squeal and hop over each other to rush out.

"Take your stuff!" he calls out. "There's no concierge service!"

Two of them are already out of sight, but the other two take their backpacks and garbage bags. Gavin pulls my boat in next.

"Thank you!" I say as he helps my girls out. We pass them their bags and knapsacks.

"I totally remember this place," I say. "And it looks exactly the same."

"Why do they call it New Beach?" Lily asks, the last one in the boat.

"Because this piece of property used to be owned by another family, and camp just bought it about twenty years ago," Prague says.

"Is that true?" I ask Gavin.

"Probably," he says. He takes my hand and helps me out of the boat.

We're holding hands, we're holding hands, we're holding hands!

Kind of.

Could my camp boyfriend be any cuter? I don't think so.

Right by the water is a clearing where we'll have our bonfire tonight, and then farther to the left is where the two tents are already set up. To the right is the path to Bunk 11, which I'm hoping the girls don't notice.

I can't believe I'm back here. Last time I was on New Beach was one of the worst days of my summer. But this time could be one of my best?

"Okay, ladies," I say. "First let's set up your sleeping bags. Three girls per tent plus one counselor! Take out your clothes so you can change right after you swim. Not your pj's! We are only putting those on right before bed. We want to keep them clean and tick-free!"

We find the tent area, and Talia and I unroll their sleeping bags and help the girls find spots for their flashlights and stuffed animals.

"Who wants to swim?" I yell out.

"Me! Me!" I hear back. The kids are already wearing their bathing suits, so they strip off any extra clothes, completely messing up our organized tents, and run into the water.

"I'm too cold to swim," Prague says, lagging behind the rest.

We step into the clearing.

"Me too," I say.

"You can help me get wood," Gavin offers.

"Get wood?" I say under my breath, and give him a look. He laughs. "Dirty mind."

"Attention, all campers and counselors," we hear in the distance. "Attention, all campers and counselors. It is now the end of Dinner Washup. Please proceed to the flagpole."

The girls all stop splashing and laugh.

"Oh yeah, we're really far from camp," Fancy says.

"I don't hear anything," I say. "Talia, do you hear anything?"

"Nothing at all," she says. "Gavin?"

"Nothing at all!"

"You guys are such liars!" Fancy calls out.

"You have to believe for it to be true," I say.

"That's what my mom says about the tooth fairy," Slugger says.

"You don't believe in the tooth fairy?" I ask.

"Of course not!" Fancy says.

"There is definitely a tooth fairy," I tell them. "She's just not interested in any of your teeth because of all the candy you eat."

Gavin snorts.

When the girls are ready to come out, we walk over with their towels and wrap them each up. Giggling, they sprint to the tents to change.

"Don't come here, Gavin!" Fancy says.

"I won't," he says, rolling his eyes.

"Sam, make sure he doesn't come!" Lily says.

"I'll guard the tents with my life," I tell them.

We hear a lot of squealing and then one by one they join us back in the clearing.

"I have to pee," Shira says. "Sam, can you come with me?"

"Sure," I say. "Who is ready to pee in the woods?"

I grab the toilet paper and one of the seven hand sanitizers Talia packed in our supply bag. "Whoever has to pee, follow me!"

"I just went in the lake!" Fancy says.

"That's so gross!" Shira tells her.

"Why is that any grosser than going in the forest?" she barks back.

"Because we're all in the water," Em says.

"We're all in the forest!"

"We don't swim in the forest," she explains.

"Okay! Whoever has to pee, follow me," I say again, and lead them to a tree that has some space around it. "This is a good spot. This is the official bathroom. Everyone watch where you step."

"No pooping!" Prague says.

"If you gotta go, you gotta go," I say. "But it might be easier to wait to poop until tomorrow morning, if you have a choice in the matter."

The girls all laugh hysterically.

"I'm peeing!" Prague says. "Easy-peasy pumpkin squeezy!"

"I can't do it with everyone here!" Em says.

"Then move more into the forest," I say.

"I'm too scared. I don't want to get a tick in my patoota."

"Your patoota?" Shira giggles.

"Yes! My patooooooooota."

"Okay, everyone close your eyes so Em can pee," I order.

"Eyes closed!" Prague says.

"Can you go?" I ask her, my eyes closed too.

"I need everyone to close their ears *and* their eyes. And someone has to hold my lion."

I hold the lion. "Okay, everyone, close your ears!" I say. "Now can you?"

"Maybe . . . almost."

We all wait. And wait.

"I did it!"

"Hooray!" we all cheer.

"But I got some on my bathing suit."

I hand her the toilet paper roll. "It's fine. Pee comes out in the wash."

"I miss our toilets," Prague says. "Our short, gross, never flush all the way toilets."

"It's only one night, girls! Now use the sanitizer!" I pass it around and then we rejoin the group.

Back at the clearing, Gavin has the fire going.

I stand beside him. "Nice flame."

"Thanks," he says.

"How many overnights do you have to do this summer?"

"About three. One for the seniors, though, which is off camp."

"Oh. Not too bad."

"I don't mind. This is fun."

The fire suddenly blazes in front of us and we step back.

"So we eat after this?" I ask.

"They play a little, and then we make hot dogs for dinner and play cards and make s'mores and then I go back to my bunk and you and Talia try to get six girls who have had too many marshmallows to fall asleep."

"Sounds awesome," I say.

"They're probably going to wake up really early tomorrow. But I'll be here by eight to help you guys get back."

"And then we just row back to camp?"

"That's it."

I smile. "Easy-peasy pumpkin squeezy."

We make hot dogs and smother them in ketchup. Talia says she's never had a hot dog before because they look gross, Gavin and I make fun of her, and she decides to try one.

"I'm a vegetarian!" she says. "But I'm starving. And I forgot the soy peanut butter. So hand one over." She chews about half. "This is as vile as I imagined."

Then it's time for the s'mores. The girls get the chocolate all over their faces and I wish I had Wet-Naps but I didn't bring any. I make them wipe their hands and faces on their towels.

Then they all take out their flashlights and we tell ghost stories.

There's one about a boy who drowned in New Beach and now haunts New Beach.

There's one about the killer loose in the Adirondacks who eats children.

"I heard a girl really did die at an overnight once," Prague says. "She was allergic to peanut butter and someone brought peanut butter and used the same knife on her bread and she didn't have her EpiPen on her and she died."

It suddenly gets a little cold.

"That's not true," Fancy says. "You're making that up."

"No, it is," Prague says. "Has no one else ever heard about that? I heard my mom talking about it."

"I heard that too," Talia says. "But that's not this camp. Or this beach."

"Still scary," Em says.

Gavin and I look at each other, our eyes wide.

"I don't want to die," Prague says, shivering.

"No one is dying," I say. "Can we talk about something else, guys?" I look at Slugger, remembering that her dad passed away.

"What do you think happens after you die?" Slugger asks.

Oh, brother. This is getting really heavy, really fast.

"I think you go to heaven," Prague says.

"Jews don't believe in heaven," Em says.

"We don't?" I ask.

"No," Shira says. "Didn't you go to Hebrew school?"

"I did not," I say.

"I do," Em says.

"You do?" Fancy asks. "You're Jewish?"

"Yes!" Em says.

"But you're black!" Fancy says.

"Hey," I say quickly. "She can be black and Jewish."

"I go to Jewish day school," Em says. "I probably know more about Judaism than you do."

"Probably," Fancy admits. "I have a Christmas tree in my house."

"Lucky," Prague says.

"We put up a Christmas tree, too," Lily says. "And a menorah. We celebrate everything, including Chinese New Year. My mom's parents are from Hong Kong."

"My mom says after my bubbe died, she came back as me," Shira says.

"That doesn't make any sense," Fancy tells her.

"Yes it does. She died before I was born and my mom thinks she's me now. In a new body. I look just like her. And act like her. We're both stubborn."

"Sam, what do you think?" Prague asks me.

"Do you believe in heaven?" Em asks.

Gavin and I exchange a look. Um. Wow.

I don't know what I believe. I don't think I believe in heaven. I definitely don't think there's an old man in the sky judging us on our actions, good or bad. But I'm not sure I should tell the kids that.

"Okay, everyone look up," Gavin says. "Who sees the Big Dipper?"

Everyone shifts and looks up.

"What's the Big Dipper?" Lily asks.

Nice way to change the subject, I think.

"Turn off your flashlights," Gavin says, and they all do.

He jumps up and points to the sky. "See over there? It's the seven stars that look like they're a pot."

"Sam," Talia says, pulling at my sleeve.

I turn to her.

"I . . . I have to go to the bathroom," she whispers.

"Do you need the toilet paper?"

She bites her lip. "Yes, but no. I have to go, go. I can't do it in the woods. I'm going to run to Bunk Eleven."

"Okay," I say. "I'll be fine. Gavin is here."

She nods and takes off running.

Gavin raises his eyebrow, and I shrug.

He continues pointing to the sky, explaining stuff, and being really cute as he does it. He explains all about stars and the solar system and the galaxy. Everyone seems to have forgotten about the death talk.

When Prague starts to yawn, I say, "Girls, five minutes until you get into your tents, okay? It's getting late."

I spot Talia coming back through the path. She smiles at everyone but sidles up beside me. "There's something wrong with me," she whispers. "I knew I shouldn't have had that hot dog."

"Are you sick?" I whisper back.

"Yes! And I can't go in Bunk Eleven! What was I thinking? They're all there! A bunk of boys! I used it for a second but then realized that *they could hear me*! I have to go back to our bunk. I'm so sorry. I'll take Pepto or something. Ow, ow ow." She clutches her stomach as she talks.

"Don't worry," I say. "I'm okay. Gavin will stay until the kids go to bed."

"What's wrong?" Gavin asks, coming over.

"Talia has a headache," I say quickly.

She smiles at me gratefully.

"I can always use your sleeping bag and stay," Gavin says.

Stay? He can stay where? Here? Where is he sleeping exactly?

"I gotta go," Talia says, and I see how pale she is. "Please don't be mad at me."

"I'm not. You gotta go when you gotta go."

She takes off, calling out, "I'll come back if I can."

"Where is she going?" Prague asks, the only one paying attention.

"She's not feeling great," I say.

I look up and Gavin is looking at me. I look away.

Just the two of us here under the stars? Is that a good idea?

He smiles.

Yes. It's a good idea. A very good idea.

* * *

After I put the kids to bed, the fire is out and Gavin is sitting on the edge of the dock. The moon is massive and lights up the whole lake.

"Hi," I say, sitting beside him, cross-legged.

"Hi," he says, smiling. "Girls okay?"

"They seem fine," I say. "Tired but cozy."

He nods. "You're really good with them."

"Thanks," I say. "So are you. You totally saved me with the Big Dipper."

He's sitting about a half a foot away from me. Not even. He smells like smoke from the fire.

"Anytime," he says.

I look up at him. My whole body tingles.

Our eyes are locked, and neither of us looks away.

Do I want this to happen?

"I . . . so . . ." He hesitates.

I take a gulp of air.

"This," he says.

Heart. Thumping.

I can feel him beside me. He is so close. He clears his throat. "If it weren't for Eli and Kat . . . would we . . . would we be a thing?"

He said it. It's out there.

"I think . . ." I say slowly. "That if it weren't for Kat and Eli, we . . . would be a thing." I can barely breathe. This thing between us is not in my head. It is real. His thigh was

172

touching mine in the hot tub. On purpose. I wondered, and now I know.

"Yeah."

"So."

He inches closer to me.

What am I doing? Is this going to happen? Is he going to kiss me?

Do I *want* him to kiss me?

My boyfriend left me for Europe! I am on a dock in the moonlight under a starry sky with a gorgeous guy who wants to kiss me! Why shouldn't I kiss him? Eli is doing who knows what who knows where, and if I'm not going to do something like kiss a guy who is not my boyfriend when I am nineteen, when am I going to do it?

The air is suddenly thick. I push thoughts of Eli out of my mind.

Gavin is so cute. He moves closer. I move closer. He is right beside me, his leg once again pressed against mine. I can't think of anything except what his lips will feel like. This is happening. There is no stopping it. It is happening right now. I close my eyes—

"Hellllllo?" we hear.

I pull back quickly, my heart racing. Shit, shit, shit.

"Where are you guys?"

I turn around. It's Janelle.

"Right here." I leap to my feet.

"Talia asked me if I would come, so I came!"

"Oh! Great! Awesome. She okay?" I straighten my shirt even though no one touched it. No one touched anything. Nothing happened.

"Yeah, she'll be fine. She downed an entire bottle of Pepto."

"I thought she had a headache," Gavin says.

"I was being discreet," I mutter.

Gavin stands. He doesn't look at me. "I guess I'll head back."

"You are the sweetest for hanging out here," Janelle says to him. "Are you coming on my overnight too? We go tomorrow night!"

"I don't think so," he says. "Maybe Morgan?"

"Talia said she would switch with me tomorrow night. So I don't have to sleep out here again, although it's kind of awesome out here so I don't mind." Her hands are waving all over the place. "Did you pee in the woods?"

"On that note, I guess I'll go," Gavin says.

"Thank you for staying with me," I say quickly.

"Anytime," he says, and then he's gone.

I show Janelle to Talia's tent and then sneak into mine. I turn over and then turn over again.

One of the girls is snoring. My heart won't stop racing.

What just happened?

Or what just almost happened?

Something just almost happened. I almost let something happen.

Did I want that to happen?

Yes. I definitely did.

But what about Eli? What's wrong with me?

I close my eyes and imagine Gavin kissing me, over and over again, knowing that if Janelle hadn't shown up, I wouldn't have said no.

WEEK 3 SCHEDULE—BUNK 6A

	SUNDAY	MONDAY	TUESDAY	WEDNESDAY	THURSDAY	FRIDAY	SATURDAY
PERIOD 1 10:15–10:45	SHOWERS	TENNIS	?	?	TENNIS	DRAMA	DRAMA
PERIOD 2 10:45–11:30	DRAMA	DRAMA	?	?	SAILING	SI	ART
PERIOD 3 11:30–12:15	NEWCOMB	DANCE	?	?	SOCCER	TENNIS	WRESTLING
12:15–12:30	LUNCH WASHUP	LUNCH WASHUP	LUNCH WASHUP	LUNCH WASHUP	LUNCH WASHUP	LUNCH WASHUP	LUNCH WASHUP
12:30–1:00	LUNCH	LUNCH	LUNCH	LUNCH	LUNCH	LUNCH	LUNCH
1:00–2:00	REST HOUR	REST HOUR	REST HOUR	REST HOUR	REST HOUR	REST HOUR	REST HOUR
PERIOD 4 2:00–2:45	SI	BASKETBALL	?	?	BASKETBALL	ART	SI
2:45–3:15	MILK & COOKIES	MILK & COOKIES	MILK & COOKIES	MILK & COOKIES	MILK & COOKIES	MILK & COOKIES	MILK & COOKIES
PERIOD 5 3:15–4:00	ART	SI	?	?	SOCCER	WATERSKI	POTTERY
PERIOD 6 4:00–4:45	SOCCER	BASEBALL	?	?	GS	GS	GS

Week 3

The next morning, Janelle and I help the girls roll up their sleeping bags, which is ten times harder than it should be. I have the most trouble with mine and most of the bag ends up spilling over the edge like a muffin top.

"Thanks again for coming," I tell Janelle.

"Anytime!" she says. "It was fun. I was just OD. I would rather be sleeping under the stars then stuck in the cabin any day. I have serious FOMO. I want to try it all! See everything! Kiss everyone!"

I laugh. "Sounds fun."

"It is," she says. "I'm sure I'll slow down eventually, but now's not the time in our lives for us to be stuck in a box, you know?"

"I think I can see what you mean," I say. We start to carry our stuff to the clearing near the water.

Gavin is sitting in a rowboat.

"Oh. Hey," I say, feeling incredibly awkward.

"Hey." He's wearing his sunglasses and I can't read his expression. Also the sun is bright so I'm squinting, which doesn't help the awkwardness.

Silence.

Okay, then.

Does he regret what almost happened? Do I?

My head feels blurry. Cottony. I need coffee.

"Do the girls need help with their bags?" he asks.

"We're okay," I tell him. "Thanks." Squint.

I hear more squealing and an "I got pee on my shoe!" and we put our stuff back in garbage bags, and then back in the rowboats.

"Come row with me, Sam!" Janelle says, and I climb into her boat.

Gavin pushes us off.

Half the girls are cranky and overtired and the other half are pretty much asleep.

"The girls in my tent all woke up having to pee in the middle of the night," Janelle says. "I thought a bear was going to get us for sure. What a night."

You're telling me.

We drop off our stuff at the bunk. Talia is still in bed.

"I am so sorry," she says, jumping up. "How did it go?"

"Fine," I say. "Thanks for sending Janelle."

"Was she super annoying?" she whispers.

"Not at all," I say. "She was great. Arrived just in time." Just, just, just in time.

"I don't know what happened to me," she says. "But I think the worst is over."

We have showers first period, which we all appreciate, then drama, then Newcomb. Newcomb is basically volleyball, but you catch and throw the ball instead of volleying it. Then we have lunch washup, and lunch. Half the girls run to the Rec Hall during Rest Hour to try out for tomorrow night's talent show, but I nap. After lunch, we have SI—swim instruction—in the lake.

Instead of going in, Talia and I sit on the dock. I can't tell if going in the water now would wake me up or if I'm still so tired I would sink to the bottom. I'm pretty sure the latter.

I watch Gavin across the lake when I know he's not looking. I've been playing a careful game of it, trying to make myself appear extremely busy when his sailboat is heading in our direction.

"Don't stop, keep going!" Marissa tells the kids.

"Strong legs!" we hear.

"Remember to blow bubbles!"

"I can be OD tonight," Talia says. "I owe you. Janelle wants to go back to New Beach so I'm here."

"Don't worry," I tell her. "I'm so tired I'll probably stay in anyway. But can you make sure the girls get Milk and Cookies and get to art? I'll meet you at the A and C. I want to try and call Eli."

More like, I desperately *need* to call Eli.

"No problemo," she says.

As soon as the girls are out of the lake and drying off, I speed-walk to get my phone and then run to the office.

I'm so glad I didn't do anything last night. *So* glad. I was being incredibly dumb. I have an amazing boyfriend! Who I love! Who loves me! Why would I almost throw it away for a stupid summer hookup? That was moronic!

My fingers ache to text Eli. To say hi. To make contact. I need to hear his voice. I open the office door, and then call him with one hand and wave to Eric with the other.

"Hey, Beautiful!" Eli says.

Ah. His voice. "Hi!"

"It's you!" he says.

"It's me! I miss you!" I sit down on the edge of the well-worn gray couch.

"I miss you, too!" he says. "How are you?"

"I'm okay," I say, but I feel like a fraud.

A huge thing happened. Even if nothing actually happened.

And I'm not going to tell him.

"How was your camping trip?" he asks.

He knows? Oh, right, I told him. "Oh. It was fine." I tell him about the rowboat and the already set up tents and rolling up the sleeping bags. I don't tell him about who rowed the boat or cooked the food. He doesn't ask. Maybe he thinks it was me. "Where are you?" I ask, changing the subject.

"Prague!"

I laugh. "No way! My camper is named Prague!"

"That's a strange name for a kid," he says.

"It fits her," I say. "So what are you doing in Prague?"

He tells me about the hostel and the synagogue they went to see, which is one of the oldest synagogues in Europe.

Eric taps me on the shoulder. "Um, Sam? I have to call the next period."

Eli's in the middle of a sentence.

"Eli? Shoot, I gotta go."

"Again? Come on! What's so important?"

Really?

"I have to get back to the kids."

"You can't wait a minute?" he asks, sounding annoyed.

"No," I snap. Does he think camp runs on my schedule? "Can I call you tomorrow?"

"Might be on the train, but I'm not sure. You can try."

Oh, gee, thanks.

Neither of us says anything. "Love you," I say.

"You too."

I end the call.

I run right into Gavin, Botts, Jill, and Josh on my way to art. They're standing at the top of the beach laughing about something.

"Hey there, Rosenspan!" Botts says. "Are you sneaking

off to call your boyfriend in the middle of the day?"

My cheeks heat up. Crap. Now the head counselors are going to think I'm blowing off my bunk. Plus Gavin knows I went to call Eli. Which isn't necessarily bad, but he's looking at the ground instead of looking at me, so maybe it is?

"Sorry," I say. "I don't normally call him in the middle of the day, but—"

"You were on your overnight," Jill says. "I get it. He's in Europe, correct? And I heard Talia . . . did not like the hot dogs."

"I heard they did not like her," Botts says.

They all laugh. Word really does travel fast. She would be mortified if she knew.

"We need to work on your cooking, Gav," Botts says.

"Apparently," he says.

"Did you guys have fun?" Josh asks.

"Um . . . me and Gavin?" I yelp.

"I meant your bunk," Botts says.

"Oh, right," I say, cheeks on fire. "Yes. We had a great time."

Gavin looks back down at the ground.

"I have to get to art," I say quickly. "The lanyards are not going to butterfly stitch themselves."

They all laugh.

I hurry up the hill without looking back.

* * *

Gavin and I don't talk to each other for the rest of the day. I'm not sure how we manage it. Or why. Are we purposefully ignoring each other? We might be.

That night he walks by my table holding a tray of spaghetti, but does not look up. Is he afraid of spilling the spaghetti? Or is he pretending not to see me?

We sit at opposite ends of the Rec Hall during Jeopardy.

He waves. I wave back.

Neither of us approaches the other.

What is happening? I don't know. Do I want to never talk to him again? Do I want to make out with him? Do I want to just be friends? I don't know, I don't know, I don't know!

We'll have to talk eventually. We're not going to not speak for the rest of the summer.

Unless that's his plan. To not speak to me for the rest of the summer.

At breakfast on Monday, I notice the head staff all whispering to each other.

"Did something happen?" I ask Talia, and motion to their table with my chin.

She squeezes a drop of hand sanitizer on her hands, rubs it in, and then looks their way.

"I bet it's color war," she says to me. "Maybe the break is tonight after the talent show."

Ah. Color war. Basically the Olympics for campers. They divide up the camp into three teams, each with a color, and we do activities against each other for two days. They try to announce color war—or break it—by surprising the kids with the announcement.

Two captains are chosen per team.

It's an honor to be chosen. Being a captain means that you're not only a great counselor, but well-liked by all the head staff.

If they chose me, it would mean that I'm actually good at this education thing even if camp isn't the same as school. And that I'm competent, even if Eli teases me about getting lost or forgetting my keys. It would mean that everyone likes me.

It seems dumb to get excited about being chosen to do extra work, but I suddenly want to be chosen as captain very, very badly.

By the time the talent show starts Monday night, there's a lot of buzz about color war breaking at some point tonight.

I try to ignore it and focus on the show. Fancy is in it. She was the only girl in our bunk to make it in. I heard her practice in the bunk, but as she sings "Roar" by Katy Perry, it makes me tear up. She's that good.

I take a million pictures and a video and plan to send it to her mom. Which is probably a mistake, but it's too cute not to forward.

During the last number, a juggling act by Botts, all the lights in the Rec Hall go off.

People scream.

Power failure?

Then the lights start to flicker.

A camper yells out, "Color war!"

Then everyone starts chanting, "Color war! Color war!"

Botts takes the microphone. "Everyone please proceed to the tennis courts!"

"They're breaking it! Told ya," Talia says to me.

The kids are all jangly with excitement, and we lead them out the side door and to the tennis courts.

"Red. Blue. Yellow. It's color war!" the head staff scream out together. Red, blue, and yellow spotlights turn on and dance across the tennis courts. Red, blue, and yellow firecrackers blaze across the sky.

Everyone cheers.

The head staff talk about the history of color war, making it sound as epic as possible to get the kids excited. Not that they need to try that hard—the kids are pretty excited. Two full days of competitions! Three teams! One winner!

I search the crowd for Gavin. I spot him to my right, the next bunk over, arm around one of his campers.

Aw, he's so cute.

But why is he not looking at me? We still haven't spoken since the overnight. Is he not thinking about me at all? Two days ago we almost made out and now he is totally over me? Is that even possible?

Why do I even care if he looks at me? I don't want to cheat on my boyfriend! I *love* my boyfriend!

"And now it's time to announce the captains of the yellow team," Priya says.

My head snaps back to the head staff.

"The captains are Brody Friedman and Ilana Morris!"

Everyone cheers. I cheer too, trying not to look at all disappointed.

"I hope we're on the same team!" Slugger says to Em.

The two captains run to join the center of the circle.

Danish takes the mic. "And the captains of the red team are: Benji Rhee and Audrey Goodman!"

Yay for Smokin' Hot Benji. Boo for me.

Only one more chance.

Maybe they didn't pick me at all. Maybe I'm not really that good of a counselor. Maybe Josh and Danish actually were annoyed that I was calling Eli in the middle of the day. Maybe no one even likes me. Not Gavin, not Talia, not Danish. Maybe when I'm not in the room, they all laugh about me and call me Porny.

Botts takes the mic. "And the captains of the blue team are: Gavin Lawblau and Sam Rosenspan!"

It's me! YES! Hooray! They called my name! AND GAVIN'S! Now we will run into each other's arms and make out immediately!

No, no, no.

We will not make out immediately. We will not make out at all. I have. A freakin'. Boyfriend! What is wrong with me?

I slowly turn to catch Gavin's expression. He smiles and shrugs. I smile and shrug back.

I AM CAPTAIN WITH GAVIN OMIGOD OMIGOD.

We both run up into the center of the court. Everyone cheers.

"Sam and Gav! Sam and Gav! Sam and Gav!"

It has a nice ring to it, though, doesn't it?

After they read out the lists of campers on all our teams and the kids are all sent to Milk and Cookies, the head staff ask the six captains to stay behind.

"Ready for this, Sam?" Gavin asks, lazily putting his arm around my shoulders. His touch makes me freeze.

"Yup," I say.

He is touching me, he is touching me.

"You looked shocked," Priya says to me.

"I am." He is still touching me.

I need Gavin to stop touching me or I am going to make out with him, and I really don't think I should make out with someone who is not my boyfriend.

I take a step away from him so his arm slides off.

"You really didn't know we were going to choose you?" Priya asks me, an eyebrow perfectly arched. "You're such an obvious favorite."

Favorite? I am a favorite? An *obvious* favorite? "I hoped but I didn't know."

"Of course they were going to choose you," Gavin says, smiling at me. "You're a killer counselor. And you look good in blue."

My cheeks heat up. He's still flirting with me!

"So, you know the rules?" Botts says. "Try not to make

the kids in your bunk who aren't on your teams feel bad. You still have to help put them to bed, and you still have to do OD if no one will switch with you. But your curfew is waived for the next two days. For organizational purposes only, you're allowed in boys' or girls' cabins. You should spend tonight coming up with a few cheers for the morning, and giving jobs to the staff members on your team. And as always, the winning captains get a five-hundred-dollar bonus."

"Really?" I say. "Fun!"

"Yes. Added incentive. Go, captains!"

"I have OD," I tell Gavin when we disperse. The colored spotlights all turn off and we're standing in the dark.

"That's fine. I'll come to your bunk. We'll hash it all out."

"My bunk?"

"Yeah."

Oh boy. Gavin. In my bunk. I clear my throat. "I . . ."

"About . . ."

We both stop.

We both laugh.

"We got a little carried away the other night," I say.

"Yes," he says.

"But I love Eli and you love Kat and neither of us wants to do anything dumb," I say.

"We don't?" he asks.

"We don't," I say.

"We don't," he repeats with a crooked smile.

Oh, boy. "Okay," I say. "Good. We're on the same page."

"Kind of," he says. "But if that's what you want . . ."

"It's what I want," I say quickly. "I think."

He smiles again. "Then okay."

Everyone congratulates me at Milk and Cookies. I love every second of it.

"Yes! You're on my team!" Janelle says, high-fiving me as we walk back to our cabin. "Oh, captain, my captain! This is going to be amazing! I am totally going to paint my face blue," Janelle says.

I am not painting my face blue. "Come on, girls, into bed!" I yell out as I step into the bunk.

"You're my captain!" Shira and Lily tell me, giving me hugs.

"I wish I was on the blue team!" Fancy says. "This sucks. I don't want to be red!"

"Lis is on your team," I say.

"But she's not the captain," Fancy says with a pout. "You're the captain."

"No color war in the bunk," Prague says. "Right, Sam?"

"Absolutely. And it's only two days, Fancy. Then everything will go back to normal. Do you guys all have clothes for tomorrow?"

"Remember, guys," Lis calls out, "everyone can also wear black and white."

"Who wants to trade yellow and red clothes?" one of them calls out.

It's a frantic swap meet for the next ten minutes. After they're settled, and after Janelle and Lis and Talia all go out for the night, I hear steps on the front porch and then a soft knock on the front door, and then it opens.

"Sam?" Gavin calls.

"In here," I say from the counselors' room. My heart is beating hard, but I try to keep calm. He is here for color war, that's all. Nothing is going to happen. This is work. We have to work.

He pushes back the sheet doorway. "Ready?"

"Let's do this," I say. I pull out the clipboard the organizers handed me on the tennis courts. I'm sitting on my bed, cross-legged.

He sits on Janelle's bed across from me and leans his head back against the wall.

"So, what are you thinking for the first cheer?" I ask.

"B-L-U-E, blue team on to victory," he says in a dry voice.

"That'll be our morning cheer," I tell him. "Well, look at that. We're half done. We've practically won."

"So this is where you live," he says, looking around our room. "Lis and Talia are in there?"

"Yup."

"No pictures of your boyfriend?"

I shake my head. "I forgot to print them out before I left. Do you have pictures up?"

He nods.

We're both quiet. I don't want to talk about Eli or Kat.

"I have a list of all the staff on our team and all the big jobs. Should we go through it?" I scan the paper. On the final night of color war, all the camp sections have to perform. The seniors do a skit. The inters do a dance. The juniors do a cheer. The CITs do a magic act. Each team does a song. We have to choose a staff member on our team who can lead them.

"Let's start with the senior skit," he says. "Allie's on our team. And she wrote it last year. It was funny. We can ask her to do it again. The performance is worth twenty points."

"Great," I say. "What about the team song?"

"We have Trevor. And he always has his guitar out."

"The basketball teacher?"

"Yes.

"Perfect."

"Junior cheer? That's only worth fifteen points."

"Janelle?" we both say at the same time.

"Done."

We pick counselors to do the inter dance, and the CIT magic act, and by the time we're finished, Talia and Lis are back, with Janelle close behind.

"Janelle! You up for the junior cheer?" I ask.

"I don't know what you're talking about, but I am up for anything my lovely leaders need me for!"

"You are a rock star," I tell her, writing her name in.

Lis nibbles on her thumbnail. "Argh, Talia and I both have to write our junior cheers too."

"We'll have the cheeriest bunk in camp," I say.

"Should we talk to everyone else?" Gavin asks. "Give them their assignments?"

"Sure. Let's do it," I say.

I grab a thick sweatshirt, stuff my feet into my shoes, and meet him on the porch. It's cold out.

"Wait! We forgot about the plaque," he says. Every year, every team has to paint a plaque. They're about the size of a laptop, and have to list the captains, the camper captains, and the organizers. Then they're hung in the dining hall. The best one gets ten points.

"Do we have anyone good?" I ask.

"Yellow will win it since Brody's the captain," he says. "But we have the pottery teacher. I bet she can draw."

"But isn't it supposed to be done by campers?"

"Suuuuuure. Campers." He turns to me. "I kind of want to win this thing. I know it's fun just to compete, blah, blah, blah, but—"

"Oh, we're winning this thing," I say. "Or we'll die try-ing."

Back in the bunk, I wash my face and then get into bed, smiling.

I am color war captain! Me! Porny! Zoe Buckman would DIE of jealousy. HA!

And Gavin and I kept it totally professional! There was no inappropriate touching or stares or anything! Even though I told him nothing could happen between us, we are united in our pursuit of victory on a FRIENDS-ONLY BASIS and we can hang out and be together all the time—but just as friends. I am so glad he is my super-hot-only-a-friend person who I have to do everything with for the next two days while I am faithful to my boyfriend even though my boyfriend was a tiny bit jerky on the phone but it's fine, because I made things clear with Gavin, and I am a very trustworthy, reliable individual.

Yeah.

The next day is intense. Instead of lining up at flagpole with our bunks, we line up with our teams. In the Dining Hall, we sit with our teams instead of our bunks.

I sit next to Gavin. He winks at me. Not the most professional, but friendly. I decide I'll allow it.

I imagine putting my hand on his knee under the table. What? No. Brain, stop imagining things like that. Stay focused. Eli is boyfriend. Gavin is co-captain. Hands to myself. I get coffee instead.

After calling freeze, Gavin says, "We should do a cheer."

"Right now?"

"Yup. Which one?"

"Um . . ."

It dawns on me that I am captain. For real. That means I have to get up and lead these people. Leading a bunk is one thing, but there are sixty people on my team. Whether or not we win—it's up to me. And Gavin. I take a deep breath.

"Let's do something everyone knows," I tell him, and stand up on the bench. "Maybe blue team, you've got the spirit?"

"Great. Blue team, stand up!" Gavin yells, and stands up beside me on the bench.

Everyone stands up. Just like that.

The bench wobbles underneath us. I grab his arm for balance.

"One. Two. Three," I say, and then together we yell, "Blue team!"

"Blue team," they all yell back.

"We've got the spirit," I call out.

"We've got the spirit," they reply.

"Blue team!" we yell again.

"Blue team!" they repeat.

"Come on, let's hear it!"

"Come on, let's hear it!"

Then together we all yell, "Na, na-na-na-na, na-na-na-na . . ."

We do the whole thing one more time and then start screaming, "B-L-U-E, blue team on to victory!"

Then we cheer loudly and sit down.

The yellow team and then the red team scramble to do a cheer next.

After breakfast, we send everyone back to the bunk for a quick cleanup.

Gavin and I head to the picnic tables for a catch-up.

"We need some way to get them quiet, too," I say, sitting right on the tabletop. "What about if we yell something and they yell it back and then they're quiet?"

"Like what?" he asks, sitting on the bench below me.

"Something that makes sense? What's blue?"

"The water? The sky?" He smiles. "Your eyes?"

I laugh. "You're making it difficult to be professional here!"

He smiles again. "Am I?"

Oh brother. "Yes! We need something besides my eyes. Blue ribbon?"

He smiles. "Blue balls?"

"No! Gavin!"

"What?" He laughs. "It's funny because it's true."

"I do not want to hear about your balls! First of all, they are not my responsibility. Deal with your own balls. And second of all, you're the one with pictures of your girlfriend all over the wall of your bunk. We agreed."

"Okay. I won't talk about my balls. That was terrible. I'm sorry. I was trying to be funny. To, like, acknowledge the elephant in the room, I guess."

"Yeah," I say. "I get it."

"Honestly, guys talk about their balls all the time when girls aren't there. JJ talks about his balls. Muffs talks about his balls. Eric talks about his balls. It's balls all the time in our cabin."

I laugh. "Be good."

"I'm just putting it in context. But from now on, polite conversation only," he says.

"Thank you. We are behaving ourselves," I say.

"But your eyes are really pretty," he says. "I meant that."

"Blue ribbon it is," I say.

Ten minutes later, we march the kids to Upper Field for opening ceremonies.

Once everyone is there, each section competes in a tug-of-war and an egg toss. We win some, we lose some. We lose the staff tug-of-war. The yellow team has the Tank, the wrestling coach. He is not called the Tank for nothing.

We do the blue team chants and cheers again. Gavin and I scream in front of the campers at the top of our lungs.

"I am totally going to lose my voice," I say.

"We're light! We're bright! We're going to win this fight!" the yellow team yells.

"Yellow looks like pee!" one of the kids yells.

"We're red! You're dead!" the red team screams.

"Blue moon!" two of the senior boys from our team yell, and then pull down their sweatpants and moon everyone across from them.

The campers howl with laughter.

Crap. The judges are not going to like that.

"Ten points from the blue team!" Priya yells. "Keep your pants on, ladies and gentlemen!"

Fair enough.

Janelle offers to put two blue lines on our cheeks like

we're football players. I accept. Gavin passes.

"Too cool?" I ask.

"Yes," he says.

"Not me!" I cry. "I'm all in."

After the opening ceremonies are done, the kids are broken up by section. Junior girls have gaga ball, junior boys have soccer, inter girls have boating races, and so on and so on.

Gaga ball is basically dodgeball but played in a circular pit, and we check on them first. Blue team wins both games. Woot!

While the kids have more competitions throughout the day, Gavin and I run through the camp cheering them on and checking on the staff who are working on the big-ticket items like the song, skit, cheer, and dance. The song needs to be done by three o'clock so we can start teaching it to the kids. Last period is a team-wide practice.

Ours is pretty good—it's to the tune of Lady Gaga—not to be confused with the game gaga—and Bradley Cooper's song "Shallow."

Basically the counselors just change the words so that it sounds like it's about camp. We go into Bunk 10 to hear it.

Trevor takes out his guitar and starts strumming and singing all the lyrics about camp and summer and friendship and home.

"Great," I say when he's done. Hopefully it'll do.

We go to visit Janelle next. Her cheer is actually adorable.

It's to the tune of "Blue Suede Shoes."

"I got you, girl!" she says.

We check on the dance team and the skit team. The dance team hasn't picked a song yet, and the skit team only has two lines so far, but they promise us that they'll finish it by end of day.

By midnight, Gavin and I are giddy with exhaustion. We kicked ass all day. We both nailed the counselor hunt—I hid in a cupboard in the A&C and he hid behind the curtain in the Rec Hall. Every time a counselor got found, Eric announced it over the intercom like we were in the Hunger Games. Regular counselors were worth five points to whatever team caught them. Captains were worth twenty.

Neither Gavin or I got found.

"I think we're in good shape," he says when we're outside my bunk. "The relay race is going to be hardcore."

The relay race involves every camper and takes about two hours. It starts at the office, with three seniors, one per team, running across camp. Then the sticks are passed to teams of kids who do various relay activities like sort a bowl of Froot Loops by colors, make a bed, or canoe across the lake. Eventually, the last camper runs to the beach, where she hands the baton to the staff in charge of making the bonfire. When they get the baton, they start the fire. About five feet in the air, a rope stretches above each fire. The first fire to burn through the rope wins the relay race.

"I'm going to run the whole thing, with the kids," he says.

"If you're up for it," I say.

"No problem," he says.

"I'll make sure everything is set," I say. "So that's it? Day one is done? Do you think we're in the lead?"

"We're definitely tied with yellow at least. Beating red for sure."

"Good," I say. "Good night, then."

"You too. Sweet dreams."

"When I say sweet, you say dreams. Sweet!"

"Dreams!"

"Sweet!"

"Dreams!"

"Omigod, we're losing it," I say.

"We really are. Blue!"

"Balls!" I say, and giggle my way up the porch and into my bunk.

Professional enough.

The next day, I'm walking up to the lookout to check on the five inter girls who are going to be making a human pyramid when my phone rings. I've been secretly carrying it around with me to snap some pictures, but had not expected it to work. Why is there no service hardly anywhere in camp, but there is service in the middle of the forest? Cell service, you so crazy.

The relay is supposed to start in five minutes.

It's Eli.

"Hello!" I say.

"Hello, Beautiful!" he says. "I was starting to worry about you! Where are you?"

"Literally in the middle of a forest. Where are you?"

"Still Prague. But leaving for Switzerland today. I was going to leave you a message. I'm so happy to hear your voice instead."

"I can only talk for a minute—it's color war," I say. "I'm captain!"

"You would love it here. It's gorgeous. How are you? Your voice sounds weird. Are you sick?"

"No, just hoarse. Lots of cheering. It's this crazy two days of competitions. Like the Olympics. I'm head of the blue team. Which is a big deal. So I haven't slept in two days because we're—*I'm*—running the whole thing. And the relay race starts in five minutes. So I have to check on the human pyramids." I know I'm rambling, but I can't stop. Once again, I am not mentioning Gavin! I'm running the whole thing? Really?

"I have no idea what you just said. Was that English?"

"Kind of."

"Last night we—"

"Attention, all campers and counselors. Attention, all campers and counselors. The relay race begins in two minutes. Two minutes until the relay race begins."

"I'm so so so sorry, I want to hear all about everything, but I really have to go," I say.

200

He sighs. "Okay. Enjoy your game."

The way he says *game* rubs me the wrong way. I'm not playing Jenga. "It's not just a game, it's my job."

"What?"

"It's my job! I'm working! I am sorry I can't talk all the time! But I'm working!"

"It's not a real job, Sam."

My jaw drops. "Are you kidding me? I have SMALL CHILDREN who rely on me. I'm helping them through what for a lot of them is their first time ever away from home. There's all kinds of social and emotional learning that goes on at camp, community building, team building—it's not just a game, Eli."

"Okay, don't snap at me."

All the stress and adrenaline comes tumbling out of my mouth. "I meant it when I said I don't get a lot of sleep here. And I'm working every second I'm awake. When I pee, I'm working. When I shower, I'm working. This color war, I have to organize huge numbers of people, and make sure the kids are happy, and working together, and deal with people being anxious and scared. I have to show them they can do it. I'm being a role model. And you never ask me about anything that's happening here. You just make jokes about bugs and whatever. You know I want to be a teacher. You know education is important to me. And this is, like, the first time I've ever gotten to do anything really related to that, besides babysitting, and I'm working my butt off, and you just call it a game."

"Isn't it a game, though? Color war?"

"Yes, but—" Suddenly, I don't feel like making him try to understand. "I have to go. The race is about to start and I need to win. I'm sorry. I love you. I'll try you tomorrow."

"Sure," he says, and I can hear the edge in his voice. "If you're not too busy."

I hang up as fast as I can, pissed off. If I'm not too busy? Seriously? After all that?

Screw him.

And just like that, bam, I'm back in the game, and Eli is on the other side of the world.

Canoe racing!

Human pyramids!

Froop Loop sorting!

Gavin runs alongside the kids the entire time. At some point he takes off his shirt.

I am not the only counselor staring. I catch all the CIT girls making googly eyes. Just like when we were kids.

I run beside him. I do not take off my shirt.

Blue team gets to the beach first! Woot! We start our bonfire. But the yellow team is right behind us! Unfortunately the Tank is not only a killer at tug-of-war, he is also great at bonfires.

Gavin is in the thick of the smoke with the other staff working on the fire, while I am getting the kids to cheer them on.

"Burn, baby, burn! Burn, baby, burn!"

"B-L-U-E, blue team on to victory!"

"Blue team for the win!"

Suddenly the yellow team and ours are tied. Both of our fires are burning and the ropes are turning black. Which will break first?

Their fire goes sky high.

Their rope breaks in half.

"The yellow team wins!" Josh yells.

Crap. Crap crap *crap.*

The yellow team is all cheers.

I look at Gavin. We both make a face.

My whole team looks sad.

"It's all right, it's okay, we'll still beat you, anyway!" Janelle shouts. She motions to the juniors to sing along. "It's all right, it's okay, we'll still beat you, anyway!"

I try to shrug off the disappointment and join her cheer.

We spend the rest of the day practicing for the finale tonight. We teach the kids the song, we check on the senior skit, the junior cheer, the CIT magic act, and the inter dance. Our skit is funny and our juniors are adorable, although teaching them the cheer is hard since the seven-year-olds can barely read. The inter dance is a hot mess. The blue team got the best inter campers on their team according to the staff, and our CIT magic show does not seem that magical. Our song is good. It could be great. It would be great. If we were not so off-key.

Gavin and I, on the other hand, are very on-key.

Instead of splitting up, we run from the beach to the dining hall together. He holds the walkie-talkie, I hold the clipboard.

We overhear the red team's junior song on Lower Field and share a look that says, *Ours is soooo much better.*

"Don't forget your water bottles!" I call out to the kids. "And your—"

"Hats!" he finishes.

We are exhausted. We are a team. We are delirious.

We push through the day until eight o'clock, when the whole camp heads to the Rec Hall.

Everyone is abuzz. Everyone is wearing their colors. We are in second place but it's all about tonight.

"Okay, everyone, quiet!" Botts says. We all scream our quiet-down cheers.

"Red!"

"Hot!" the kids yell back.

"Blue!" we yell.

"Ribbon!" our kids yell back.

And finally:

"Mellow!"

"Yellow!"

First up is the junior cheer. Which is pretty much just a song, but cheered. The yellow team goes first. Even though it's the opposing team, I can't help but think the kids are adorable. Especially Prague and Em. They sing a version of "Here Comes the Sun." Their noses are painted yellow.

There are lots of jazz hands. Everyone oohs and aahs.

Talia does the movements in front to help the kids along. It is seriously cute.

Next come our juniors! They sing—and by sing I mean scream—the words to the first minute of "Blue Suede Shoes." It is super cute and short, and involves kicking their feet up and spinning. Lily does three perfect cartwheels across the stage. We totally won this one. Janelle killed it.

I am so proud I feel like bursting.

I wrap my arms around Janelle. "You are THE BEST."

"Of course I am!" she says back.

Next up are the inter dances, which we for sure lose, and then the senior skits. Finally, it's time for the team song.

We're last.

"Let's do this!" Gavin cries.

We pile onto the stage. We wait for the first few notes of "Shallow" on the piano. One. Two. Three.

The juniors sing, the inters sing, the seniors sing, and we all sing our hearts out. We sing about best friends, and time going too fast, and blue skies.

On the final chorus, my eyes fill with tears.

"We'll miss the days, we'll miss the nights.

Here we're not alone

So much we share, we'll see you next year

Blue Springs is our home."

Cheesy, yes. But so good. This summer is the best. Camp is the best.

Why did I miss so many years of it? Because of one mean girl? I wish I could tell my eleven-year-old self what I know now. A nickname is just a nickname. You don't have to let it define you, or run away from it either. It's not you—it's her. Stay strong. There are true friends out there. Find them. Focus on them.

And I know that even though I can't tell my eleven-year-old self that, I can tell my campers that. I can show them. I am showing them.

Time *does* go so fast.

It feels like I just got here, but on the other hand, like I've been here forever.

After our song is done, we all cheer like crazy. Then the red team starts to cheer and the yellow team starts to cheer and everyone is stomping on their benches and on the floor and the room is alive with noise and happiness.

"B-L-U-E! Blue team on to victory! B-L-U-E! Blue team on to victory!"

"We are red! The other teams are dead!"

"Yellow! Submarine! Yellow! Submarine!"

I spot the head staff sneaking out of the room, presumably to tally the points. My watch says it's already ten. It's going to be a late night.

A few minutes later, Jill comes onstage and motions to us to quiet everyone down.

"Red!"

"Hot!" the kids yell back.

"Blue!" we yell.

"Ribbon!" our kids yell back.

And finally:

"Mellow!"

"Yellow!"

"All teams!" Jill calls out. "Please make your way to the pool to find out who wins!"

"The pool?" I say to Gavin. "Why?"

He shakes his head. "That doesn't sound good."

The teams squeeze through the doors and we all head to the pool, laughing and giddy with nerves. We congregate on the pool lawn.

"Here's what's going to happen," Danish says. She is using a megaphone. "The six captains are going to stand on the edge of the pool. Six members of the head staff will stand behind them. On the count of three, the two winning captains will be pushed into the pool!"

Seriously? Everyone except for the captains cheers.

"So if we win, we lose, and if we lose, we win?" I say to Gavin as we make our way toward the pool with the other captains. I glance down at my favorite jeans and my electric-blue sweater.

"Should we all take off our shoes just in case?" Ilana asks.

"We definitely should."

The six of us kick off our shoes and socks.

"Maybe we should just all get completely naked," Brody says.

"There's no way that's happening," Audrey says.

"I would, but it's really cold," Gavin says.

"You think it's going to be warm getting out of the pool all wet?" Brody asks.

"You don't have to worry about that," Smokin' Hot Benji tells him.

"Now I don't even want to win," I say.

"Yes we do," Gavin says.

"Yes we do," I agree.

"Let's do this!" Priya says, her voice reverberating through the megaphone.

Everyone cheers.

"Step back, guys!" Jill says.

The six of us all stand by the deep end of the water.

Danish stands behind me.

Botts stands behind Gavin.

"Tell me somebody brought towels," I say.

"That would have been smart," Priya says. "Unfortunately, we did not."

Botts takes the megaphone. "And the winner . . . of this year's color war . . . is . . ."

My heart races. I have never been pushed into a pool! I want to be pushed into the pool! I want to win! I will be very disappointed if I don't get pushed into the pool!

But I also don't really want to get wet.

". . . The BLUE TEAM!"

I feel Danish's hands on my back and the next thing I know I'm falling face-first into the water. And it's cold! Ah!

Actually, it's warm, but it's still shocking. But this means I won! I won color war! I am the best captain ever!

I pop up from under the surface and hear the deafening cheers from my team outside and then Gavin is hugging me and screaming, "We won! We did it!"

"We did it!" I scream, trying not to be pulled under.

The other captains jump in too.

Gavin pulls me close and I feel the water on his skin, and his breath on my neck.

We hold on to each other way longer than we should.

Janelle brings me extra clothes, so after the kids go to a super late Milk and Cookies, the other captains, Gavin, and I take turns using the pool showers.

Gavin is in the one next to me.

On the other side of this curtain, Gavin is naked. Naked, naked, naked Gavin.

Naked, soapy Gavin.

Keep it professional.

Professional, naked, soapy Gavin.

"Can we get some food?" Audrey says afterward. "I'm starving."

"Me too," Gavin says.

"It's already eleven," Benji says.

"But Jill said no curfew for any of us tonight," I remind them.

"I have the keys to the kitchen," Botts says. "And I know where the good stuff is."

"Booze?" Gavin asks.

He shakes his head. "Ice cream sandwiches."

Brody and Ilana head back to their bunks, but the rest of us follow Botts through camp and to the kitchen. He unlocks the door, and then turns on the light. "I'll show you where the snacks are kept."

We go into the cupboard and find all the cookies and snacks.

"Yessssss," I say. "I found the black and whites! These are the best." I bite into one. Ah. Heavenly. "Do you think I can take a glass of milk?"

"I can do better than that. Take a glass of chocolate milk," Botts says.

"Yes, yes, yes," I say.

Audrey laughs.

"You want?" I ask Gavin.

"Sure," he says.

I pour us both glasses. "To us!" I say.

He clinks with me. "To . . . us," he says.

Our eyes lock.

My heart starts to race again.

One kiss wouldn't be the end of the world. I can kiss him *one* time, and then I'll say, we can't do this, I have a boyfriend and you have a girlfriend, and he'll pull away and agree with me, and then we'll laugh and shake it off, and it will be five minutes of fun (hot, smoldering fun) and then it will be over. What happens at camp does not have to affect real life.

It's not like I would ever even see him again! He goes to school in Maryland!

He puts his arm around my shoulder. "We did it."

"We did," I say. I put my head on his shoulder.

"Tomorrow is going to be so weird," Audrey says. "I've been running a team for two days and now I go back to dealing with just my bunk. So boring."

"Do you like your bunk?" I ask.

"They're assholes," Audrey says. "Hilarious assholes. But assholes. Girls get meaner as they get older. I should have asked for juniors, but . . . I don't want lice."

"My girls don't have lice!"

"Yet." She laughs and yawns. "I need to sleep."

"I need to lock up," Botts says, and we all follow him out of the kitchen.

The three of them wave as they head toward Upper Field.

"Are you tired?" Gavin asks.

I am, but I'm also not. And I think the question actually means, do you want the night to be over?

I don't.

"No," I say. "Wired, actually. Oh, that rhymes. When I say tired, you say wired! Tired!"

"Wired?"

"Tired!"

"Wired!"

I laugh. I am giddy. I am nervous. I am charged with electricity.

"I'm not tired either," he says. "Winning was really fun. Losing would have been a bummer."

"But we won!"

"You won," he says. "You were a great captain."

"Thank you!" I say. It's nice to be appreciated. "So were you. You ran the whole relay!"

"We were a great team."

"Yeah," I say. "We were."

We're standing on the Dining Hall porch, facing each other. The light is on overhead. "Where should we go next?" I ask. "Should we break into the art room? Eat all the art supplies?"

"I'm not sure how tasty the paint will be."

"I bet the clay is delicious."

Since the A&C is underneath the Dining Hall, we are there in two seconds. I sit down on the bench on the porch. Below us is the waterfront, and we can see the moon reflecting in the lake.

It's just the two of us. Alone. I can barely breathe.

He sits down right beside me, almost touching me, and we're both looking straight out at the lake.

"Hi," he says.

"Hi," I say back.

"I really want to kiss you," he says.

"I really want to kiss you too," I say. "But I . . ." My words trail off.

His lifts his hand and his fingers graze the top of my arm. My whole body is alive.

I should move. I should stand up. I should say, *We shouldn't do this.*

He runs his thumb to the tips of my fingers.

My whole body feels like it's going to explode.

I look up at him. His mouth is inches away from mine.

"We can kiss, but that's it," I say. "Okay?"

"Okay," he says.

"Okay," I say again and press my lips against his.

Everything explodes. He kisses me softly at first, and then his hand is on the back of my neck and pulling me into him and my hands are on his back.

I'm pulling him against me and leaning backward on the bench and now he's on top of me. He feels so good on top of me and we're still kissing. His tongue is soft, and I am kissing someone who is definitely not Eli. He is someone new and different and it should freak me out, but it doesn't because it feels *so* good.

Now my legs are around him and I am pulling him closer and we are still kissing and I don't want it to stop. But it has to stop. Because I am not going to have sex with him. That would be taking this too far. But wow do I wish I were wearing less clothes.

We keep kissing and kissing, and pressing our bodies against each other. Until a million hours later when my lips are raw, and we're just lying there.

"So that happened," he says, and I laugh, and he laughs.

"That was . . . fun," I say.

"It was really fun," he says.

"We should probably go back to our bunks, though," I say. "It must be super late."

"Yeah." He sits up and then pulls me up too. "You okay?"

"I'm good," I say, and I mean it. He takes my hand and we start to move back to the main road, when I stop. "Wait," I say. "Maybe I should walk by myself? In case anyone sees me . . ." My voice trails off.

Just saying that implies a whole issue that we are going to have to talk about. No one can see us. Because we're not supposed to be doing this.

"Ah. Okay. That makes sense. I'll give you a two-minute lead," he says. He leans over and gives me a soft, quick kiss on the lips.

I run the whole way.

When I get to my bunk, my heart is racing. I am not sure if it's because of my little sprint, or what just happened. Probably both. I quietly open the front door and make my way to the bathroom. Then I sneak into the counselors' room. Janelle is out cold. I don't hear Lis or Talia. I take off my bra and jeans and sweatshirt, but leave on my T-shirt and get into my bed.

I can still smell him on me. I can still feel him on me. I close my eyes, thinking of him and smiling.

Danish knocks on our counselors' room the next morning. "Morning, winner!"

My eyes open. Did I dream that? Or did I really just hard-core make out with Gavin?

I have a flash of him lying on top of me. Art porch. I feel both sick and excited.

"Sam, you can stay in bed a little while longer if the others will watch your kids," Danish says.

"Got 'em, Sam," Talia says. "You should sleep, champ!"

"Thanks." I pull my covers over my head. My heart is racing, but I don't want to get out of bed. I let them go to flagpole and pretend to be asleep.

When the bunk is quiet, I push my covers off.

What did I do? What did I do?

I get out of bed and go to the bathroom. I sit on the tiny toilet and take a deep breath.

I cheated on Eli.

Why did I cheat on Eli?

Suddenly a million questions are buzzing through my mind. Am I a terrible person? Do I have to tell Eli? Do I want to tell Eli? Do I want to break up with Eli? Do I love Eli? How could I love Eli if I made out with Gavin? Do I want to make out with Gavin again?

My head hurts.

I flush and wash my hands, and then stare at myself in the mirror. My lips look different, like they've been stung. Plumper. And my chin and the area around my lips is red. Like it's been rubbed by sandpaper. Gavin should have shaved.

I wash my face to calm it down.

215

Since everyone is at breakfast, I take my phone with me and stand in the spot that I know has internet.

I look at my phone for the first time in almost a day.

Eli: I'm sorry about yesterday. I know this job is important to you. It's just really hard to never talk to you! I miss you!

Eli: Did you win? I hope you won.

Eli: In Switzerland! It rained the whole day. So bored. Miss you.

His texts make me feel worse. I'm not sure what to write back. Miss you too? Miss you so much I made out with someone else? Hi! I cheated on you! Hope you're having fun!

But let's just put this into perspective. It was only once. Gavin and I just kissed. It's not good, but what's the point in telling Eli? He'll never find out. No one else here even knows him. I can pretend it never happened. It's not like Gavin is going to tell anyone. He's cheating on his girlfriend too!

Hi, I write. *Sorry about yesterday too.* I am not sure what else to say. Oh. *I won color war!* The second biggest thing that happened last night.

When I'm back in the bunk, the kids are back. There is a paper plate and a croissant on my bed.

"Aw, thank you!" I say.

"You're welcome," Talia says. "There's a cup of coffee on your shelf."

"You are the best."

216

"Hardly," she says. "But we have freakin' tennis next and I can't do it alone."

"I'm all yours," I say.

"Thank goodness."

I spend all of tennis nervous for sailing, which is second period, but it starts to pour in the middle of tennis so we all run back to the bunk. Our rain schedule says we have Games in the Bunk, which might be the best activity ever. Except for sailing, which would have been better. Maybe? Part of me doesn't mind hiding.

I teach the girls how to play the card game Crazy Eights. I'm half paying attention, half wondering what will happen when I see Gavin again. How do I act? Do I say something? Like, "This can't happen again"? Unless I want it to happen again. I shuffle and deal. Do I want it to happen again?

I finally see him at lunch. He's wearing his fluorescent-yellow rain jacket, which I've noticed before but now makes my heart jump.

He catches my eye as soon as he walks in.

He smiles. It feels like every drop of blood in my body rushes to my face. I smile back.

One of the kids pulls him over to his table and he winks at me before following him.

I'm careful not to look at him again. I don't want him to think I'm obsessing. Which I totally am.

Does he feel the same way I do? Maybe I'm just some random girl he can make out with. Maybe he makes out with other girls all the time. Maybe he's made out with other counselors this summer.

Maybe he's a total creep. Maybe I'm a total creep. Maybe he's going to tell all the guys here that I'm a huge slut who cheats on her boyfriend. Am I huge slut who cheats on her boyfriend? I definitely cheated on my boyfriend. Why am I such an asshole?

"What the hell is up with you?" Talia asks. "I just yelled freeze and you didn't even notice."

"Sorry," I say. I look around the table and see that the kids are indeed frozen. I am super spacey today.

"Hey," Botts says, coming up beside me.

"Hey," I say back. And then I wonder. Does *he* know? Would Gavin have told him? No. Maybe?

"Are you coming to my cottage again this day off?" he asks.

"Oh. When are you taking off?"

"Tomorrow night."

"Is that okay?" I ask Talia.

"Totally," she says. "You need a day off."

"Great," I say. "I'm in. Fun! Thank you for inviting me."

I don't ask if Gavin is coming too. But I am really, really hoping he is.

I don't see Gavin the next day. When his table is empty at dinner, I realize he must be on his overnight.

We really need to talk about what happened. Don't we?

I assume that I'll get to talk to him at the cottage at least, but when I get to the office at six p.m., he's not there. It's just Botts and Priya and Smokin' Hot Benji.

"I'll drive," Botts says.

"No Gavin?" I ask, trying to sound cucumber-cool.

"No, he's taking tomorrow night instead. He has to go into the city."

Why would he have to go into the city? Is he meeting someone? Who? Another girl? Or maybe it's Kat? No, she's still in Paris. I think. I hate that I'm even worrying about this. Why do I care? Why didn't he tell me?

I sling my backpack over my shoulder. "I need sleep."

"You are looking kind of tired," Botts says.

"Hey!"

"I'm kidding. Kind of. Let's go. You can go straight to sleep."

I manage to stay up for a delicious dinner of steaks and baked potatoes and a dip in the hot tub.

"Who wants to watch a movie?" Botts asks.

"Me!" I say.

"Sure," Priya says.

Smokin' Hot Benji shrugs.

"Okay, meet me in the living room in twenty," Botts says.

Botts turns off the outdoor lights, and the four of us go back inside.

I take a quick hot shower and put on my leggings, a bra, and a sweatshirt and head downstairs.

Botts is already making popcorn in the microwave. He's

wearing flannel pants and a Boston Red Sox T-shirt. "What do you want to watch?" he asks.

"Do you have the latest Star Wars?"

"Do I have the latest Star Wars?" he asks. "Are you kidding? I have every Star Wars! You like Star Wars?"

"Of course I do. I'm Rey for every Halloween. But I haven't seen the latest."

"And why were you not at the theater on opening night?"

I shrug. "Eli is not that into Star Wars."

"So? He wouldn't go with you?"

"He didn't want to fight the crowd."

"Nooooo! Opening night crowds are the best. You could have worn your Rey costume! Next time we'll go together and I'll dress up too."

"As who? Darth Vader?"

"Don't be ridiculous. Han Solo. Obviously. I have the perfect vest."

I laugh as he sets up the movie.

I look up toward the rooms. "Do you think they're coming down? It's been a while."

"Um . . ." He looks toward the room and smiles. "Possibly not?"

My eyes widen. "Priya and Smokin' Hot Benji? No way!"

"Maybe? I don't know. I can see it."

"Sure," I say. "Why not?"

* * *

My eyes start to feel heavy about halfway through the movie, so I spread out on the couch, pulling a cashmere blanket over my legs. Priya and Smokin' Hot Benji never show so I have a lot of room. It's a fabulous couch. A super soft couch. A couch of marshmallows.

Maybe I'll just take a little snooze.

When I wake up, the credits are rolling and the clock on the DVR says 11:02 p.m.

"Oops," I say.

"Don't worry," he laughs. "I'll watch it again with you tomorrow. Go to bed. I'll close up the house."

I blow him a kiss and climb into my super luxurious bed. I text Eli that I'll call him in the a.m. and fall fast asleep.

The next morning I wake up at eleven. I scroll through my phone first and go to Instagram. Eli's last picture was taken in Juan-les-Pins, France. He and his cousin are on the beach together. I scroll through the comments.

Love that place! Are you going to Barcelona?

Then there's a, *Great pic! Best night!*

Posted by someone named Sydney.

Who's Sydney?

I flip over to her profile, which is public.

Her latest post was today, and it's also in Juan-les-Pins.

And Eli, my Eli, is in the photo!

Wait, what?

Five of them are standing on the beach together! And she—this Sydney chick—is wearing a bikini!

Who is this Sydney chick?!

I scroll a few photos down and right in front of me is another picture of her, some other girl, and *my* Eli's face pressed together in a picture, smiling for the camera! In Switzerland!

What the hell? Didn't he specifically tell me that it was raining in Switzerland and that he was *so bored*?

He doesn't look *so bored*. He doesn't look *so bored* at all. He's smiling and drinking and he looks like he's having a great old time being *so not* bored in Switzerland.

And now Sydney's in France with him too? For real, who is this girl?

Fine. Whatever. It's not like I have a right to get mad, even if something did happen.

I look up Gavin's profile. It takes me a few minutes to find him, but there he is.

I scroll through his pictures. He doesn't post a lot. Although he's in camp, and we're not supposed to be online. But still. He hasn't posted once all summer. His last photo was in May. It's the one Lis showed me of him and Kat.

Part of me hates that she's so beautiful.

But on the other hand, now it makes me feel powerful.

Being with *me* is worth risking his relationship with this beautiful girl.

Wow, what a seriously messed up way of thinking.

I should call Eli. I really, really, really should. I press his name.

"Hey, stranger," he says, answering.

"Hey, stranger to you," I say, my voice cold.

"I miss you."

"I . . . miss you too." I do miss him. Kind of. I'm a little mad at him, though.

"Where are you?" he asks.

"At Botts's place. Day off. I slept in. You?"

"You spend a lot of time with this Botts character," he says.

Ha. Botts is the one he's jealous of? "We're friends," I say. "And he has a really nice house."

Maybe it's a good thing that he's jealous of Botts. He won't realize what he should really be jealous about. "Where are you?" I ask.

"In my room, too. South of France. You're alone? Can we FaceTime?"

"Um, yeah. Sure."

Great, now he's going to look at me. I shake the worry off. He can't tell. It's not like I have hickeys on my neck. And the stubble burn has worn off.

My phone buzzes with a FaceTime video request. I accept.

"Hey, Beautiful," he says.

"Hi," I say, and I smile. "Look how tan you are! And scruffy!"

He laughs and touches his chin. There's a white wall behind him. He could be literally anywhere, for all I know.

"You're pretty tan too," he says. "You look great."

I smooth my hair out and sit up. I try to hold the camera so that it's at a good angle and I don't have a double chin.

"You'd love it here," he says. "I wish I were in bed with you right now."

"Eli!" I say, then I whisper, "You're on speakerphone. I don't know who else is in the house." I look outside and see that everyone is at the lake.

No one is here. Should I tell him what happened? No. There's no point in doing that. It's so easy just to pretend it never happened. What would be the point in saying anything anyway? It was clearly a one-time thing. It built up and then it happened and now it's done. It's not like we slept together. We don't even live in the same city. Gavin didn't even tell me he was taking a day off without me! He just left!

Gavin, Gavin, Gavin.

Eli, Eli, Eli.

Sydney, Sydney, Sydney.

"So who are you in France with?" I ask.

"My cousin."

"That's it? Just the two of you?" I ask. I try to keep my face blank.

"And some other people I met in Switzerland. "

"Oh? Really? Where are they from?"

"Australia. And some Americans."

Interesting that he does not mention that any of them are women. Lie by omission? I don't press, mostly because I don't want him to press. About anything.

He shows me his hotel room, and I show him where I'm sleeping.

"I fly in on the twenty-seventh," he says. "Only two weeks left! Are you still okay to take a day off on the twenty-eighth?"

We coordinated the day off in advance, since it was the last day off we're allowed to take, and his first day back. "Yes, but are you sure you're going to want to drive all the way up to camp? I know you'll be tired. Or I can come meet you in the city. Or I'll be home the next week."

"No, if that's your last day off, then I'll come then. We can go somewhere near camp so I get more time with you," he says. Which is thoughtful, and selfless, and really sweet.

Except I don't really want him anywhere near camp. Better to keep the worlds separate. But I don't want to say anything that sounds suspicious.

"Okay," I say. "I love you."

"I love you, too."

I do love him. I really do. He's sweet and caring and, yeah, he doesn't really appreciate my job here, but I don't really get what he's doing there. In two weeks we'll be together again and then I'll visit him in Greenwich after camp, and then we'll be at school again and camp will be a hazy memory.

Eli is real. Gavin is a sexy mirage.

What happened with him was a one-time thing. And now it's over.

225

We pull up to camp at six p.m. to see Gavin driving out.

My heart stops.

He honks twice. He's driving someone's car. I'm not sure whose.

Botts honks back.

I have another day without him. I'm relieved. I'm disappointed. But at least, if he's not at camp, I can't hook up with him.

WEEK 4 SCHEDULE—BUNK 6A

	SUNDAY	MONDAY	TUESDAY	WEDNESDAY	THURSDAY	FRIDAY	SATURDAY
PERIOD 1 10:00–10:45	DANCE	WRESTLING	ART	SI	NEWCOMB	TENNIS	EXTRA CLEANUP
PERIOD 2 10:45–11:30	SI	DRAMA	GAGA BALL	DANCE	BASKETBALL	SI	PAPER CHASE
PERIOD 3 11:30–12:15	CANOEING	SOCCER	TENNIS	POTTERY	CANOEING	ARCHERY	SHOWERS
12:15–12:30	LUNCH WASHUP	LUNCH WASHUP	LUNCH WASHUP	LUNCH WASHUP	LUNCH WASHUP	LUNCH WASHUP	LUNCH WASHUP
12:30–1:00	LUNCH	LUNCH	LUNCH	LUNCH	LUNCH	LUNCH	LUNCH
1:00–2:00	REST HOUR	REST HOUR	REST HOUR	REST HOUR	REST HOUR	REST HOUR	REST HOUR
PERIOD 4 2:00–2:45	FROG HUNTING	BASKETBALL	KAYAKING	BAKING	ART	POTTERY	VISITING DAY!
2:45–3:15	MILK & COOKIES	MILK & COOKIES	MILK & COOKIES	MILK & COOKIES	MILK & COOKIES	MILK & COOKIES	VISITING DAY!
PERIOD 5 3:15–4:00	ART	SI	NEWCOMB	TENNIS	SOCCER	WATERSKI	VISITING DAY!
PERIOD 6 4:00–4:45	GS	GS	GS	GS	GS	GS	VISITING DAY!

Week 4

Even though I've decided it's over with Gavin, I still spend most of Sunday thinking about him.

Except during frog hunting. Frog hunting is all-consuming.

Danish finally put it on the schedule.

We all put on our rain boots, wear clothes we don't mind getting dirty, take buckets, and go to the marshy area beside the beach. We run into Botts on the way.

"Omigod, you're going frog hunting?" he cries. "I want to come too! I haven't been in years! How did I not see that on the schedule!"

"So go put on your boots!" I say. "Hurry!"

He meets us ten minutes later at the marsh.

"The trick is to be really quiet," I tell everyone. "And not make any sudden movements."

"I'm not touching the frogs," Talia says.

I catch two, Botts catches one, and the girls all take turns holding the buckets.

At the end of the activity we return the frogs to the marsh. No frogs are injured in the activity.

"That was so gross," Talia says, squirting her hands with hand sanitizer again. In the last forty-five minutes she must have used the sanitizer every three to four minutes.

But the activity was as fun as I remembered. The frogs were definitely as slimy.

And we all get covered in mud.

Thankfully, Gavin is not there to see me.

Jill snaps a picture of the nine of us. "This is totally going on the website tonight," she says.

We smile for the camera and hold up our buckets. I fully expect a text worrying about warts from Fancy's mom.

I take the girls for emergency showers. I have to break it off with Gavin tonight and I need to smell good to do it.

Evening Activity is Win, Lose, or Draw, and Gavin sits down right beside me on the bench in the Dining Hall while the kids are winning, losing, and drawing.

"Hi," he says quietly.

"Hi." I keep my tone serious. We can't talk for real here, but I don't want to sound too flirty since I'm going to end it. And I am. It's over. I think.

"How was your day off?" he asks.

"Good," I say, keeping my eyes on the kids. "I went to

Botts's. How was yours?"

"It was . . . shitty, actually. I spent the day with my dad at Sloan Kettering."

Wait, what? I turn to him. "The cancer place?"

"Yeah," he says, his eyes sad. He sighs.

"I'm so sorry," I say, taking a breath.

One of the kids yells, "It's *The Wizard of Oz*!" and everyone cheers.

"Me too," Gavin says to me. His shoulders slump. "He has colon cancer. It sucks."

"I had no idea your dad was sick," I tell him, out of breath.

"He is. It's kind of recent. Since May. I'm not dealing with it well."

"It's not an easy thing to deal with," I say, my heart hurting for him. "My dad was sick too. He's okay now, kind of, but it was hard. It's still hard. I'm here if you want to talk."

Suddenly I don't just want to talk. I want to put my arms around him. I want to hold him. I want to take care of him. He needs me. I want to kiss him all over and tell him everything is going to be okay.

He nods. "Yeah. That would be good. I've been wanting to talk to you. . . . I was going to text you, but I don't even have your number. I'm sorry I haven't been around."

"You should have my number," I say. "I'll give it to you later. I'm here tonight if you want to talk. Do you have OD?"

"No," he says.

There's more cheering at the front.

"Me neither," I say.

"Want to hang out?" he asks, knocking his knee against mine.

"Okay," I say. I say it so quickly, I don't even give myself a chance to think about it.

"It's so nice outside," he says. "We can take out a canoe?"

I laugh. "Really? In the middle of the night?"

"You're with boat staff," he says. "You're safe."

After Milk and Cookies, I take the kids back to the bunk and help them get ready for bed. Janelle has OD and she's letting the girls on both sides of the bunk try on her tube tops.

"Just what we need, eleven mini Janelles," Talia mutters.

"Omigod," Lis says. "She'd have an army."

"It would be the cutest army ever," I say.

"Or the skankiest," Talia says, and Lis laughs. She's very busy writing her name on the wall in black Sharpie. I've spotted her name in at least seven locations in this cabin alone.

"Come on," I say. "Be nice."

What would they think of me if they knew where I was going?

Skanky for sure.

But right now I care more about what I'm supposed to wear to go middle-of-the-night boating. A swimsuit? Will we end up in the water? Probably not. Just in case, I put on a bikini under my sweatshirt and leggings. I change super fast so my co's don't ask me what I'm doing. Going boating with Gavin in the middle of the night does not sound unsuspicious.

As soon as I'm ready, I hurry down to the beach and find him sitting on one of the benches.

He smiles. "Hey. Ready? I grabbed us two life jackets."

"Okay," I say. "And you're sure no one will care? That we're taking out a canoe?"

"No," he says. "Boating staff does it all the time. We just try and be quiet about it."

We take off our shoes and make our way toward the water. The moon and stars are out in full force.

The boat rocks as I get in, but I sit down on the seat at the front of it, facing the wrong way, toward him.

I hold on as he pushes the boat out and then jumps inside. He's facing me and kneeling, his back against the wooden bar in the center. He paddles us into the middle of the lake.

We're face-to-face. My legs are stretched out in front of me, almost touching his knees.

The lake is quiet. It's just us and the fireflies.

"So," he says. "We've been missing each other the last few days."

"We have been," I say. "How was your canoe trip?"

"Less fun without you."

I laugh.

"How was your day off?" he asks.

"Less fun without you," I tell him. The water is glass-still except for the ripples from his paddle. "This reminds me of the song," I say.

"Which one?"

"The one about the boy and the girl in the canoe."

"No idea what song that is. Sing it."

"I have a terrible voice," I say.

"Oh, I know," he says. "Co-captain."

I jab his knee with my toe. "You really don't know the song?" I ask.

"C'mon, sing for me. Sing!"

I clear my throat.

"Just a boy and a girl in a little canoe,
With the moon shining all around."

I pause.

"That's it?"

"Oh, there's more. You want the whole song?"

"I do!" He moves his knee up an inch so that it's touching my foot.

"As he glides his paddle
You couldn't even hear a sound
And they talked and they talked
Till the moon grew dim—
He said you better kiss me
Or get out and swim."

"Ouch!" he says.

"So what you gonna do in a little canoe
With the moon shining all a—
Boats floatin all a—
Girls swimming all around!"

"So he forces her to kiss him?" he asks. "Is that why all the girls are in the water? Because all the boys are creeps? That's messed up."

"That is an excellent question. I seem to remember another ending too—*What the heck, let's neck.* So in that version the girl kisses the guy to avoid going in. Highly problematic. Maybe I shouldn't teach this song to the kids."

"Probably not," he says, but he hums the tune. Then he puts the paddle across the canoe behind him.

He gently traces his thumbs up my ankles. Oh, boy. Yes.

"You didn't feel pressured the other day, did you?" he asks.

"Me? No," I say. "Confused, yes. Pressured, no."

"Yeah," he says. "Me too. Although not that confused. More, really, really attracted to you."

My heart zooms. "I've never cheated on Eli," I say. "Or anyone. Or, like, anything. Never a test, or homework. I did once steal a candy bar from a 7-Eleven. But it wasn't intentional. I was holding it and forgot I was holding it and walked out."

"You're such a goody-goody," he says, smiling. His thumbs are on my knees.

"I ate the candy bar. I could have gone back and returned it, but I didn't. Just totally ate it. It was a Twix."

"Can I kiss you again?"

Yes. No. Yes.

"No pressure," he says. "But you look incredibly hot right now."

My lips and body burn.

"Okay. But we're not telling . . . them," I say. I don't want to say their names. "Right?"

"I am not telling anyone." He's leaning over me now, and his hands are on my hips, and he's lowering me onto the floor of the canoe.

The boat rocks with our weight.

"We can't even tell our co-counselors," I say. "Or anyone at camp. Who knows who's connected to who."

He nods. "This is just between us."

"It's so wrong."

"Yes." His lips are against my neck.

Suddenly my arms are around him and his hands are in my hair and we're fully making out again.

We're in the middle of the lake, under the stars and the moon, and I'm kissing the hottest guy at camp and I'm so turned on and all I'm thinking is that this is the sexiest thing I've ever done, and what's the point of anything if I pass this up.

I pull away. "But still only kissing," I say, and then put my tongue back in his mouth.

He winks at me the next morning at flagpole. It's our thing, the wink.

I accidentally-on-purpose bump into him in the food line at breakfast.

He runs his finger down my leg at lunch.

Every minute I vibrate with excitement. Even when he's not there, I'm thinking about him.

When we can get away with it, we sneak away from the crowds and find different places at camp to make out.

We stick to kissing *only*.

Until Rest Hour behind the Upper Field bleachers, where our tops come off.

But that's the limit! Second base!

Until the Lower Field bleachers. Where my jeans come off, but not my thong.

From then on, underwear definitely stays on! That's the rule!

Until his counselors' room. Where his boxers disappear under his comforter.

We still don't have actual sex. Everything else, yes. But not sex. Sex is the line. Everything else is kind of cheating, sure, but having sex with someone else is the worst kind of cheating.

If Eli somehow found out, I could say, but I never slept

with him! I never slept with anyone but you!

And it would be 100 percent, technically true.

It's pouring out. Lightning and everything. It's ten thirty at night, and instead of going to Slice, we're all packed into the Counselors' Lounge. Gavin, Muffs, Lis, and I are sprawled on the carpeted floor in a circle, playing Hearts.

"Where's JJ?" I ask. "OD?"

"Yeah," Muffs says. "Apparently with Brody. . . ."

"Oooooh," I say. "Interesting."

Gavin's hand is in the Doritos bag and I reach mine into it at the same time.

He runs his thumb down the center of my palm.

Mmmm. Maybe we can sneak off somewhere. Tonight would have been a great one for one of us to have OD. I feel bad that I'm not in the bunk, actually. The kids are probably terrified by the storm.

"Who's sitting in your bunk?" Muffs asks. "Janelle or Talia?"

"Talia," I say. I take a chip out of the bag, eat it, and then slowly, very slowly, lick the spices off my fingers.

Gavin readjusts on the floor. Ha!

"Anyone keeping her company?" Muffs asks.

"No," Lis says. "She's definitely on her own."

"What's her deal?" Muffs asks. "She never hooks up with anyone."

"Maybe the guys here are too dorky for her," Lis says.

"Maybe she's into girls," Muffs says.

"No," Lis says, looking surprised. "At least I don't think so. I really don't think she's into anyone."

"Everyone's into someone," Muffs says. He stares at Lis when he says it. Lis turns red, and bites her thumbnail.

"No," I say. "That's not actually true. Some people just don't experience sexual attraction. Like, their sexuality is asexuality. Welcome to the twenty-first century."

"Okay, New York City," says Muffs.

Botts chooses that moment to walk in. He is wearing a giant blue poncho. "In the CL," he says into the walkie-talkie. "Everyone is fine on Upper Field."

Lis turns even redder.

"You like Botts?" Muffs whispers. "Still? Seriously?"

"Keep your voice down," Lis mutters.

The walkie-talkie crackles. "Everyone fine on Lower," we hear Priya say.

"I heard Priya is hooking up with Benji," Muffs says.

I nod, pretending I didn't know.

"He is Smokin' Hot Benji," Lis says.

"Why don't I get a nickname?" Gavin asks.

"Grumpy Gav?" Muffs says.

"Gorgeous Gav," I say, batting my eyelashes.

Everyone ooooohs, and I worry I went too far.

"I had a nickname," I say.

Lis looks up. "I thought we're not allowed to talk about that."

I look at Gavin. I shrug. "Zoe Buckman used to call me Porny. But I'm over it."

He laughs. "Porny? Why?"

"Because of my big boobs," I say. "She was jealous, what can I say?"

"She wasn't the nicest," Gavin says.

"Didn't you go out with her?" I ask.

"For like a week."

The door bursts open with basketball teacher Trevor on the arm of Janelle. They are both soaked and laughing, their clothes sticking to their bodies.

"Anyone have a change of clothes?" Janelle calls out.

"Just take it off, we don't mind," Lawrence says from the couch.

I see Allie glare at him from the other side of the room. I'm not sure if she and Lawrence are on or off this week.

"Is Janelle hooking up with Trevor now?" Muffs asks.

"I think they're just friends," I say.

"She has a lot of 'friends,'" Lis says under her breath. "Talia's afraid she's going to give us crabs."

"I've had it twice, it's not as bad as you think," Muffs says.

"Very funny," Lis says and plays a card.

It's Rest Hour. Gavin and I are walking to the office together to call our significant others. I'm going to call Eli and he's calling Kat. To say hi. We figured we might as well keep each other company. I can't decide if we're being practical or sociopathic. A little bit of both?

"We're not going to sit next to each other while we talk, are we?" I ask.

"Don't be ridiculous," he says. "Too distracting."

"So I'll sit inside, and you sit on the steps outside?"

"Good plan."

I push the door open to the office. "What's up, Eric?"

"The sky," he says. "It is up, up, up."

Okey dokey.

I wave to Gavin outside. He waves back. I call Eli's number and wait for him to answer.

"Hey," he says.

"Hi."

As we talk, I watch the back of Gavin's head through the window in the door. The muscles in his neck are moving but I can't tell what he's saying. Then he turns to the right and I can see that his jaw is tightening.

I wonder what happened. Maybe she's leaving him for a French billionaire? But he wouldn't even care. Because he has me!

"Sam?"

"Yes," I say, snapping back to my phone call. "Sorry. I couldn't hear you for a second. Interference. What did you say?"

"That I won money!"

"Huh?"

"We went to Monte Carlo! And I played poker and won four thousand euros!"

"What? Seriously?"

"Yes!"

"That's wild." Is Eli now a French billionaire?

"I know! It was fun. The casino was gorgeous. So fancy. And so many castles in Monaco! And you would not believe the cars that were lined up everywhere. Out of control."

"I'm confused. Did you move over to Monaco?"

"No, we just went for the night. We didn't stay there."

"Who did you go with?" I ask.

"A whole crew. The Australians and some Americans. Oh! Wait! One of the girls' boyfriends is at your camp too. I forget his name. Devin? His girlfriend is named Kat."

I almost drop the phone. What?

Eli is with Kat?

"Really?"

"Yes! Small world, huh? I think she said he was a color war captain too? You have to know him. Devin?"

I feel vaguely sick. "I . . . yeah. Gavin. I think you mean Gavin."

Is Eli *Kat's* French billionaire?

"She's here for a few days too. She's friends with Sydney, a girl I met in Switzerland. They go to the University of Maryland."

How is this even possible? Eli and Kat are hanging out in Europe? Eli and Kat went to Monte Carlo together?

What, what, *what is happening*?

She's friends with Sydney? Instagram Sydney?

I'm in a haze for the rest of the phone call—I think I say I love you, but I'm not sure.

Once I hang up, I see that Gavin is still on his phone, so I click straight to Instagram.

Eli posted a picture last night of a big group of people. I spot Kat right away with her gorgeous hair. Eli's arm is around her. *Eli's arm is around her? What the hell?* They are standing against a railing with blue water in the background. There are ten of them in the picture, all smiling and glamorous. Eli wrote, *Amazing night in Monte Carlo.* And then he even hashtagged it! #strikingitrich #noregrets #monaco. I don't know what to do with this.

No regrets? No *regrets*?!

I can't help it. I laugh.

He is having the best summer ever. With Instagram Sydney! And Kat!

He has no regrets? Not even about leaving me for an entire summer?

What else isn't he regretting? Is he hooking up with Kat? Or Sydney? Or someone else?

Am I angry? I don't even know.

The door opens and Gavin steps inside. He's off the phone.

I jump off the couch.

"Omigod," I say. "You are not going to believe this."

"What?" he asks, not looking me in the eye.

"You are *really* not going to believe this. Let's go outside."

We step outside the office and close the door.

He forces a smile. "Is it that Kat is in Monte Carlo with your boyfriend right now?"

"Omigod, yes! I mean . . . what are the freakin' chances?"

"How did that happen?" he asks.

"It seems like Eli met some Americans in Switzerland, and one of them is some girl named Sydney—"

"Kat's best friend. She goes to our school."

"Right. So Sydney went to the South of France with Eli and his cousin and they must have invited Kat . . . I don't know. Small world?"

"You could say that." He looks a bit shell-shocked.

I feel a bit shell-shocked.

"Should we . . . walk back?" I ask.

"Okay," he says.

He puts his sunglasses back on. We walk in silence for a few minutes.

"Maybe they'll fall in love," I say.

He turns to me. "Who?"

"Eli and Kat!" I laugh.

If he cheats on me, then I don't have to feel bad about any of this. Then I was justified. Am justified. If he's cheating on me, then I'm doing nothing wrong,

"That is *not* going to happen," Gavin snaps, and I see his neck muscles tense.

"Okay, so they probably won't fall in love," I say quickly. "But they could hook up. It's not impossible. They're all together, in a glamorous place, a million miles away from us. It's easy to get caught up in the moment."

Very easy.

I should know. So should Gavin.

He shakes his head.

"I'm kind of joking," I say, "but wouldn't that make everything easier? If they hook up, then we're all even. We get to not feel guilty about this. Don't you want to not feel guilty about this?"

"I don't feel that guilty," he says.

"You don't?"

He stops and turns to me, but I can't see his eyes. "I don't. I don't know why. I know I should. But I don't."

I'm not sure what he means. That he doesn't think there's anything wrong with cheating? That he doesn't care if Kat finds out? That he doesn't care if he loses her? That he really cares about me?

I don't ask him to explain. I'm not sure I want to know the answer.

"Laundry's back!" I call out later that night. "Let's go, every-one, let's go! And then put your stuff away and get into bed!" I'm on OD tonight and Gavin is coming over any minute. Lis and Talia are both on their day off and Janelle is . . . I don't know. But she put on a tube top and took off for the night.

Once a week we leave all our laundry on the porch in our individual laundry bags, and a van comes back with all of our clothes mixed together. It's our job to sort them.

I empty all the clothes onto Prague's bed, very carefully. The clothes come back folded, but you have to find the name tags to see who the piece of clothing belongs to.

I call out the kids' names, and they run up to get their stuff.

"Yes!" Lily says. "Clean undies! Finally!"

I agree. I am running low on all my cute ones. All I have left are my period ones, and I don't want Gavin seeing those.

"Who's Emma Carleton?" I ask. "Oh! Slugger! I forgot you had a real name." I throw her a pair of sweatpants.

"Emma F.!" I call out, and toss her a yellow T-shirt.

"Um . . ." She holds it up against her body. It is half her size.

"Did you grow or did it shrink?" I ask.

"I think it shrank," she says. "By, like, a lot."

"It's not the world's best laundromat," I say.

"Oh! I know!" Em says. She takes out her stuffed lion and dresses her in the now itty-bitty shirt. "Pajamas for Ms. Lion!"

When we're done, I usher them into bed and then change into a clean thong and my cutest leggings and tank top. Not that they'll stay on for long.

The girls are asleep. Gavin is in my bed. All our clothes are off with the exception of my clean thong and his boxers.

He somehow elbows the shelf I share with Janelle and it crashes to the ground. All of our stuff is on the floor. Tissues. Tampons. Janelle's purple hairbrush. A box of condoms.

"Oooooh, condoms," Gavin says, picking up the box.

"They're not mine," I say quickly. I push the shelf back up and start rearranging the stuff that fell off.

"I figured," he says. "Since we haven't had sex. Janelle's, I guess?"

"I assume so," I say.

"The box is opened," he says, giving it a little shake.

"I'm guessing she's used some of them, then."

"Good for her," he says. He pauses. "Do you think she'd mind if we used one?"

"We are *not* using her condoms," I say. "That's our rule. Our only rule. No sex. Sex is too far."

He returns the box of condoms behind the tissue box, and climbs back into bed beside me. He puts his head on my pillow and looks into my eyes. "That's not our only rule."

"It's not?" I ask.

"No," he says. He kisses me lightly on the lips and then pulls back, our eyes locked. "No falling in love. That would really be going too far."

There are butterflies in my stomach. "No falling in love," I repeat softly. "Got it." I want to add, *And no tensing your damn neck if I mention the possibility of Kat falling in love either.*

246

There's a knock on the doorframe.

"Crap," I whisper. They were all asleep twenty minutes ago. "One sec! Hide," I tell Gavin. I pull my T-shirt over my head and step out of the counselors' room.

It's Fancy.

"What's wrong?" I ask. Please let her not have gotten a peek of the mostly naked guy in my bed.

"I don't . . . I think . . ." She vomits all over the floor. And me. And the door sheet. Then she starts to cry.

"Oh, sweetie," I say. I grab the garbage pail and pull it over to her. "More?"

She nods. And vomits more in the pail. And more. I see the burgers we had for dinner as well as this evening's milk and chocolate chip cookies.

I rub her tiny back as she sobs and pukes, sobs and pukes.

I hear the window opening in my counselors' room. What is he doing? Is he sneaking out? I guess that's smart?

"What's going on?" Slugger says, stepping into the hall-way. "Oh, gross."

A second later there's a knock at the front door to the cabin. "Hello?" Gavin says. "Everything okay in there?"

He is totally dressed and standing at the front door. Aw. Cuteness. He wants to help.

"Hey," I say, opening the door. "I have a sick kid."

"Oh no," he says. "Sam, should I get the doctor?"

"I need to take her to the infirmary," I say.

"I can stay with the kids," he says. "Until you get back."

"Okay," I say. "Slugger, get back into bed. Gavin will stay on the porch until I get back, okay?"

"Okay," she says. "Is Fancy going to be okay?"

"She's going to be fine," I say as she heaves again into the garbage pail. "Just go to bed, please."

I take Fancy's hand and lead her carefully to the infirmary, which luckily is not that far from our bunk.

I ring the doorbell, and Dr. Harris answers in sweatpants, a T-shirt, and glasses. I hear a *Law & Order* episode in the background.

"What do we have here?" she asks, bending down to Fancy's level.

"A very sick kid," I say.

The doctor puts her hand on her forehead. "A fever too. You don't feel too good, do you?"

Fancy shakes her head.

"You want to bunk with me tonight?" the doctor asks.

Fancy's head shakes even harder. "Not alone! Can Sam stay with me?"

"I . . ."

"You don't have to," Dr. Harris says. "But we do have an extra cot."

"Tell you what," I say. "I have to clean up the bunk and then as soon as one of the other counselors gets back, I'll come stay with you. How's that?"

She nods. "Thank you."

"Let's get you some medicine," the doctor says, taking her hand.

I get back to the bunk at around midnight. Gavin is sitting on the porch reading my copy of *The Interestings.*

"I borrowed a book," he says.

"No problem," I say, surprised. I didn't take him for a reader. "I finished it already. You can have it. Did any of the kids wake up?"

"Nope," he says.

"Did anyone see you here?" I ask.

"No one even walked by," he says.

"Good," I say. "Less explaining."

"We're allowed to be friends," he says. "There's no rule against that."

"I know," I say. "And now I have to clean up the vomit."

"I did it already," he says.

"You did?" I open the door. The vomit on the floor is gone. "You did! You didn't have to do that."

"I was here anyway. I used the paper towels in the bathroom. I wasn't sure what to do with the door sheet, though. Laundry or toss?"

"Laundry," I say. "It's not our bunk's turn, but I'll run it over as an emergency. And I'll wash the garbage out tomorrow too. And I'll go shower as soon as one of my co's gets home. I'm sure I smell fantastic."

"Smell? I don't smell anything," he says, smiling.

"Sure," I say.

"No, it's true!"

I laugh. "Thank you. And sorry our night was interrupted."

He shrugs. "It happens. And there's always tomorrow. I

think I have OD. You can come visit me."

Since no one is around, I lean over and kiss him lightly on the lips. "Perfect."

I take down the sheet, and throw it and my clothes in my laundry bag. I'll stop by the laundry and see if they can sneak my stuff in, or if they mind if I do it myself. I'm waiting in my bathrobe when Lis, Talia, and Janelle get back.

"What the heck happened here?" Lis asks.

"It smells like dead fish!" says Janelle.

"Vomit," I tell them. "A whole lot of vomit."

Talia shivers. "Gross, gross, gross, gross. We have to sterilize everything." She takes hand sanitizer out of her purse and squeezes some onto her hand. She hasn't even touched anything yet.

"Was it one of mine?" Janelle asks.

"One of ours ate three burgers at dinner," Lis says. "It was for sure her."

"No," I say. "It was Fancy. And she was so sad looking. Poor baby."

"Are you going to tell your BFF?" Talia asks.

"Huh?"

"Her mom!" Talia says. "Your texting buddy."

"Oh God, no," I say. "Do I have to?"

"Not yet," Lis says.

"I'm going to shower," I say, "but then I promised Fancy I'd sleep in the infirmary with her."

"That's the worst!" Lis says. "Why would you do that? Is there air-conditioning in there?"

"No. But she was crying! She asked!"

"You're too nice," Talia says.

"Maybe," I say as I leave them to shower. But I don't think so.

I spend the next day with the bunk, but visit Fancy during Rest Hour and Free Play. She gets to watch movies, so she's not too bored. She sleeps most of the time. I decide to text her mom and just accept that I'll be deluged with replies. The infirmary has Wi-Fi.

I'm not wrong. Her mom sends about seven hundred texts.

Fancy's Annoying Mom: What color was her vomit?

Fancy's Annoying Mom: Chunky or clear?

Fancy's Annoying Mom: Do you think she has a peanut allergy?

Fancy's Annoying Mom: Can I FaceTime her?

Fancy's Annoying Mom: Please? Just for five minutes.

Fancy's Annoying Mom: One minute.

Fancy's Annoying Mom: Thirty seconds.

Fancy's Annoying Mom: Please please please I'm losing it.

Clearly. Finally we let her talk to Fancy, which makes her mom, if not Fancy, feel better.

"I'm fine!" Fancy tells her. "Sam and the doctor are taking care of me. Calm down! I'll see you in two days!"

Saturday is Visiting Day. I am kind of excited to meet Fancy's mom in person.

I text Eli a few times, but I don't have a chance to call him. Which is kind of a relief.

I tell him I don't have Wi-Fi in the infirmary. So now I'm officially a cheater *and* a liar.

The rest of the bunk makes Fancy a get better soon card in art.

When I'm not with Fancy and the bunk, I'm finding time to secretly make out with Gavin. In his counselors' room. Behind our bunk. In our bunk when no one's in it.

"You know I'm gonna get sick and then you'll get sick too," I say.

"I know," he says. "Totally worth it."

I get a killer headache on Friday afternoon.

Gavin brings me chicken soup. Talia's hand sanitizing goes into overdrive.

"Where did you get this?" I ask, impressed by his sweetness.

"I called in some favors," he says.

He sits on the end of my bed and plays with my hair when no one's looking.

Saturday is wild.

The kids are off the wall with excitement.

Partly to see their parents, but mostly because visiting parents means more candy.

252

"I asked for licorice!"

"I'm going to eat a million brownies," says Fancy, who has her appetite back.

"My parents are divorced, so I'm getting twice as much!"

"Tonight's going to be bonkers," Talia tells me.

"I'm excited for the brownies," I say.

"I'm excited for the tips," Talia says.

During the last staff meeting, they told us that we are allowed to take tips. But you have to turn them down at least once. They acted out the process for us.

"Thank you so much for taking such good care of my kid!" Priya said, and tried to hand Botts something.

"Oh, I couldn't," Botts said.

"But I insist! You've earned it!"

"Well, okay, thank you!"

The morning is all about cleanup. There's a paper chase through the camp, where all the kids run around and try to pick up as much garbage as possible. Whoever collects the most bags of garbage gets a sundae party later this week.

Then we all clean up our bunks and porches.

Everyone has showers the morning of Visiting Day. We take the girls up right before lunch. Juniors have the last slot.

"Okay, no joke, girls, everyone has to wash their hair today!" I yell.

"I don't want to!" screams Fancy. Now that she's well again, her spunkiness has returned.

"No choice!" Talia says. "Today is a must-wash day!"

"Am I done?" Slugger pops her head out of the shower.

I glance at her hair, which is both soapy and slick with conditioner. "No," I say. "Another rinse. Next!"

I knock on the next stall. "Who's in this one?"

"I am!" I hear. It's Prague. "Not done yet!"

"Lily, where are you?" I ask.

"In here!" she says from the last shower.

"Did you take out your braid this time?"

"Um . . . no!"

I roll my eyes. "Take out your braid!"

"Okay!"

"Before you wash it!"

"Oops!"

Now Talia rolls her eyes. "They're seriously helpless. Don't their parents teach them anything?"

"Everyone remember to look for ticks!" I yell out. "On your feet and armpits! I'll look behind your ears! I do not want your parents finding ticks on you!"

"Now am I done?" Slugger asks again, sticking her head out. She has a little conditioner on her ear, but that's it. "Good enough," I tell her.

I double-check on Shira. Last week, I noticed that her shampoo had never been opened.

When they are all done, we march them back to the bunk and get them dressed in their camp T-shirt and shorts. We brush all their hair. We check behind their ears for ticks.

"They better not give us spaghetti for lunch," I say.

"Maybe we should have them wear other T-shirts and then change them?" Talia asks.

"We just refolded all the clothes in their cubbies."

"I know, but it's so risky."

"Okay, girls, take off your camp shirt, put it on your bed, and put whatever shirt is at the very top of your T-shirts on. Whatever that is. I do not care if it doesn't match. Do it very, very carefully!"

We are glad we did, because they manage to get cream cheese and bagel all over themselves. Smears of cream cheese. Everywhere.

"Why are children so filthy?" Talia asks, and pulls out the hand sanitizer.

At 2:00, the kids are standing on the porch. At this very moment, all the parents have arrived, driven onto Upper Field, and are waiting for Eric to announce the beginning of Visiting Day. All the kids are on their porches, ready to run.

"And Visiting Day starts . . . in . . . three . . . two . . . one! Happy Visiting Day!" There's a loud horn sound.

The kids shriek and take off.

Shira slips and falls right on her face.

"Kid down," Talia says. "Kid down!"

I hurry beside her. "Are you okay?"

Tears stream down her face.

I pick her up. Her shirt is dirty and her knees are skinned. Crap. I take her back into the bunk, clean her up. I put her in a plain white shirt instead of the camp shirt.

She takes off again. "Don't run!" I yell.

She slows down but then runs again.

"If she goes down another time, we're out of shirts," I say.

Talia sighs. "There goes our tip."

As instructed, we stay in the bunk to greet the families. Kids want to show their parents where they sleep, and they are adorably excited for their parents to meet us.

It's super funny to see the parents after knowing the kids for so long. Shira has her dad's big ears but her mom's height. Slugger looks nothing like her mom, who is tiny and bird-like. Lily looks identical to her mom, but has her dad's curly hair.

Prague's parents don't show up.

They're in Greece and couldn't make it back.

"I'm sorry, sweetie," I say, running my fingers through her hair.

"Whatev. They didn't make it back last year either. They're a little self-involved."

I laugh even though my heart breaks.

"If it makes you feel better, my parents didn't come either," I tell her. I hadn't invited them. It would have been tough for my dad in his walker, and my mom just complains. She sends at least three texts full of complaints to me every week.

"You're a counselor!" she says. "It's different."

"True. I'm kind of jealous that Talia's parents are here though." They are currently sitting on her bed.

"They're kind of adorable," she says.

"They really are. So will you hang out with me all day? Keep me company?"

"Sure," she says, lacing her arm around my waist. "I don't want you to get lonely."

Talia sanitizes her hands between parents.

Fancy's mom corners me on the porch.

"Thank you for taking such good care of my baby," she says to me. "She loves you."

"Aw, thanks." Then she awkwardly hands me a wad of cash.

"Oh, not necessary," I say.

"You slept with her in the infirmary," she says. "It's necessary. Please."

Good point. "Thank you!" I say, trying to be cool about it but not really succeeding.

I check to see what she gave afterward. "She gave me two hundred bucks! Holy shit!"

"And yet she only gave me fifty," Talia says.

"Her daughter did vomit all over me," I say. "And she's sent me about seven hundred texts."

"Fair enough," Talia says. "Although I got lice from Mara Stevens last year, and I got nothing from her folks."

"We only get the tips at Visiting Day, is the problem," Lis

says. "Parents don't see staff at bus drop-off. Next time get lice in the first half of the summer."

When there is only thirty minutes left, we walk to Upper Field to collect the girls from the Rec Hall.

They are all crying. All of them. Every single one. Even Prague.

Some of the parents are crying too.

"It's okay, everyone," I say. "You're crying because you love each other! But there are only two weeks left. And then you're back together again. And the last two weeks are the best weeks of camp. We still have mini-golf and Superbowl!"

"Once one goes, they all go," Talia says. "I should have warned you. Visiting Day is the worst."

"Porny?" I hear. "Is that you?"

My skin crawls. That voice. Please, no. I turn around. The short black hair, pointy chin, and beady eyes are unmistakable.

It's Zoe Freaking Buckman. What the hell is she doing here?

"You came back to camp?" she asks gleefully.

I spot her brother, twelve-year-old Bennett, standing beside her. Ah. She came to visit him. For Visiting Day. Of course. She is not here to torment me.

"My name is Sam, actually," I say, my voice shaking. "How nice of you to come visit."

Why am I being nice to her? I should slap her across the

face. I should tell her that she is a horrible bitch. I should tell her that she may have tried to squash me, but that she didn't succeed! I'm back! I'm strong! I won freakin' color war! I have a boyfriend AND I'm hooking up with her precious Gavin! I win! She loses! B-L-U-E, Sammy's here for victory!

"I'm good," she says lazily. "I'm studying film at UCLA. I live in Silver Lake. Do you know LA at all? I'm just on the East Coast for the week. It's like time is frozen here! Nothing has changed at all. You, Botts, Gav, Priya, the Tank! Everyone is exactly the same. So adorable!"

Nothing has changed at all? She thinks I've been here the whole time? Is she freaking kidding me? And Gav? She calls him Gav? Who does she think she is?

I hate you, I hate you, I hate you! I want to scream.

"Why'd she call you Porny?" Prague asks.

Suddenly I notice that all six of my girls are standing beside us. With their parents.

I freeze. I rack my brain to try to think of an explanation. Is there a word that rhymes with porny that would make sense? Borny? Corny? Horny? No. "I don't know," I say finally. I put my hands on my hips. "Why did you call me Porny, Zoe Buckman? I really hated it."

Everyone looks at her. She takes a step back and shrugs. "I don't even remember," she says, before giving me a half smile and turning away.

That's it?

Yeah. That's it.

Porny is dead.

I put my arm around Fancy and Em, and lead my girls back to our bunk.

WEEK 5 SCHEDULE—BUNK 6A

	SUNDAY	MONDAY	TUESDAY	WEDNESDAY	THURSDAY	FRIDAY	SATURDAY
PERIOD 1 10:00– 10:45	DANCE	TENNIS	A&C	SI	NEWCOMB	DRAMA	A&C
PERIOD 2 10:45– 11:30	SI	DRAMA	GAGA BALL	DANCE	BASKETBALL	SI	SI
PERIOD 3 11:30– 12:15	ARCHERY	SHOWERS	SOCCER	SOCCER	SHOWERS	DRAMA	SHOWERS
12:15– 12:30	LUNCH WASHUP	LUNCH WASHUP	LUNCH WASHUP	LUNCH WASHUP	LUNCH WASHUP	LUNCH WASHUP	LUNCH WASHUP
12:30– 1:00	LUNCH	LUNCH	LUNCH	LUNCH	LUNCH	LUNCH	LUNCH
1:00–2:00	REST HOUR	REST HOUR	REST HOUR	REST HOUR	REST HOUR	REST HOUR	
PERIOD 4 2:00– 2:45	DANCE	BASKETBALL	SAILING	BAKING	CANOEING	A&C	
2:45–3:15	MILK & COOKIES	MILK & COOKIES	MILK & COOKIES	MILK & COOKIES	MILK & COOKIES	MILK & COOKIES	MINI-GOLF
PERIOD 5 3:15–4:00	A&C	SI	NEWCOMB	TENNIS	SOCCER	WATERSKI	
PERIOD 6 4:00– 4:45	GS	GS	GS	GS	GS	GS	

Week 5

"Do you think anybody has noticed us?" I ask. Gavin and I are at the staff party and the lights are low and a super-slow song is playing. We're pretty much right in the middle of the dance floor, but we're keeping our bodies a few inches apart at least.

"No," he says. "Everyone is a little drunk, I think. And possibly high."

There were definitely some flasks being passed around earlier, out of sight of the head staff. Also there was a definite whiff of pot, too.

"Are we going to Botts's for our day off?" he asks.

"Sure," I say. "That will be fun. Did he invite you?"

"Yeah. Said he would invite you, too."

"I'm in."

I look around to see where my co-counselors are.

Talia, JJ, and Muffs are talking in the corner. They are

glaring at Brody. I guess that's over.

Smokin' Hot Benji has his hands up the back of Priya's shirt.

Janelle is grinding on . . . Lawrence.

Allie's not going to like that. Where is she? I spot her on the other side of the room whispering with Audrey, one of the color war captains.

At least I know what she's whispering about. And it's not me and Gavin.

OMG. "Botts is dancing with Lis," I whisper.

"Good for him! She's great. Maybe she'll come on our day off too. Keep him distracted so he doesn't figure us out."

"Ooh, good plan."

"I bet he'll be visiting your cabin tonight. . . ."

"I'll let you know," I say. I can't help but feel jealous. Unlike Gavin, Botts is head staff and can just visit any bunk, no problem. Plus, he's single! But not me! If Gavin were spotted in my bunk in the middle of the night, everyone would be talking about it the next day. Allie would tell Kat. Kat would tell Eli.

We probably shouldn't even be dancing.

We definitely shouldn't be close dancing at least.

We have to be so vigilant.

If we don't want people to find out.

Unless we want people to find out?

"Look at Botts and Lis," he says.

I watch them. They're getting closer. And closer and closer.

"They're kissing! OMG, they're kissing!" I whisper.

Gavin whispers in my ear, "I wish I could kiss you right here."

"You can't."

"I know."

"We're in the middle of a staff party."

"I know."

"Unless we don't care," I say. "Do we care?"

He takes a step back and looks me in the eye. "I don't know."

Neither of us says anything for a minute. We continue dancing.

Lis is beside herself with excitement in the bunk after. "He kissed me! While we were dancing!"

"I saw!" I say, but my mind is still buzzing from what Gavin and I said at the staff party. That maybe we don't care if Eli and Kat find out. What does that mean? Are we going to break up with them? Are we going to be together for real? Is that what we wanted? Did that make any sense? Camp is over in less than two weeks!

"He's a really good kisser," she says. "Like, amazing."

He is? I mean, I'm not totally surprised. I bet he'd be a great boyfriend. I try to focus on Lis. "So what happens now?" I ask her. "Is he coming to the bunk later?"

Talia groans. "I need earplugs. And an eye mask. Or maybe I'll go sleep in the cubby room."

"Do you think Lawrence will come by?" Janelle asks.

"Him too?" Talia asks.

"Lawrence is really hot," Lis says.

"Right?" Janelle says. "And funny!"

I hesitate. He's a little too full of himself for me. "He rubs me the wrong way," I say carefully.

"Hopefully he'll rub me the right way," Janelle says.

I snort-laugh.

I catch Talia making a vomiting motion when Janelle isn't looking.

"Just be careful with him," I say. "Is he really coming here tonight?"

"No, I told him I was too tired. But maybe when you're on your day off . . . we'll see."

When we wake up the next morning, neither Botts nor Lawrence nor Gavin has come. I wasn't really expecting Gavin. But Lis is heartbroken.

"Why didn't he come?" Lis asks as she nibbles on her fingers.

"Maybe because he's not skeezy?" I ask. "Showing up in someone's bunk in the middle of the night is skeezy!"

"Or I'm a bad kisser," she says. "Either or."

I spot Botts at the picnic tables on the way back from lunch and sit beside him. "Hello there, stranger," I say. "So what happened? We were kind of expecting a late visit."

"Were you all waiting up with flashlights?" he asks.

"No," I say. "But Lis may have been."

"I don't know," he says. "I thought about it. But . . . she's staff! I shouldn't be hooking up with staff!"

I laugh and let the sun warm my face. "What are you talking about? You should be hooking up with campers?"

"No, I just mean . . . I'm kind of like her boss."

"You are not her boss. And Priya is hooking up with Smokin' Hot Benji! He's not head staff either. Lis is eighteen. She's only a year younger than you. Do you like her?"

"I do. But . . . I don't know. I'm not in love with her or anything."

"It's a summer fling!"

"But I don't want a summer fling! I want the real thing."

"But you barely know her! You can't be in love with her already!" I sigh. "Does this mean you're not inviting her on our day off tomorrow?"

"I don't know," he says. "Maybe I should invite her? See what happens? You think I should invite her?"

"Yes," I say sternly. "I do."

Gavin and I make out in the gym that night after Milk and Cookies.

"So, tomorrow . . ." he says. His voice trails off.

I am lying on a foam mat. "Yeah?"

"Should we . . . stop at a drugstore?"

"Why? Are you out of conditioner?" I ask. "I am almost out of conditioner."

I think of when I met Eli. But then shake it off.

"No, I am not. I meant . . . maybe we wanted to get other stuff."

It takes me a second, but I realize he means condoms. "No! That's too far! We talked about this. No sex. Remember?"

"I remember," he says. "I was just hoping that maybe we're over that."

"We are not over that."

"Okay," he says quickly.

"That's the line."

He nods. "Got it. Still the line."

"You're okay with that being the line, right?" I ask.

"Of course I'm *okay* with it. I would just rather be having sex than not having sex. And since we have another day off tomorrow . . . I just thought I would bring it up. In case you really wanted to have sex but you just didn't want to borrow one from Janelle."

"Borrow?"

"You know what I mean."

"I do. But see, if I asked to borrow a condom, then she would know I was having sex with someone. Someone who is not my boyfriend. And we haven't decided that we want anyone to know yet. And I kind of think that if we did want anyone to know, we should tell our significant others first. Not that we've decided that."

"All good points. Although, if you did want to borrow a condom, you could say that you were making water balloons. It's been done."

"Why not just use a regular balloon?" I wonder.

"Condoms are more accessible?"

"Not to us."

"Got it. No condoms."

"No sex. That's our rule. Sex is bad."

"Sex with you would not be bad," he says.

I kiss his lips. He tastes like oatmeal cookie. "You're right. Not physically speaking, of course."

Botts invites Lis to come on our day off after all. At Rest Hour, she flutters around the counselors' room debating what to pack. Which swimsuit? Which jeans? Which underwear?

I am debating the same thing. I really wish I had thought to bring at least one sexy outfit to camp. Like the black lace nightie I bought at Victoria's Secret. But why would I have? I had not expected to dress sexy. At all.

He will probably spend most of the night in my bed. He'll have to sneak back to his own room at some point. But still. It's going to be the first time we spend most of the night in a bed together. We can fall asleep together. How nice will that be?

At flagpole, the two of us hike to the office. Lis is coming with me in my car. Gavin, Smokin' Hot Benji, and Priya are going with Botts. It's just the six of us. Couple central.

"I might throw up," Lis tells me as she climbs into the front.

"Do you get carsick?"

"No! I'm just nervous. Do you think he's expecting something to happen?"

"Probably," I say. "But don't feel pressure or anything. He won't kick you out of the canoe."

"Huh?"

"Never mind," I say.

"I'm a virgin," she says.

"Oh. Okay. I didn't know that."

"I'm not sure I want to have sex with him."

"Then don't! You barely know him. You don't have to do anything with him. Just get to know him."

"You don't think he's expecting me to have sex with him, do you?"

"No, I definitely don't," I say. "Botts is a good guy. And if you do decide to hook up or whatever, it's totally fine to say that you're not going all the way. I've done that." I just did it, in fact. "Maybe don't have too much to drink or smoke tonight if you're nervous. And remember, I am just down the hall if you feel uncomfortable *at any point*." Not that I want her interrupting me. But there's a lock on my door. I can always make Gavin hide in the closet.

She talks and talks until we pull up outside his massive house. "Omigod, this is his *cottage*? Never mind sleeping with him, now I want to marry him."

Everyone but Lis drinks at dinner. We barbecue and they make the same amazing burgers.

Gavin and I get a little tipsy.

Gavin and I get handsy when we get tipsy.

We try really hard to keep our hands off each other, but it's hard.

His fingers trail down my back at dinner.

I rub my leg against his in the hot tub. I guess we're legsy as well as handsy?

At midnight, when we are walking back to my room together and we are in the hallway, Gavin stops and pushes me against the wall, and we are kissing and it is so good and I'm giggling and then I hear Botts say, "Hey, Rosenspan, do you want to try watching Star—" and then his voice stops.

We look up.

Botts is staring at us.

Gavin takes a step back.

"Oh," Botts says.

"Um," I say.

"Well," Gavin says.

"Okay then," Botts says, trying to look anywhere but at us. "I was not expecting that. I'm going back to my room now."

I feel sick. Botts saw.

He turns around and walks back to his room.

Gavin and I both stand there.

"Shit," I say.

"Shit," Gavin repeats.

I motion for him to follow me into my room.

"How bad is that, you think?" I ask.

Gavin is running his hands through his hair. "He won't say anything," Gavin says.

"To anyone?" I wonder.

"I don't think so. I'll ask him not to. It's not like he knows Kat."

"Or Eli."

He nods. "Right."

"But I don't want him to tell Lis either. Or Allie. Or anyone. Do you think he thinks we're horrible?"

"Maybe he didn't see anything," he says, sitting on the edge of the bed.

"He saw," I say.

"Yeah?"

I nod. My heart is racing. Why were we making out in the middle of the hall? How dumb, how careless.

Neither of us says anything for a few minutes.

"I don't think it's that big of a deal," Gavin says finally. "He's my friend. He's your friend."

But there was something about the look on his face. "He seemed upset."

"Why would he be?"

I shake my head.

Gavin takes a step closer to me. "Where were we?"

"Yeah?" I'm not sure how I'm feeling about this.

He shrugs. "Yeah?"

"I don't know. I feel weird now."

"The other day we weren't even sure if we cared if anyone knew," he says.

"I know. But now someone does. It's different." It's real.

"Do you want me to go back to my room?" he asks. He puts his hand on my shoulder.

"No," I say quickly. Everything feels a little dizzy. "Let's just lie down for a minute."

He lies down next to me on the double bed and puts his arm around me.

Maybe it's not that big of a deal. Botts doesn't know Eli. He doesn't know Kat. He's our friend! Maybe he's happy for us! Wouldn't he want his two friends to be together?

We're quiet for two minutes until Gavin runs his hands through my hair and I feel my body responding. So Botts saw. What's the worst thing that could happen? He announces it on Instagram? He's not going to do that. And even if he did . . . does it really matter? Am I really going to pretend none of this happened with Eli? How would I go back to normal? And maybe I want to be with Gavin. For real.

"You okay?" Gavin asks.

I nod and my lips find his.

"I borrowed one of Janelle's condoms," I whisper. "Just in case." Truthfully, I have three.

"Borrowed?"

I elbow him.

He tries again. "You did? Really?"

"Yeah. Do you want to?" I ask.

"Very much yes."

He kisses me harder.

Botts is acting overly enthusiastic the next day, but not looking me in the eye. Does he think I'm a horrible person?

"Good morning, Sam! How did you sleep last night?" he booms from the kitchen. "We're making French toast and turkey bacon. Are you starving?"

My cheeks burn. What's he trying to say?

It's not like we're rubbing it in his face. Gavin fell asleep in my bed, but left around six in the morning to go back to his room. By the time I got up, he was already in the kitchen, making coffee. Priya's door is still shut. She must still be asleep. I'm assuming with Smokin' Hot Benji.

Botts can't possibly know we had actual sex. We were very quiet. I think? As quiet as you can be during sex, I guess.

But it wasn't *just* sex. It was *good* sex. And so different than with Eli. Not better, not worse, just different. With Eli, it's sweet and gentle. With Gavin, it's sexy and new.

"I slept very well, Botts, thanks for asking."

"This is like the nicest house ever," Lis says. "Can we just stay here the rest of the summer?"

I wonder what happened with the two of them last night. She didn't come knocking, so hopefully all went well.

"What?" Botts asks. "And miss the Superbowl? And my kids go to the water park. The last two weeks of camp are the best."

There are only two weeks left? I shake my head. Less than two weeks. Eleven days. The summer went fast.

If there are only eleven days left, then Eli is coming back in five days. On Sunday.

"But we can all come back for our last day off," Botts says. "You guys in? Sunday night?"

"Maybe," says Lis. "You in, Sam?"

"I . . ." I hesitate. The plan is that Eli is flying back to NYC on Sunday, which means that he can come up to see me for my last day off. Next Monday is the last possible day to take a day off and we coordinated it. He'll see me and then he'll drive back to Connecticut to see his parents for two weeks. I'll come visit him for a week, and then I'll spend just a few days with my parents before meeting him back in New York.

"Actually, next week I'm taking Monday/Tuesday. I already coordinated it with Danish."

"What are you doing?" Lis asks innocently.

Botts freezes. Gavin drinks his coffee.

"I'm . . . well, Eli is coming up to see me."

Gavin chokes.

"Oh, yay!" Lis says. "He's coming home finally! That's great. I can't wait to meet him. Is he coming up to camp?"

There is no edge to her voice, and I can tell Botts didn't say anything to her. I didn't think he would, but good to know for sure.

Botts smirks. "Eli, huh? How *is* Eli? Is he enjoying his

274

trip around the world?" He is not going to make this easy, I can tell.

"I believe he is," I say sharply.

I look over at Gavin, who is looking at me. He fakes an extra-large smile.

Botts turns to Gavin. "And when is Kat coming back?"

"Not until the end of August."

"I bet she's having a great time too," he says. "But not as great as you guys are."

"Probably not," I say.

"Omigod," Lis says, pulling me into a hallway after breakfast. "What is going on?"

"What do you mean?" I ask, heart pounding.

"Why did he invite me here if he wasn't going to make a move?"

"Oh, Botts."

"Yes, Botts," she says. "Nothing happened. We were sitting alone in the hot tub, and then he was like, oh, I have to go to sleep, I'm super tired. And he left! Who does that when they're in the hot tub with a girl they've already kissed? But then this morning he invited me to come back. When he said come back, he meant me too, didn't he? What do you think the deal is?"

"I honestly don't know," I say.

"Did I sound dumb last night or something? I didn't drink or smoke or anything. I wanted to be completely sober. But

Botts is so smart. I feel like he probably thinks I'm too dumb for him. Or too silly. Do you think I'm silly?"

"No, not at all," I say.

"Can you find out if he likes me or what?"

"I . . ." I really don't want to have a personal conversation about anything with Botts right now. And this is so eighth grade. "I'll see what I can do."

"Thank you!" Lis says. "You're the best."

"You guys are not going to believe what happened," Talia says the second we get back to the bunk. Actually, the second we get back to the bunk we are swarmed by children who want the Munchkins we've brought back, but the second after that, Talia pulls us into the counselors' room. She sticks her head out into the hallway to see if anyone else is around.

"What is it?" Lis asks, eyes wide. "Tell me, tell me!"

"Craziness," she says, laughing manically. "Total craziness."

"What?" Lis asks. "You're killing us!"

"Janelle hooked up with Lawrence last night," Talia whispers.

"Okay," I say. "We were expecting that, right? Are they a thing?"

Talia shakes her head. "No, they're not a thing! He just hooked up with her because . . . why not! She hooks up with everyone!"

"Did she tell you?" I ask. "Were they here?"

"Yes! They were here! She put up a sheet between our

areas at least. But I could tell what was happening. It was way worse than with Jamon. She was super noisy and gross about it!"

"So why is this such a scandal?" I wonder. "Does Allie know?"

"Oh, she definitely knows. And she's mad. Everyone knows. But that's not the crazy part." Talia's eyes are gleaming. I cannot for the life of me figure out what she is so excited about, but it makes me feel slightly sick.

"Ready?" Talia asks.

"Just tell us," I say.

"He asked her to"—she lowers her voice—"masturbate for him and she did and used *her hairbrush!*"

Lis gasps.

We all look at the purple brush that is oh so casually lying on her windowsill.

"And *then* he went back to his bunk and told Lenny and Max about it," she finishes.

"How do you know?" I ask.

"Because I saw Max on the beach and he asked me if I saw it! And then he told me about it!"

"Poor Janelle," I say. I feel sick to my stomach. Janelle trusted Lawrence. They were together, and she trusted him, and he completely betrayed her. Now the whole camp is probably talking about her.

"Poor Janelle?" Talia says. "Poor me! I had to hear the whole thing."

I clench my fists. "I'm sorry she did it in the room when

you were here, and it definitely makes me feel differently about the hairbrush, but it's not *that* big a deal. Couples do stuff together when they have sex. They try things out."

"They're not a couple!" Lis says.

"That doesn't make Janelle wrong for doing it," I say. "She was sharing herself with him!"

Seriously, who cares that she masturbated in front of him? I mean, really. Who. Freaking. Cares? And so she used a brush. Big freaking deal.

People love to talk. People love to judge. But I mean, that's what couples do. Try to please each other.

But still. This is going to be a problem for Janelle.

"How many people know?" I ask.

"It's spreading," Talia says. "And she is so clueless and—"

Talia's sentence is interrupted by Janelle throwing open the sheet and bouncing inside in one of her trademark tube tops. "You're back!" she says. "Hiiiii! How were your days off? I can smell the powdered sugar!"

We all freeze.

"Great, thanks," Lis says quickly.

I don't know what to do. Do I say something? But what would I say exactly? The very fact that I know is going to make her feel horrible. "It was good," I say slowly. "How was . . ." I hesitate. "Your day?"

"Totally exhausting. We had soccer, which was a total shit show. Our girls cannot block a ball. But General Swim was fun. It was so hot that I went in."

I nod.

Eric comes on over the loudspeaker. "Attention, all campers and counselors. Attention, all campers and counselors. It is now the end of Dinner Washup. I'm hungry. Are you hungry? Please proceed to flagpole."

"There's lots more, but I'll fill you in tonight!" she says with a wink. She grabs a sweatshirt off her bed. "Let's round up the troops!"

Talia and Lis are smirking to each other as they follow Janelle out of the cabin.

I can't help but wonder—is there any chance that Talia was the one who told everyone? Or that she made it up? Is she pulling a Zoe Buckman?

No. She wouldn't do that. Would she?

Gavin and I are walking to the Counselors' Lounge after Milk and Cookies. "What's wrong?" he asks me.

I sigh. "Did you hear about . . . what happened?"

"I did," he says. He doesn't even hesitate.

"I figured. She has no idea that anyone is talking about her," I say. "I hate it."

"He's a jerk," Gavin says.

"I can't believe he told everyone. Or Talia told everyone."

"Why would she do that?"

"Why does anyone do anything?" I ask. I hesitate. "How do we know that everyone isn't talking about *us*?"

"Because *I* am not an asshole. And no one knows. Besides Botts. And he doesn't know what he knows."

"We don't know that we've never been spotted. Someone

279

could have seen *something*. Everyone could be gossiping about us behind our backs."

"True. But if everyone was talking about us, we would hear it. And we could always deny it. If we wanted to. No one knows what happens between us except us."

"I guess," I say.

"And anyway, no one really cares. Even about this brush thing. By tomorrow everyone will be over it."

But he's wrong. By the next night, all the counselors in camp know. Or at least it feels like that.

Lis and Talia stand even farther away from Janelle than they normally do at flagpole. Before she was the annoying co-counselor. Now she is genuinely a leper. Allie and her friends are clearly whispering about her on the other side of the flagpole circle.

At dinner, I go to the kitchen to get the lasagna, and then sit beside Talia.

"Ugh," Talia mutters, taking a bite of her faux–peanut butter sandwich and jutting her chin at Janelle. "She is so gross."

"She is not gross," I snap. "Who cares what she does?"

"Everyone." Talia shrugs. "I'm just glad I didn't see. My eyeballs would be scarred."

"He's the one who's gross," I say finally. "Why would he tell his friends?"

"Guys always tell their friends."

"No, they don't," I say. "Not if they're decent guys."

"Lawrence is a jerk. She should have known he'd be a jerk."

My head hurts. "So now it's her fault that he's a jerk?"

"You know what I mean," she says with a shrug.

I don't. And I do.

But seriously, what the hell did *Janelle* do wrong? Besides hooking up with a guy she thought was hot and getting intimate in her own way? He doesn't even have a girlfriend!

"Why is he allowed to do whatever he wants but she's the one everyone is whispering about?" I ask.

Talia laughs. "Because he's Lawrence and she's a weirdo."

I help myself to a second piece of lasagna. "So if he was a weirdo, and she was . . . Allie, then everyone would be whispering about Lawrence?"

"If Lawrence *pleasured himself* in front of Allie with *a brush*, then yes."

"Are you kidding me? Guys always have their hands down their pants," I say. "Look at Bunk Two! Five guys have their hands down their pants right now! And we're at a meal! We're literally eating and boys everywhere have their hands down their pants right in the Dining Hall!"

Talia just laughs. "At least they're not eating with their hands."

Three boys from Bunk 2 pick up pieces of French bread. With their hands. Oops, make that four. Oh, wow, all five.

I turn to Talia and eye her meaningfully.

After the meal, Botts taps the microphone to get everyone's attention.

"I hope everyone enjoyed their lasagna!" he says. "Do you want to hear what tonight's activity is?"

Everyone cheers.

"It's Ugly Counselor Night!"

Everyone cheers louder.

"What does that even mean?" I ask.

"It means the kids dress one counselor from every bunk up really ugly," Talia says. "Guess who we're dressing up?"

"Don't choose Janelle," I say.

"Why not? It's just a game. And she'll love it. Do you want to do it?"

Part of me wants to be a good sport and save Janelle, but I've been where she is, and I never want to be there again. I cannot be there again. I can't take a chance that anyone would be laughing at me instead of with me.

Janelle is still clueless.

At Free Play, the girls dress her in rain boots and a yellow feather boa that comes from who knows where, and tease her hair and cover her face in clown makeup, giggling the whole time.

After Eric calls the activity, they lead her to the Rec Hall by the hand, while giggling hysterically. Every bunk has one poor counselor dressed up.

The whole camp is in the Rec Hall for the activity. All the Ugly Counselors wait backstage while the kids get settled.

The lights flash on and off. Here we go.

Dance music comes on, and Josh takes the microphone.

"Welcome to Ugly Counselor!" he calls out. "Who will

be the ugliest of the ugliest?"

Everyone cheers.

The junior boy bunks go up first. Muffs's face is painted purple and he is wearing a raincoat and a plunger on his head, which does not seem hygienic at all.

Danish laughs next to me on the bench.

Janelle is next.

"Next up, we have Janelle from Bunk Six!"

My girls all cheer.

Janelle prances across the stage and shimmies.

The rest of the campers start cheering as well, getting louder and louder.

"Use your brush!" I hear.

I freeze. Shit.

There are laughs throughout the senior boy section. Lawrence's bunk.

His campers know too?

"Use your brush!" someone else calls out, and suddenly the entire back section is chanting, "Use your brush! Use your brush!"

No, no, no.

What do I do? I have to stop it. This is the worst. The worst. They could easily be chanting *Porny*.

I touch Danish's arm.

Onstage, Janelle seems oblivious to the chanting. Or maybe she can't hear over the loud music.

"We have to stop them," I say. "The boys."

She listens. "What are they saying?"

"They're telling her to use her brush."

Danish looks at Janelle and then back at me. "I don't get it. Because her hair is messy?"

"No," I say, putting my head down. "Because she apparently masturbated with it in front of Lawrence."

Danish closes her eyes, looking pained. "Shit," she says.

"Yeah."

"And he told everyone."

"Yeah."

"What a fucking asshole," she says.

I have never heard her swear, ever.

"She doesn't know that everyone knows?" she asks.

"No," I say.

The chanting continues. "Use your brush! Use your brush!"

"Dammit," Danish says. She motions to Josh to move it along.

"Thank you, Janelle!" he says. "Next up, we have Bunk Five!"

Danish goes to the back of the room and I see her whispering to Priya and Botts.

"What did you say?" I ask when she comes back.

"I told them what was going on. And told him to threaten their staff that they would all be zapped with OD if any of their campers uttered anything about a damn brush again."

The show continues. After all the counselors have their turn, they return onstage. Josh calls them out one at a time and asks for applause.

I hold my breath for Janelle. There is a lot of applause.

And a lot of laughing. She turns around and shakes her butt, totally obliviously. Everyone whoops and hollers.

"Crap," Danish says.

"At least they're not saying anything about a brush," I whisper back.

No one else gets as much applause as Janelle, so she is declared the winner.

"Are you going to tell her?" I ask Danish when the event is over and the kids are sent to Milk and Cookies.

She nods. "I would want to know. Wouldn't you?"

"Yes," I say. I would.

Danish motions for Janelle and the two of them head out of the side door. I take a deep breath and follow my kids to the Dining Hall.

Janelle and Danish don't return to the bunk until after curfew. Lis and Talia are in the bathroom so it's just me in the counselors' room.

Janelle's eyes are red, like she's been crying. She's still wearing her Ugly Counselor makeup, outfit, and teased hair. She sits on her bed and leans her head back against the wall.

"You okay?" I ask. I debate putting my hand on her shoulder but I leave it on my lap.

She shrugs but then shakes her head no. "I'm embarrassed. And mad. This place is . . . fucked up," she says.

"Yeah," I say. "It really is."

She looks me dead in the eye. "I wish you would have told me."

"I'm sorry," I say quickly. "I didn't know what to say."

"Who told you?" she asks. "Talia?"

I nod.

She sighs. "I'm not sure why she and Lis dislike me so much."

I don't respond. It's hard to explain to someone that they're just different.

"Was what I did so wrong?" she asks.

"No, of course not. He's the wrong one," I say. "He's a jerk."

"I just didn't expect him to . . . tell people." Her eyes tear up. "I'm a moron."

"You are not! There is nothing wrong with trusting someone."

"Clearly there is," she says.

She stands back up and strips off her clothes, wraps a towel around herself, and grabs her shower bucket.

Talia opens the curtain and she and Lis stand at the entranceway.

"You're showering now?" Lis asks. "It's after curfew."

"Yeah," Janelle says. "I don't care." She picks up the brush, waves it at both of them, pops it into her shower bucket, and pushes her way out the door.

"Danish told her," I say.

Lis watches her go. "Told her what?"

"That everyone knows," I say.

Talia nods. "Good. That should teach her a lesson."

"Don't be a bitch," I say. "She shouldn't have done it with

you in the bunk, but there's nothing wrong with hooking up with a cute guy or three. And Lawrence was a total ass to her. And tonight, the entire camp was a total ass. Her bunk-mates don't have to make it worse."

I walk out of the counselors' room to check on the girls and make sure they're okay.

The next day, I walk to the office to check my messages at Rest Hour. I don't have any from Eli. Or Fancy's mom. She seems to have calmed down since Visiting Day.

Eli's lack of texts is the more concerning issue. We haven't written each other in a few days. Is he so busy traveling or is he in bed with someone else?

I have an excuse. I don't always have Wi-Fi. But what's his?

Last I saw, he was in Portugal. It's his last stop. In three days he's flying back to New York. In four days he's coming to see me.

I check his Instagram. He doesn't have new posts but he's tagged in someone else's posts. I look at them.

I see pictures of him on the beach with a group. With women in bikinis. Do women just wander around willy-nilly in Europe in bikinis? Well, not willy-nilly, I suppose. Vajayjay-nilly?

I look back at the pictures he posted.

Is he trying to tell me something?

Maybe he is. Maybe he isn't. I can't decide if I want him to be hooking up with someone or not.

I debate if I should write him. Yes. No.

He is cavorting with women in bikinis. He is not texting me. He is not calling me. He is definitely hooking up with them. Of course he is. He is a nineteen-year-old guy!

What if this is how we end things?

We both just stop communicating with each other? Do I want to end it? No. Maybe. Why am I hooking up with Gavin if I don't?

I stare at my phone. I put it away. I pick up the kids' mail and head back to camp.

Saturday afternoon is mini-golf day for the junior section.

All the juniors, and all the junior counselors who are not specialists—so, no Gavin—get onto a bus. I make sure all my kids are accounted for and grab the seat next to Danish in the front. Janelle sits in the back, and Muffs sits across from her. As usual, he is wearing his earmuffs. Janelle laughs extra loudly at something he says. How does he even hear in those things?

Lis and Talia sit together and start whispering. Danish does a quick bunk check, and away we go.

"You're taking Monday/Tuesday?" she asks.

"Yeah. That okay?"

"Totally. It's the last day off. Then we're in the home stretch. I can't believe another summer is almost over. My last one, probably."

We hit a bump and we both jump in the seat. "Really?" I ask.

"Yeah. I finish grad school next year. And I have to get a real job, I think. What about you? Would you come back?"

"Maybe," I say. "I had a good summer. Mostly."

"Yeah," she says. "Me too."

She smiles. Then she takes out her phone, so I do the same.

I have a bunch of texts from Eli.

Sorry I've been MIA—weird Wi-Fi.

Sure, I think.

Then:

At airport! Land in NYC tomorrow and then driving up to see you the day after that! You can leave at 6? Will pick you up.

With a shock, I realize he's still coming.

He never said he wasn't. But it will be so strange to see him here. Two days. Two days until I see him.

What will I do about Gavin? Will I introduce them? Eli will expect it since he is now friends with Kat. Or sleeping with Kat. Or sleeping with Kat's best friend. Or just friends with Kat.

Can I avoid introducing them?

Will Gavin want to meet Eli?

Or will he make himself scarce?

Should I break up with Gavin before Eli gets here?

Or will I get back with Gavin after Eli's visit?

I think I might be a terrible person.

I put my phone down and look out the window.

Eventually, the bus pulls up in front of the mini-golf.

Danish jumps up. "Okay, girls, everyone be careful! And

289

have fun! And stay with your groups! And be mindful of your putter. Last year a girl got hit in the head and had to go to the hospital and get stitches."

"Ouch," I say.

I imagine having to write Eli a note. *So sorry, I can't make it. One of the girls has to get stiches. Can't get away, she needs me too much.* Then I wouldn't have to face him with my terrible betrayal and my lies and I wouldn't have to decide if I love him or not and I wouldn't have to decide if I trust him or not and I wouldn't have to decide about Gavin, I could just be a great camp counselor and NOTHING ELSE.

Omigod, what's wrong with me? I am fantasizing about one of my campers getting hit in the head!

I shake it off, and head out for some mini-golf and ice cream. Eli is coming to camp. And I'm going to see him.

WEEK 6 SCHEDULE—BUNK 6A

	SUNDAY	MONDAY	TUESDAY	WEDNESDAY	THURSDAY	FRIDAY	SATURDAY
PERIOD 1 10:00– 10:45	POTTERY	TENNIS	SI	SUPERBOWL	SUPERBOWL	DRAMA	POTTERY *ONE COUNSELOR STAYS IN THE BUNK TO PACK WITH CAMPER
PERIOD 2 10:45– 11:30	SI	DRAMA	DRAMA			SI	DANCE
PERIOD 3 11:30– 12:15	SHOWERS	NEWCOMB	SHOWERS			TENNIS	GAGA BALL
12:15– 12:30	LUNCH WASHUP	LUNCH WASHUP	LUNCH WASHUP	LUNCH WASHUP	LUNCH WASHUP	LUNCH WASHUP	LUNCH WASHUP
12:30– 1:00	LUNCH	LUNCH	LUNCH	LUNCH	LUNCH	LUNCH	LUNCH
1:00– 2:00	REST HOUR	REST HOUR	REST HOUR	REST HOUR	REST HOUR	REST HOUR	REST HOUR
PERIOD 4 2:00– 2:45	DANCE	BASKETBALL	CANOEING	SUPERBOWL	SUPERBOWL	ART	SOCCER
2:45– 3:15	MILK & COOKIES	MILK & COOKIES	MILK & COOKIES	MILK & COOKIES	MILK & COOKIES	MILK & COOKIES	MILK & COOKIES
PERIOD 5 3:15– 4:00	A&C	SI	SOCCER	SUPERBOWL	SUPERBOWL	WATERSKI	DOUBLE GS
PERIOD 6 4:00– 4:45	GS	GS	GS	GS	GS	GS	

Week 6

"So today's the big day," Gavin says.

It's one a.m. and he's lying next to me in my bed, since my counselors' room is empty. Lis and Talia have the day off. They went home together. Botts took off two days earlier. He invited Lis to come, but she told me that if he wasn't interested in her, then she would just go home. I haven't actually asked him about it—I'm kind of avoiding him.

Anyway, all three are gone. And Janelle took off about a half hour ago. She went to Bunk 5, I'm guessing, to see Muffs. When Gavin saw her there he headed straight here, knowing my room was empty. Now the kids are all fast asleep and the lights are off. We haven't even kissed, but I'm lying in the crook of his arm under my covers.

"Today's the big day," I repeat. "He's driving up."

Neither of us says anything.

"Is it going to be weird?" Gavin asks.

"I don't know. I feel weird."

"If he's going to try and beat me up, I would love a heads-up."

I laugh. "He would never beat you up," I say. "I'm not going to tell him. And he's not that . . . passionate."

"No?"

"No," I say. "He's more of an even Steven kind of guy."

"I am not an even Steven kind of guy," he says. "I tend to only like a few things but get kind of obsessed with them."

"What's Kat like?"

"She falls in love with everything," he says.

I wonder if I'd like Kat. Ugh. I bet I would.

We talk about his dad and my dad. I tell him about how unhappy my parents are. How I never want to be stuck in a relationship that isn't right.

We don't talk about what I'm going to do tomorrow.

I don't know what I'm going to do. Isn't what's happening with Gavin a sign that Eli isn't the right person for me? Or is it just a sign that I'm a terrible girlfriend?

Eventually, when it's about four a.m., I fall asleep with my head on his chest.

We wake up with the light spearing in through the sheet covering the window. It's probably only an hour later, but it feels like a decade.

Janelle is in her bed.

I'm glad we are fully dressed. I'll tell her we were just talking.

I shake Gavin awake. "It's morning," I whisper.

"Shit," he says. "Bye." He's about to kiss me goodbye, but sees Janelle asleep in the bed beside us and pulls away.

He disappears out the door sheet. I hear the cabin door open and softly close and the porch creak under his footsteps.

"I wondered why his bed was empty when I was in Bunk Five," Janelle says, flipping over to me. "Don't worry, I didn't see anything."

"Nothing to see," I say. "Nothing happened last night," I say quickly. This time it's not even a lie.

"No judgment," she says. "I *was* in Bunk Five."

"With Muffs?" I ask.

"No way," she says. "I'm not getting in the middle of that triangle too, thank you very much. I was with Eric. He has really good pot."

I push away my plate of mac and cheese. I can't eat. I feel too nauseous.

Eli is coming, Eli is coming, Eli is coming.

"How excited are you?" Danish asks.

"Look at her. She can't sit still," Janelle says.

"She hasn't seen him in six weeks!" Danish exclaims. "Where are you guys staying?"

"I don't know," I say. "He said he booked something."

I pack during Rest Hour. I continue to feel slightly sick

through basketball, SI, and finally General Swim. I am grateful that we don't have sailing today.

As soon as GS is done, I think I might really throw up. And it's not just because of Gavin. I am excited to see Eli. I really am. I'm not just telling myself that. Am I? I miss Eli. But I also like Gavin. But am I in love with Gavin? No. Maybe? I can't wait to see Eli. I'm afraid of seeing Eli. Can he tell I cheated by looking at me? I can't stop sweating.

I hurry the kids back to the bunk, and quickly run to the shower. Then I put on jeans and a cute top, and quickly apply eyeliner. My hand shakes, and I make myself look like a raccoon.

Get it together, I tell myself.

I fix it. There.

I take a deep breath and grab my backpack.

Ready.

I see Gavin and Botts on my way to the office. They're standing in the middle of the road, above the beach. Of course they are.

Botts whistles. "Looking good, Rosenspan."

"Thanks," I say, hitching my backpack on my shoulder.

"Eli's at the office," he says.

I stop. "Already?"

"Yeah." He holds up a walkie-talkie. "He just pulled up."

Gavin raises an eyebrow. "Have fun."

"Um. Thanks?" This is awkward for everyone.

I wave as I walk by. I want to touch Gavin, to let him

know that I am thinking about him, but I don't.

I walk fast to the office and when I am almost there I start to run.

I feel like the kids on Visiting Day.

He's leaning against the hood of his gray rental car, and he's wearing a blue shirt I don't recognize with jeans I do. Did he get taller? He's tan. His hair is longer than usual. It's Eli, it's Eli. My Eli.

I throw my arms around him, and he's kissing me, and I'm kissing him, and he smells like soap. He smells like *him*.

My eyes prick with tears, but I'm smiling because I'm so happy to see him. "Hi."

"Hi, Beautiful," he says. He's smiling too.

"You're here," I say.

"I am."

"You came to see me!"

"I came to see you," he says. "So this is camp, huh?"

"Yup." My arms are still around his neck.

"Can I get a tour?"

"Oh! I don't think we're allowed." It is probably allowed, but I already feel like my worlds are colliding. I don't want Gavin and Eli to meet. My life might explode.

"Okay. I want to get you alone, anyway." He takes my hand.

"Where are we going?

"Saratoga Springs!" he says. "Wait until you see the hotel. I was going to book a B&B but after I won the Monte Carlo money, everyone was teasing me that I had to get us something fancy. So I did."

"I just have to check out," I say. "Gimme a sec."

I hand him my backpack and then run into the office to tell them I'm leaving.

"Your boyfriend?" Eric asks.

"Yup."

"Have fun," he says.

"I will," I say, and fly out the door.

We get in the car, and Eli hits the gas, his hand on my leg.

As soon as he pulls out of camp, he pulls over onto a side road. At first I wonder why—is he going to tell me something? Ask me something?—but then he kisses me again.

We kiss for a while. He kisses differently than Gavin. His lips are softer. He's more hesitant, sweeter.

He wouldn't be kissing me like this if he had hooked up with someone else, would he?

Can he tell that I've been kissing someone else by the way I'm kissing him?

"I can't wait to get you into bed," he says, kissing my neck.

"To the hotel!" I say.

"Actually, I made us a dinner reservation at seven, so dinner first and then the hotel. Can you wait that long?"

"A dinner reservation? A fancy hotel? Who are you?"

He laughs. "I am romancing you!"

The restaurant is just down the street from our hotel, so

we park at the hotel and head straight to eat.

The restaurant is nice—we get a table outside. Eli orders two glasses of wine, and we both casually show our fake IDs.

"The best part of Europe was not needing these," Eli tells me when our waiter turns around.

"Were you guys just drinking the whole time?" I ask.

"There was a lot of drinking," he admits. "It was hard keeping up with Yosef. He's a bottomless pit."

I want to ask about the girls I saw in the pictures. Sydney. Kat. But I don't. I ask about Yosef. About the cities. About the museums. About everything else.

Am I just going to sleep with him and pretend that nothing's wrong? Yes. I think I am.

The restaurant is beautiful. The food—especially after all that camp food—is really good. Eli takes my hand across the table. I am excited and nervous and happy to see him and a little tipsy and filled with guilt. I am feeling everything all at once.

"My treat," he says. "Thank you, Monte Carlo."

"They don't take euros here, you know," I tease him.

"I have a credit card, thank you very much."

"Was Monte Carlo your favorite part of the trip?"

"Maybe," he says. "Definitely a highlight. It was nice to feel like I was part of a group."

He takes my hand as we walk into the hotel. We check in, giggling.

"I feel so grown-up," I say. "We've never stayed in a hotel together."

But then I realize that he has stayed in hotels—well, hostels—for the last month. So maybe it doesn't feel so special to him.

Back in the room, we start kissing right away. There are so many feelings rushing through me. Excitement. Guilt. Confusion. Love.

"Did you bring condoms?" I ask. I could have borrowed a few more from Janelle, but I didn't even think of it. At some point, she's going to notice.

He nods, taking off my shirt.

We climb under the covers and we're kissing again and it feels so good to be with him, but it also feels really good to be lying down on a clean, well-made bed.

"Let me massage your back," he says.

I turn around and feel his hands around my shoulders and back and it feels so good. His fingers are so gentle.

And suddenly I am so tired. Really, really tired. Like exhausted. I barely slept last night and my heart has been racing all day and now I am with Eli. I had wine. Too much wine.

Soft sheets.

Tired eyes.

I'll close them for just a second.

I open my eyes. The hotel room is bright. It's morning. It takes me a few seconds to process what happened. Eli was giving me a back massage and I fell asleep.

I fell asleep!

He drove all the way here to see me, like four hours, and I fell asleep!

Crap, crap, crap.

I snuggle up to him in bed. I can feel him tense.

"I'm sorry," I whisper.

He doesn't answer.

"Really sorry," I say. I feel horrible. For falling asleep. For not telling him the truth. For everything.

"You fell asleep," he snaps. "How could you fall asleep?"

"I am really, really, really sorry," I say, and I mean it. "Why didn't you wake me up?"

"Why didn't you stay awake?" He lies on his back. "I just don't know how you could possibly fall asleep. All I've been thinking about for the last five weeks is having sex with you. Are you even excited to see me?"

"Of course I am! But camp is exhausting," I say. "I was just . . . tired. And the sheets here are so clean! And the bed is soft! And I don't know. I'm sorry. It's not about you. Kiss me." What did I do? I'm horrible. *How could I have slept with Gavin? Do not think about Gavin!*

"I need to brush my teeth."

"I don't care about your teeth." I slide on top of him and kiss his neck again until he puts his arms around me. I kiss him on the mouth. "I'm really sorry. You taste perfect. Let's try again."

I feel him harden underneath me.

"Okay," he says. "But I'm still mad."

"I know," I say. "You have every right to be mad."

This time I stay awake. And it's nice. Sweet and gentle and good.

After showering, we get brunch and then spend the day walking around Saratoga. There's a cute Main Street, and we walk into the bookstore, and antique shops, candy stores, and cafés. I pick up artisanal lollipops for the kids. I am not sure why they're artisanal, but they're lollipops and all children like lollipops.

We hit the road back to camp at four thirty.

"I'll be back next week," I say as he pulls up to the office. "Last day of camp is Sunday, but then staff has to stay until Monday. Are you driving to Greenwich tonight?"

"Actually, I'm going back to Saratoga Springs," he says.

"You are? Why?"

"There's a horse race tomorrow. Might as well go. I'm gonna stay tonight and tomorrow to watch and then drive back Wednesday morning."

"Don't put all your winnings on one horse," I say.

"Why not?" he asks. He kisses me. "When you know, you know."

I force myself to smile. "Right. So I'll see you next week?" My plan was to go home for a few days after camp, then to spend a few days at his parents' house with him before returning to school together.

"Unless you want to make a run for it now?"

Part of me does. I shake my head. "Next week."

"'Kay." He kisses me again. "Love you."

"You too," I say. I hop out of the car, sling my backpack across my shoulder, and close the door.

I'm feeling down for the rest of the night. The kids all hug me when I come in, but they mostly just want to know if I brought them back anything. I hand out the artisanal lollipops.

"After dinner," I say. "But not right before bed."

Luckily Gavin is MIA the whole night. I spot him at dinner for two minutes, but for some reason he's not at Evening Activity.

The junior section is playing Wheel of Fortune in the Rec Hall, and when Danish dismisses everyone to go to Milk and Cookies, I have a hard time getting up off the bench. Janelle stands and stretches her arms above her. It's just the three of us left in the room.

"How was your day off?" Danish asks me.

I don't know what to say. And suddenly I feel so entirely overwhelmed that I burst into tears.

"Oh, honey," Janelle says, sitting on the bench beside me, and rubbing my back.

"What happened?" Danish says. She sits on the other side of me. "It'll be okay. Whatever it is."

"I . . ." I start sobbing even more. Before I know it, my face is dripping with tears and snot. "I don't know what I'm doing. Janelle already knows this, probably, but—"

302

Janelle hitches up her red tube top. "I do?"

I nod. "He was in my bed."

Her eyes widen. "Ooooooh. I do."

"I've been hooking up with Gavin," I say.

Now Danish is the one to say, "Oooooooooh."

"Yeah."

"Okay. It happens," she says. "Did you tell Eli?"

"No," I say. "But honestly, I kinda thought that he had been hooking up with these girls in Europe!"

"Was he? Is that why you hooked up with Gavin?"

"Maybe?" I say. Then I shake my head. "No. I totally don't know what Eli was doing. I just wanted to hook up with Gavin. Which makes me a horrible person, doesn't it? I'm a horrible person."

"You are not a horrible person," Danish says. "You're a human person who is nineteen and who has been away from her boyfriend for five weeks."

"Expecting someone to be monogamous at our age is silly," Janelle says. "You're not married! You had a summer apart. It's only natural that you might have feelings for someone else."

I cry some more.

"Do you have feelings for Gavin?" Danish asks.

"I don't know," I say. "I'm definitely attracted to him. And he thinks I'm funny, and good at stuff, like being a counselor, and color war, and all that. And he helped when Fancy vomited, and he thinks this job is important, when Eli thinks it's just fun and games. Eli was mad all summer that I couldn't call, or that I was tired. But maybe that doesn't matter. And anyway, Gavin has a girlfriend! It's a mess. And also, I think I really am in love with Eli. So what do I do now?"

Danish puts her hand on my shoulder. "If you love Eli, just stop messing around with Gavin. Pretend it didn't happen. Eli never has to know if you don't want him to know."

"But I don't like lying," I say.

"Then tell him. You can tell him and apologize and see if he'll forgive you. Then you'll know if he's for real."

I wipe my nose on the back of my arm. "Why would he forgive me?"

"Because he loves you?" Danish says. "Because he wants to be with you? Because he left you for the summer and understands that these things can happen? Or maybe he did hook up with someone and now you guys are even and can move on."

I nod.

"I also think . . ." She hesitates.

"Yeah?"

"I think you need to think about what *you* want. And how *you* feel. Sure, maybe you hooked up with Gavin because he's hot and because he's here and because you were a little pissed off at Eli for leaving you for the summer. But maybe you also weren't totally happy with your relationship with Eli."

I nod. "I'm really confused."

"Life is confusing," Janelle says and laughs. "That's part of the fun."

"You'll figure it out," Danish says. "I know you will. And anyway, I have a great distraction for you tonight. Super-bowl break at midnight. We're waking up all the kids."

"What is a Superbowl break?" Janelle asks.

"It's like color war, but only two teams, and we play foot-ball for two days!"

"Fun!" Janelle says.

"Two days of football?" I groan. "That's so much foot-ball. Is that where Gavin is tonight?"

She smiles. "He's helping build the float. You'll see."

We all stay up since we know about the break. And at eleven fifty-five, Botts and Marissa come stomping through the hallway of our bunk. They are blaring "We Will Rock You" from one of their iPhones and screaming, "GET READY FOR THE SUPERBOWL!"

Some of the kids jump out of bed and the others hide under their covers.

"Getting them back to bed is going to be painful," I say.

"Do we get a sleep-in tomorrow?" Prague asks.

"Nope," Marissa tells her.

"This is going to be fun," Janelle says.

"Everyone to the football field!" Botts cries out.

"Everyone take a sweatshirt!" I order as we usher all the kids to the football field.

A few of them run ahead, and I take the hands of the sleepy ones.

We surround the football field and wait for Marissa to take center stage. She grabs a megaphone. "We are so excited for Superbowl XX!!! Time to announce our captains!"

Everyone cheers. "For the Wolves team, wearing gray, we have Trevor Rudgers and Nora Steinberg! And for the Tigers, wearing black, we have the Tank and Janelle Moden!"

I spin to look at Janelle. She looks vaguely shocked but then throws her arms up in victory.

"Go, Janelle!" I scream. She is co-captain with the Tank? She is going to win FOR SURE.

She runs up to the center of the field.

I look to see where Lawrence is. He's watching her. I look for Allie. She's whispering to one of her co-counselors.

Whatever.

They divide the teams. Gavin's on mine. He comes up to me after they call out the rest of the teams, and puts his hand on my waist in the dark.

I flinch. I realize it's the first time I have not wanted him to touch me.

"Hey," he says.

"Oh. Hey." I take a step back. I don't know what I want.

"How was your day off?" he asks.

"It was . . . good. Weird."

He doesn't say anything. "Can you meet me in like an hour? At the beach? I want to hear about it."

"I . . . I'm actually exhausted," I find myself saying. It's not a lie. "Can we talk tomorrow?"

"Yeah. Sure." He shrugs, and I watch him disappear into the night.

The next morning, Janelle's alarm goes off at seven a.m. and she's dressed in black shorts and a black tube top and jumping around in excitement.

I spot Gavin at flagpole but try not to look at him. I am not sure what to say. I'm not sure what I want.

So of course, I end up directly behind him in the hot breakfast line in the kitchen.

"Hey," I say. "Sorry about yesterday." I'm not sure why I am apologizing. But I can't just avoid him.

"It's fine. I was wiped, too."

"Do you want to talk at Rest Hour?" I ask.

"I have to make an office run," he says.

Calling Kat, he means. "Okay," I say. "Another time."

He nods.

I get my large bowl of scrambled eggs, two serving spoons, and head back to my table. And I can't help but wonder—is it over? Just like that?

I practice with the girls on my team all morning.

Janelle pops by to watch mid-practice, and she's smiling and cheering like crazy. "You guys are rock stars!" she says. "You're going to smash the other team! Totally smash them!"

She looks so happy, and I'm thrilled for her.

After lunch, I am splayed across my bed resting when I hear the cabin door open. "Hello? Sam, you there?"

It's Gavin.

Lis and Talia both look over.

I jump off my bed and push open the sheet. "Hey," I say. "What's up?"

"Can we talk?"

"Sure, let's go outside," I say. His eyes are red. He looks upset.

The Lower Field bleachers are empty, so we head to those. My heart is racing—did he tell her? Did she freak out?

I wait to sit down before I ask, "What happened?"

"She . . ." He takes a deep breath. "She broke up with me."

I gasp in surprise. "You told her?"

"No," he says, his knee bouncing. "I didn't say anything. She did! She kissed some guy."

"Wait. She did?" My heart speeds up. "Was it Eli?"

"What?" He looks up at me. "No. Not Eli. Alain. Some French guy," he says, and his voice turns bitter.

I feel a wave of both relief and disappointment. "I did not see that coming."

"Me neither."

My heart stops. "Did you tell her? About me?" If he told her, she could be messaging Eli right now.

He shakes his head. "No. I didn't say anything about you or about anyone."

308

"What do you mean, anyone? Was there someone besides me?"

He shakes his head quickly. "No, no, I meant about me being with anyone. I didn't tell her anything. She was just saying all this stuff on the phone, about how she couldn't help the way she felt, and she hadn't known if this Alain would like her back, and she still cares about me, and how they kissed last night and she wants more. So, she broke up with me because she wants to be as honest as possible and not lead me on when her feelings have changed. She's probably fucking him right now."

The word makes me jump. It sounds so crude. Also, she broke up with him because she *wants* to hook up with some other guy? Wants to? Not did? Is she the most righteous person ever?

Or am I just the worst?

"I know I'm a hypocrite," he says. "I have no right to be mad at her. I have no right to feel like shit. But I am. And I do. She's just . . . I've never met anyone like her. I can't believe she broke up with me. I can't believe it's over."

Ouch. Wow. Now I can't stop thinking about Kat. Kat who did the right thing. Kind of. She called her boyfriend and was straight with him before anything major happened. She could have just slept with Alain and no one would ever know, but she didn't.

Kat did the right thing. I should have done the right thing.

"I think I'm going to need to tell Eli," I say.

He closes his eyes. "Great."

"Not, like, today. At some point. I don't think I can stay with him if I don't. And I want to be with him. At least I think I do."

I do love him. And I hate the idea of him not loving me anymore. "I'll try to leave you out of it," I say.

"Whatever. It doesn't really matter now anyway, does it?" He sighs. "This sucks."

"I need to get back to the girls." I stand up. I don't really need to get back to the girls. I just don't want to be sitting here with him right now.

"See you later," he says.

"Yeah."

On my way back to the bunk, I feel the tears roll down my face. I don't even know why I'm crying.

Danish is stepping up to the bunk at the same time. "You okay?"

"No," I say. "I think I need to tell Eli."

She nods. "I understand. Are you going now?"

"Going where?"

"To tell him. I thought that's what you meant," she says.

"No, I meant at some point. Like after the summer. Eventually."

But there is something so freeing about the idea of telling him . . . right now. There is such a heavy weight on my chest. The idea of letting that go . . . "You don't mind if I leave? I'll be back soon. Tonight."

"I'll cover you. Head staff is basically off today and

310

tomorrow anyway. Camp is over in four days. Can you be back by curfew?"

I nod. "You sure?"

"Absolutely."

I'm not even sure what my plan is, but after grabbing my phone and my wallet, I hurry to my car. I text as I walk.

Are you still in Saratoga Springs? I have a few hours off. Can I come see you?

Three dots.

Of course! All good?

I hesitate and then type.

Not really.

He's sitting on a bench in front of the hotel when I drive up. I park and sit beside him.

"Hey," he says. He puts his hand on my knee. "What's wrong?"

"I . . ." My voice closes up. "I don't know how to tell you this, so I'm just going to say it. I hooked up with someone at camp. I'm sorry. I should have . . . I don't know what I should have done. Not done it. Told you. I don't even know why I did it. He was there and you weren't. That's not the only reason. I think I was mad at you for going away and then you didn't seem to be taking my job seriously and then you didn't tell me about the girls you were traveling with . . . I'm sorry. I'm really sorry. I love you. I didn't realize how much I messed up until I saw you."

He looks like someone punched him in the stomach. "I . . . I don't know what to say. Are you saying you were with someone else and it's my fault?"

"No. Yes." My head is spinning and my hands are freezing. "I didn't mean to blame you. I think I convinced myself that you were hooking up with people over there—"

"I wasn't," he says dully.

"I know. I just thought . . . or I wanted to think . . . I don't know. I was confused. But it's over." I can't catch my breath. "I want to be with you. And I need you to know that it's over."

He puts his hands on the bench, as if he's steadying himself. He looks woozy. "I would never have touched someone else. I love you. I loved you."

The past tense makes me feel like someone punched *me* in the stomach.

"I'm sorry. I'm so sorry." I suddenly feel desperate. "Do you think you could forgive me? It's over. For real, it's over. I'm sorry. So sorry."

"I don't know," he says. "Are you going back to camp?"

"What?"

He crosses his arms and glares at me. "Are you going back? Tonight."

"Yeah. I have to go back."

"I don't want you to see him."

"I won't be with him," I say quickly. "But I have to see him. I work with him."

"No. Don't go back." He shakes his head again and again and again. "If you want us to have a chance of getting back together, don't go back. Stay here with me."

"I . . ." I was not expecting this. "Eli, I have to go back. It's my job. And my stuff is there."

He stands up and looks back at the hotel. "Then there's nothing to say. We're over."

No, no, no. "I know you're mad," I say. "I know I hurt you. And I'm so, so sorry. Can we talk when I get back?"

"I don't know," he says. He stands up and fidgets with his phone. "I need to go."

He's crying. I made him cry. I can't believe I made him cry. I feel myself start to cry too. What did I do?

I sit on the bench, and watch him walk away.

I have to stop the car a few times to catch my breath, but I make it back to camp by eight. As I pull into the parking lot, I see the kids crossing the road in the distance. They must be going to the CL for a movie. I can't face them right now. I lean my head on the steering wheel and wait.

What am I doing? How could I have done that to him? I made him cry. I made someone I love cry! What is wrong with me? I start crying again.

About two minutes later I hear a knock on the glass.

It's Botts.

I roll down the window. "Hi," I say, my voice faint.

"Playing hooky? Where did you go?"

"Danish said it was okay. I . . ." My voice trails off and I start to cry again. "Everything is okay, I just . . ."

"Oh, crap, Sammy, I'm sorry. Come here, come here." He opens the car door and helps me out. I'm still crying so he hugs me. I cry into his blue hoodie.

"Let's go somewhere," he says.

"Where?" I ask.

"What's your favorite place in camp?"

"I don't know," I say. "The softball field?"

"Of course it is," he says. "Come on."

I lie on my back across the bench behind home plate, and he sits beside my feet.

"I'm guessing this is somehow related to your boyfriend drama?" he asks.

"It is," I say. One of my arms dangles to the ground, and I lean the other against my forehead. "I just . . . I told Eli. About Gavin. And now he hates me. And I don't even know why I did what I did! I just got so caught up in this place! I love it here! I love the kids! And the staff! And I think Eli just doesn't understand me or what this place means to me! I tried to explain but he doesn't get it and I know that isn't an excuse for what I did. And then he broke up with me." I start crying again. "I just can't believe I would do something like that. Not the telling, the . . . Gavin. Omigod, the look on Eli's face. I'll never get it out of my mind. I'm such an asshole."

"You can't be so hard on yourself."

"I can, actually. Eli was in Europe all summer and didn't hook up with anyone else!"

"Yeah, maybe, but Gavin has the whole broody thing going on. And those abs! I mean, you're only human."

I laugh, but shake my head. "I ruined a great thing."

He picks up a baseball off the ground and tosses it from hand to hand. "Maybe your relationship wasn't that great," he says. "I don't know. Maybe you wouldn't have been looking for something else if you were so happy. Like, look at Danish and her girlfriend. They talk every night. Danish never looks at anyone else, and Marissa practically throws herself at her."

"What? Marissa?" I remember that Marissa is Danish's ex.

"Yeah. You haven't noticed?"

"No," I say.

Was I happy? I think I was when we were together. "I guess I've changed a little since I came to camp. I'm not the same person I was in June. In some ways for the better, and in some ways for the worse. I don't want to be the kind of person who cheats on her boyfriend. It's just not who I am. Or maybe it is. Maybe I have to get used to the idea that this is who I am. Someone who cheats on her boyfriend just because a guy is hot. A guy who *also has a girlfriend*! Ugh, I'm the worst."

"You're not the worst."

"You looked at me like I was the worst. When you saw us. Gavin and me."

"I did not."

"You did!"

"I did not. I was just"—he hesitates—"surprised."

"Yeah. Me too."

He laughs.

"Thank you for not telling anyone," I say.

"I would never do that to you," he says.

"So what happened with . . . Lis?" I ask. "Not my business?"

He shakes his head. "She's just not the right person for me. And I guess I knew it. I hope I didn't hurt her feelings."

"She'll be okay," I say.

"What, you think I'm that easy to get over?"

I laugh. "Summer's done. She'll move on."

"Leaving a trail of broken hearts wherever I go," he says. "That is what I'm known for."

We hear the sound of children laughing from the road.

"I guess the movie is over," I say. "We should go back."

"Any guy is lucky to have you. You know that, right?"

"I guess." I sit up and spin to face him. "Thanks, Botts."

"Anytime, Rosenspan. Anytime."

My girls are all walking back to the bunk, getting milk and cookies.

"Sam!" Prague screams, wrapping her arms around me. "I've missed you terribly! Where have you been?"

"Just dealing with some stuff, my dear," I say. "How was the movie?"

316

"Great!"

"Boring!"

"Slugger fell asleep!"

"You all need a good night's sleep," I say, putting my arms around them. "Tomorrow's a big day."

Back at the bunk, Janelle is running to the shower. "I stink," she calls out. "But today was so much fun!"

Lis and Talia are both sitting cross-legged on Talia's bed.

"Hey," I say.

"What happened to you?" Talia asks. "Why was Danish covering?"

I don't want to get into it. "I had to deal with something. But I'm staying in tonight if you want to go out. You have OD, right?"

"Oh," Talia says. "Thanks. I'm so tired, though. Lis and I were going to crash anyway."

I strip off my clothes and put on sweats and a T-shirt.

"Did you see Janelle and her tube tops at practice today?" Talia says.

"She really needs to invest in a sports bra," Lis says.

Talia laughs. "And a razor."

I can't deal with this right now. "Can you guys just stop? It's enough."

"Excuse me?" Talia asks.

"The bitchiness. The cattiness. I can't listen to it anymore. So she wears tube tops. Big freakin' deal. And why does she need to shave her armpits? The guys don't! She

317

shouldn't have to shave them if she doesn't want to!"

Lis looks scared at my outburst, but Talia rolls her eyes.

"Don't pretend she's not a freak," Talia says.

"So what if she's a freak!" I say. "Everyone's a freak!"

"We're not," Lis says.

"Lis, you've signed your name in at least fifteen spots in this cabin. Why? And Talia! You use too much sanitizer. Like way too much. There's no way that much sanitizer is good for you."

They both glare at me.

"And, look, I'm a freak too, okay!" I say. "I'm freakin' *Porny*! And I messed up the most important thing in my life for possibly no reason! And I kind of love frog hunting! Which is a really weird thing to love! And I'm very bad at folding! So big deal if Janelle likes tube tops! And her hairbrush! So WHAT?!"

I hear the front door open and I stop.

Janelle comes into the counselors' room.

"Hi," I say. I take a deep breath. "I'm going to brush my teeth," I say, and head to the bathroom.

The last day of Superbowl is busy.

Our girls' game is in the morning. We beat the other team. I manage to avoid talking to both Lis and Talia the whole time, too. I feel gleeful that we beat them.

Since Gavin is with the boys all day, I somehow manage to avoid talking to him.

318

We win inter boys, senior girls, and CIT boys, too. It all comes down to the staff game, which is Evening Activity.

Not all staff has to play, so I sit it out. So do Lis and Talia.

But we have the Tank. And Janelle. And we win the game. And the whole Superbowl. Janelle is so ecstatic when a bucket of water is poured over her and Tank to declare them the winners that I start to cry, but this time out of joy. Well, mainly.

On Friday, the second to last day of camp, it rains all day.

The kids are all inside the A & C while the four of us—me, Talia, Lis, and Janelle—are helping clean up the A & C porch.

I try to forget about what happened here with Gavin and focus on the cleaning. It doesn't help that the four of us are barely talking. There are beads everywhere; and for the record, Janelle and I have picked up twice as many beads as they have. Janelle doesn't seem to notice any of this—she is still on a high from winning Superbowl and she's humming "We Are the Champions" to herself.

But suddenly the rain changes from a drizzle to a downpour.

"Wow," I say. "This is intense."

"Yeah," Lis says. "Definitely intense. Can't we make up before the end of camp?"

I look up at her and can't help but laugh. "I was talking about the rain," I say.

Talia sits down and sighs. "Both are pretty intense."

"What are you guys talking about?" Janelle asks.

The three of us laugh, and we all sit down.

"I'm sorry," Talia says suddenly. "Janelle? I know I was a total bitch this summer."

"Me too," Lis says quickly. "You were a great co-counselor and I did not appreciate you."

Wait, what? Am I in the Twilight Zone?

"You were both bitches," Janelle says, and looks back and forth between them. "While I was nothing but nice to you."

"You're right," Talia says, her voice soft. "I'm sorry."

"We're sorry," Lis adds.

Janelle holds for a beat. She looks at Talia and then at Lis and then back at Talia. She opens her mouth and then closes it. Then she shrugs. "I try not to hold grudges. They're bad for the soul. Gimme a hug!"

She lunges toward them both and wraps her arms around them.

Lis hugs her back while Talia pulls away a bit.

"Too much?" Janelle asks.

"No, it's fine," Talia says.

"I'm a little shocked here, ladies," I say.

"We talked about it this morning," Lis says. "And we decided apologizing was the right thing to do."

"The weird thing is . . ." Talia hesitates. "I don't know why I was so mean. I think it was because it was so easy."

"Um . . . not sure what to do with that," Janelle says, biting her lip.

"I don't know either," Talia says, and sighs again. "The girls I went to high school with were bitches. Locked me in a bathroom stall once for about three hours. Left a dead mouse in my locker."

"Shit," I say.

"Yeah." She shrugs. "So when I started coming to camp, I just . . . I don't know."

"Thought if you made fun of other people, no one would make fun of you?" Janelle asks.

Talia nods. "Maybe. Like a strike first thing. You're not the only person I've been an asshole to. But I'm sorry."

"Me too," Lis says.

"But maybe it's not just about you being an easy target. I think we're just so different. You're just so *out there* with your guys and your brush and your tube tops. And the truth is, I'm not . . . I'm just not that into guys."

Ah. "Do you like girls?" I ask.

"No," she says. "Not like that. I don't like anyone like that. Not the way you—not the way everyone—seems to."

"Everyone's different," I say.

"Yeah," she says. "Sometimes I just wish I weren't."

"I'm sorry for the things I said yesterday," I say. "About the hand sanitizer and the wall signing. You're not a freak."

"No, you were right," Talia says. "I am. But we all are in our own way. I just need to relax about it, maybe."

"Eric gave me some of his pot," Janelle says. "Want to try that? Very relaxing."

I laugh. "Have you forgotten we are in charge of the welfare of children?"

"Goody-goody," Janelle says, and blows me a kiss. "But fine. You'll have to come visit me in Canada. Pot is legal there."

"Deal," Lis says. "Will we get to meet your half sister?"

"Maybe. I don't introduce her to just anyone, and you guys are still on probation."

"Fair enough," Talia says. "I'll try and behave."

"And on that note," Lis says, jumping up. "I am going to get some paint, so I can write all of our names in that empty spot right next to the door."

I stand up, too. "Let me help." I motion to the storm around us. "It looks like we'll be stuck here for a while."

On Saturday, Talia packs up the kids one at a time, while I take them to activities. They leave out their shower stuff, a fancy outfit, one pair of pj's, and an outfit to go home in. The bus leaves at ten a.m. Since the counselors are all staying an extra night, we'll pack ourselves up then.

"Are you sure you don't want to switch?" I ask. "I don't mind packing."

"I am much more organized than you," she says. "And you are a much better counselor than me."

The kids are sad to say goodbye to their friends, but it's

322

been six weeks and they are only eight and nine. They miss their families and are excited to go home. They can't wait to see their houses, pet their dogs, hug their cats, and sleep in their own beds.

They pass around their addresses and parents' emails and promise to stay in touch. They promise to come back next summer.

We go through the lost and found. We recycle the empty shampoo bottles. We help them untape their pictures from the walls. They write their names everywhere with Sharpie.

I write my name beside my bed. *Sam Rosenspan slept here.*

On the last night, dinner is a banquet. Everyone gets dressed up in their fanciest outfits and we head to flagpole. They ask Ben and Lacy, the two youngest kids at camp, to lower the flag. "Walk, don't run to dinner!" Jill says afterward, and the kids all run.

There are white tablecloths on the tables for dinner, and the plates are set out. Oooh, pretty. Then there are three courses—salad, then steak or chicken, and finally cake.

Instead of calling freeze, we tell the girls that this time the counselors will stack. They clap but help us clean up anyway.

After dinner, we're told we have a short twenty-minute Free Play, and then we are to head to the Rec Hall. As soon as we get to the Rec Hall, the lights dim, the screen is pulled down, and we go right into the slideshow.

Nostalgic music like Green Day's "Good Riddance (Time of Your Life)" plays as pictures from the first day of camp scroll across the screen. Awww! It's the girls getting off the buses! We all scream, "Lily!" as we see her walking down the road, smiling. Pictures go from day one through the first few weeks, and I love seeing candid shots of my girls. Playing softball. Eating Milk and Cookies. POTH!

Suddenly there are pictures of color war—of me and Gavin whispering and cheering.

"Go, blue!" someone yells.

The final color war picture is of us being pushed into the pool. The look on my face is pure shock and bliss.

I look over at Gavin, and he is looking at me. I smile. He smiles back.

I guess we'll always have color war.

I look back at the screen and watch the pictures of the dance show, and Visiting Day. And there we are frog hunting! Woot!

My girls clap and scream out each other's names as they appear on screen.

When the Superbowl pictures are done, the slideshow comes to an end.

The screen stays down, and we go right into a Sing-Song even though it's Saturday. Jill plays the piano, while the words to all our favorite camp songs appear on screen, and everyone sings together.

We start with "Leaving on a Jet Plane," and then move into "House at Pooh Corner," "Hello Muddah, Hello Fadduh," "Hey There Delilah," "Closer to Fine," "One Tin

Soldier," "Summer Nights," and "Breaking Up Is Hard to Do." Finally we start singing "Stay (at Camp)," the final song. Everyone sings their parts.

"Why can't we stay at camp,
Just a little bit longer.
We want to make our friendships,
Just a little bit stronger.
And the counselors won't mind—"

All the counselors yell out, *"We won't mind!"*

"And all the campers won't mind—"

The campers yell out, *"We won't mind!"*

"And all the good times that we share and all the people
that we care about . . . one more time!"

We sing the song over and over again, and everyone is jumping on the benches and hugging, and the kids are crying because they don't want to leave.

I'm going to miss this place. I came not just because it was a job, but because I wanted to prove to myself that I could make it here.

Sure, it didn't go exactly the way I planned.

I lost a part of me.

But I gained a part, too. I learned to stand up for myself. And for other people. And that maybe I want different things than I thought.

And that I'm a freakin' amazing counselor after all.

Just like we greeted them on the first day, we put the kids back on the bus. Although this time we hug them tightly first.

They pound on the windows and wave goodbye.

We keep waving until the buses are down the road and gone.

"Now what?" I ask Lis.

"We pack up," she says.

After we pack, and eat, and then pack some more and eat some more, we all head to Upper Field for a final bonfire. I flash back to the bonfire we had at pre-camp. Everything has changed so much. How will it feel to be all alone in my room at my parents' house after this? No one to talk to at all times?

Muffs is sitting next to Lis. Is that her hand on his knee? Interesting.

Talia is sitting next to Janelle.

Gavin sits down beside me while everyone sings "Leaving on a Jet Plane."

"Hey," he says.

"Hey," I say back. "How's it going?"

"It's okay. Want to go for a walk?"

"Sure," I say. We haven't spoken in days.

We head down to the beach, passing counselors as we go, saying hi.

It doesn't even matter if anyone wonders about us anymore, since we're both single.

"Want to sit on the dock?" he asks.

I nod. We take off our shoes, leave them at the lifeguard chair, and walk to the end of the creaking dock. We sit down and dip our feet into the water.

"So what happened with Eli?" he asks.

"I told him," I say. "He broke up with me and I haven't heard from him since."

"Sorry," he says.

"Me too," I say. "Any word from Kat?"

"Nope. Radio silence."

"Are you going to try and get back together?" I ask.

"Maybe? I don't know. It's not like this other guy lives in Maryland. And it's not like I was an angel this summer."

"Right."

"What about you?"

"I texted him a few times, but it might be out of my hands."

"I guess you regret it, then," he says. "What happened with us."

"I . . ." That's a good question. "I don't know, actually." I laugh. "I had a really good summer. One of my best summers ever, possibly."

He laughs. "Me too." He scoots closer to me. "So. We're single now . . . what do you think?"

"I thought you wanted to get back together with Kat?"

"I don't know what I want," he says.

I hesitate. It really was an amazing summer. But it's over now. And if I do have a chance of getting back together with Eli, I want to be able to say honestly that nothing happened with Gavin after I saw him.

The thing about Gavin—I like how he sees me, and who I am with him, but I'm not actually sure I necessarily like *him*. He's kind of into himself. He cares too much about how he looks and what people think, and "being cool." I guess I'd rather have someone who doesn't care about that stuff, because that's the person I'd like to be, even if I don't always manage it.

He's a cheater too. Not that I'm one to talk.

"Friends?" I finally ask.

"Sure," he says. "If you can resist my charms, here in the moonlight."

"I can resist them," I say. And I find that it's true.

My duffel is already in my car, which is parked right outside the bunk. Now that the campers aren't here, we're allowed to drive up to our bunks. Lis, Talia, and Janelle already took off, but I am doing one final check through the cabin one last time to make sure I haven't accidentally left anything behind.

"Hey," Danish says. "Heading out?"

"Almost," I say.

"So, aren't you glad you came back?" she asks me.

"I am," I say. "Thank you for giving me the job."

"You were a great counselor," she says. "And I recommended you to be head of juniors next year, if you're interested in coming back and replacing me."

"You did?" I ask, pleased.

"I did. I think you'd be terrific."

"Thank you!"

"You're welcome. Stay in touch, 'kay? We should get together in New York."

"I would love that," I say. I give her a hug, grab my backpack, and get into the front seat of my car. I am going to my parents' to spend a few days with them before going back to school. I am not looking forward to their fighting, but it's only a few days. And then . . . sophomore year. NYC. Here we go.

Seven Months Post-Camp

I pass Washington Square Park, the wind blowing through my hair. It's still pretty cold out even though it's March.

I can't believe I haven't seen him since August.

It feels like we've seen each other—we've talked and texted and of course I follow him on social media. But we haven't *seen* each other.

The texts and calls have gotten a little flirty too. Since he's going back to camp, and I'm going to be head of juniors, it's possible something might happen. . . .

I am just about to turn the corner onto Waverly Place when I bump straight into the last person I expect to see in New York City—Gavin.

"Oh!" I say. "You're here! What are you doing in New York?"

He looks just as surprised to see me as I am to see him.

He's wearing a hat and a leather coat—weird to see winter Gavin. Today of all days. Especially since I haven't seen Gavin since the end of camp either.

"I'm actually here with Kat for the weekend," he says somewhat awkwardly.

"Oh! Wow. You guys got back together."

"We did," he says. "For now. She's doing a year away next year. So we'll see." He smiles.

"Where's she going?" I wonder if it's back to France.

"Montreal. McGill. She's going with her friend Sydney."

"Oh! Janelle is going to McGill next year, too." Small world.

"No way. So," he says, stuffing his gloveless hands in his pockets. "What happened with you and Eli?"

"Me and Eli?" I repeat. "We didn't get back together. We're trying to be friends, but . . ." We are not friends at all, actually. We say hello when we see each other, but that's it.

At least I no longer feel a lump in my throat when I talk about him. Or see him. I'm sad that he's no longer in my life, but it's easier than I expected.

I messed up. He couldn't forgive me. But I'm okay. He was a great first boyfriend, and he made me feel loved and beautiful, but that doesn't mean he's the right person for me forever.

I've dated a few people since the summer, but no one longer than a couple of weeks. I've been concentrating on my classes, and kicking butt on NYU's intramural softball team, and doing student teaching at a public elementary school on the Lower East Side. I spend my free time exploring the city with Emily and Lauren.

"I heard you're not going back to camp," I say to Gavin.

"I'm not. I have a summer job that pays good money, at an investment bank. In New York, actually. Who did you hear that from?" he asks.

"Botts," I say. "I'm actually on my way to meet him now. He's in town for the weekend, too."

"No way," he says. "So, are you around this summer? We could hang out."

"I'm not, actually. I'm going back to camp. I'm head of juniors."

"Ha! Funny."

"It was so nice to see you, but I have to go," I say. I give him a quick hug and keep walking.

I push open the door to the restaurant.

Botts is waiting for me at the bar, and his face lights up in a huge smile.

"Hey, Rosenspan," he says. "Wow, you look good."

He looks good, too. Taller than I remembered. He's sunburned across his nose, and I bet it's from his job teaching skiing to little kids on the weekends during the winter.

"You look sunburned," I say.

"And are you glad to see me?" he asks.

"I'm very glad to see you," I say.

"Good," he says. "Because I'm very glad to see you."

He pulls me into a hug. He feels solid and warm and genuine. He smells like soap and the suede of his jacket.

I hold on to him a little longer than intended.

The summer is only three months away.

~~6~~ months until

~~5~~

~~4~~

3

CAMP BLUE SPRINGS

Acknowledgments

Thank you thank you thank you to:

Kristen Pettit, my awesome editor! Thank you for your patience and brilliant insights.

All the amazing people at HarperTeen! You are the best, Clare Vaughn! Thank you for all your hard work. Thank you to Aubrey Churchward, Alexandra Rakaczki, and Jessica White. Also thanks to Farrin Jacobs and Jen Klonsky who both believed in this book a million years ago when I first pitched it.

My amazing team: Laura Dail, best agent ever. Samantha Fabian, new queen of foreign rights. Lauren Walters, my incredible designer and super reader. Caitlen Patton, assistant extraordinaire.

Austin Denesuk, Berni Barta, and Matthew Snyder at CAA.

My critique partners! E. Lockhart and Lauren Myracle, I love you both and wish we could just cowrite everything together. Thank you for reading this as an early, crappy draft and for making it so much better. Hard pass on the fake teeth.

Love to my fab friends who read drafts or chunks of this book or just kept me company while I wrote: Jess Braun, Christina Soontornvat, Karina Yan Glaser, Courtney Sheinmel, Rachel Feld, Anne Heltzel, Jen E. Smith, Katherine Hartman, Mitali Dave, Logan Levkoff, Maverick Cortes, and Alyssa Stonoha.

To Wingate Camp née Pripstein's! Unlike Sam, I was lucky to find my summer home when I was nine and fortunate to spend ten sun-filled, blissfully happy summers there. Cory Pecker, Ronnie Braverman, Laurie Weisman, Josie Glaser, Dahlia Monk, and of course, Jeremy Rubin: Thank you for all your schedules, help, insights, and for letting me come back for "research." Wingate inspired only the best parts of Blue Springs. Love to all my former bunkmates, especially my summer BFFs Mel Fefergrad and Ronit Avni. Bunk 9 forever.

More love and thank-yous to family, friends, writers, and others: Elissa Ambrose, Aviva Mlynowski, Larry Mlynowski, Louisa Weiss, Robert Ambrose, the Dalven-Swidlers, the Dattilios, the Heckers, the Finkelstein-Mitchells, the Steins, the Wolfes, the Mittlemans, the Bilermans, the Greens, the Takefmans, Courtney Sheinmel, Anne Heltzel, Lauren

Myracle, Emily Bender, Julia DeVillers, Julie Buxbaum, Elizabeth Eulberg, Robyn Spector, Targia Alphonse, Lauren Kisilevsky, Stuart Gibbs, Rose Brock, Aimee Friedman, David Levithan, Adele Griffin, Leslie Margolis, Maryrose Wood, Tara Altebrando, Sara Zarr, Ally Carter, Jennifer Barnes, Alan Gratz, Penny Fransblow, and Maggie Marr.

And so much love for my amazing husband, Todd Swidler, and my girls, Chloe and Anaballe. I love that I get to do sing-songs with you.